Hurricane Season

Hurricane Season

Stories from the Eye of the Storm

Karen Bjorneby

SOURCEBOOKS LANDMARK™
AN IMPRINT OF SOURCEBOOKS, INC.™
NAPERVILLE, ILLINOIS

To Peter, always

Stories in this volume have previously appeared as follows: "Hurricane Season," *Story Quarterly*, 2000; "Angels in White Dresses," *New Orleans Review*, 1998; "The Goat," *Press*, 1998; "War Games," *The Nebraska Review*, 1998; "Burning Desire," under the title "Dry Cleaning," *Rosebud*, 1996; "Flamingo," *Farmer's Market*, 1992; "Defying Gravity," under the title "Gravity," *Descant*, 1992; "The Hands of the Evangelist," under the title "Evangel," *Louisiana Literature*, 1991, *Clifton Magazine*, 1991, *The Sun,* 1993.

Published by Sourcebooks, Inc.
P.O. Box 4410, Naperville, Illinois 60567-4410
(630) 961-3900
FAX: (630) 961-2168
www.sourcebooks.com

Library of Congress Cataloging-in-Publication Data

Bjorneby, Karen.
    Hurricane season: stories from the eye of the storm/by Karen Bjorneby.
        p.cm.
        ISBN 1-57071-853-9 (alk. paper)
United States—Social life and customs—20th century—Fiction. I. Title.

PS3602.J67 H87 2001
813'.6—dc21

                                                    2001031333

Printed and bound in the United States of America
        LB   10 9 8 7 6 5 4 3 2 1

Acknowledgments

I owe thanks to many people, in many classes and workshops, particularly to the members of the Palo Alto Wednesday Night Group who shared their knowledge, friendship, and encouragement as I wrote and rewrote these stories. I thank my agent Kathi Paton for her continued support of my work, and my editor Hillel Black, for gently, insistently, and with great insight pushing me to travel further. Most especially I thank Tom Parker, for wisdom; Bob Levy, for heart; and Irv Yalom, for courage.

Table of Contents

Hurricane Season

My little wooden house sat between water, on ten-foot stilts. Ocean in front, narrow finger of inland waterway behind. A thousand years ago I'd had a carpenter-lover build me a dock back there. I'd bought a small aluminum fishing boat. Now at night, I liked to motor out into the middle of the river, smoke Winstons, and drink more gin than was good for me. I'd toss the dead cigarettes at whatever rippled beneath the black water—porpoise; manatee; sea monster. I wasn't a meteorologist, I was a painter. A painter who'd lost her eye for light. But it didn't take much eye to know the storm rushing in from the Atlantic was going to be a big one. Evacuating was the smart thing to do. Drive seventy miles inland to Orlando with a totebag full of paperbacks and a bottle of Tanqueray, and wait. Or at least pack a sleeping bag and take my chances across the river at the shelter in the elementary school, between concrete walls.

But I stayed. Not because I wasn't smart. Not because I wasn't afraid. I stayed because it would be just like God to let me imagine escape and then crush me like a snail on the highway. I stayed because I just didn't give a damn.

I was forty years old. In the last three years I'd lost every single person I loved. My mother and father both to heart attacks, one right after the other. My eight-year-old son to a shooting in a mini-mall. My husband to his grief. Or to my grief. Or to bitterness or to blame or to just plain weakness.

This is the way I figured things. Either there was no

God, or there was a God and he was an evil shit, or there was a God and he was as powerless as the rest of us.

So fine then. Bring on the storm.

The last weather report I'd heard it was a hundred miles off shore. Far enough. I had time yet to cross the highway and take a look. I put on a yellow slicker and boots, but I didn't bother with a hat. I had spiky black hair not even a hurricane could ravage. But as soon as I stepped outside, the wind whipped it into black snarl. I had to shove myself across the highway. Flying sand as loud as a thousand hornets stung my cheeks, my hands, my eyes.

But the ocean was beautiful, in a terrible way. Green and purple foam swirled wildly. The sky boiled gray and yellow froth. The beach was a mess. Tangled kelp, shredded jellyfish, scraps of shipwreck scraped off the sea floor. Waves scooped up mouthfuls of earth and spewed them up the beach. I stood on top of the dunes shielding my eyes with my hands and felt the tug of riptide running beneath my feet. Each time the waves fell away, that hollowed well of time and water made me want to dive in headfirst and let the ocean carry me where it would.

Then I saw, not a hundred feet down the beach, a scarecrow boy getting ready to do just that. And I thought, shit. Shit, shit, shit. He unbuttoned his shirt, and the wind yanked it off him. He stripped out of his jeans, and the storm shrieked away with them. He dropped his wristwatch in the sand, and the sand buried it.

Maybe he was a surfer. I tried to tell myself he was a surfer. He looked like a surfer. Longish, dirty blond hair, reedy body, long, long legs—two knock-kneed streaks of tan. A crazy surfer out to catch the biggest wave of his life.

Except he didn't have a board.

I shouted to him. The wind just laughed into my face

and scattered my words over the beach. He stood there at the water's edge, his hair blowing all around his head. He didn't bother brushing it out of his eyes. A quick darting wave rushed over his feet and he leaped back. But then he squared himself and waded in.

What to do, what to do? I plowed through the wind-scooped sand—there had to be something I could throw to him. A length of plank. A coil of rope. A ragged hunk of splintered tree washed from God knows where, the Canary Islands, or the Cape of Good Hope, or the Slough of Despond.

But anything I could throw to him would only be hurled right back at me.

He'd waded in deeper. Water foamed at his knees. The ocean lunged; he faltered. It sank back; he pressed forward. One gray finger of wind cupped my ear and whispered: leave him.

But then the storm fell into a moment's silence and the water carried real sound to me: he was crying. I could see the rattling scallops of his spine, the wracked staves of his shoulders. What the hell else could I do? I threw off my slicker, tugged off my boots and my jeans, and splashed in after him.

Cold knifed straight up my legs into my stomach. I clenched my teeth and breasted through a breaking wave. The wind shoved its fist in my mouth. I swallowed seawater. I gagged. He was out so far now all I could see of him was his head bobbing up and down on gray water. The weight of water pulled at my arms. Spray slashed my eyes. A wave crested over him and he was gone. I kicked forward, hard, fighting thick water to that eddying spot where he'd vanished. Feeling my own self being swallowed in crashing tide: no. No. He couldn't vanish that fast. Knowing that he could. Knowing that I could, too. We were out a long way. My thighs cramped into rock. My belly was filled with seawater. My lungs burned with salt and fire.

Then he surfaced, and the wilding ocean rolled him right to me. I grabbed on to him. His skin was slippery and cold and I wrapped my arms around his skinny, writhing body and I clamped my wrists together and I held on while the ocean tried to tear us apart.

He hit me. He shook his weedy, wet hair and yelled. I kicked my legs, kicked him, tried to swim us to shore. He hit me again, and then I was mad. Who the hell did he think he was? Who the hell did he think I was? He hit me one more time, and I bit his shoulder and he cried out and then quieted. Rioting wind and wave tossed us toward land. We scraped over sand and pebbles and broken glass and poisonous strings of man-o'-war and tumbled up onto the beach like two dead husks.

I knelt on dry sand and vomited.

He lay limp and blue as an eel.

I crawled over to him. I pointed at the highway. I shouted into cold streaming wind: my house!

I couldn't hear his answer, but I could read his lips: leave me alone. His hair wreathed his head in green vines. My teeth marks scarred his thin, blue shoulder.

I tried again: I'm alone! I need help!

His lips said: I don't care.

I sat back on my heels. I thought: fuck you, then. Pain thrummed in my wrists and my legs jellied as I tried to stand.

But I also thought: I can't just leave him here. If I could do that, I didn't need this storm. If I could do that, my decisions were already made. He was so young. Eighteen, nineteen. If I could only get him to my house. If I could give him something to eat.

I bent over him. I placed my hands on either side of his face and leaned in as close as a lover. I whispered down into his eyes: help me. Then I'll help you. I have pills. Plenty.

He looked up at me, slow and careful. His eyes were dark tunnels of blue. I held myself perfectly still against the following wind. I let him look straight through my eyes, straight through their barren gray that never lied and seldom flinched and were as empty of light as his.

What kind? he demanded. Exactly? He demanded this like he knew what he was demanding.

I didn't want to tell him, exactly. They were mine. They were hidden. But my throat was torn. The wind had turned white and viscous, the ocean thrashed nearer and nearer, the clouds had hardened to iron. There wasn't much time. I put my lips to his cold ear. I tasted sand and sweat and salt. I whispered: Seconal. Percodan. Valium. Gin.

His eyes paled. His mouth moved: why?

I sat up. I shouted: I had to kill a dog!

He squinted at me: you crazy?

I nodded my head, big exaggerated nods. I ignored the burned strain in my wrists and hauled him up. Standing, he was thin and bleached and docile. The wind scooped us both across the highway.

But when he saw the choppy, sloppy river and my sad, sagging house in front, he stopped. He pointed at the stilts: how high?

What difference did it make now? He knew what I knew. If we were high enough we'd make it. Otherwise, we'd be swamped. We climbed the stairs to the porch. As soon as I turned the knob the wind slammed the front door open. Then he and I both had to wrestle it closed again.

Inside it was cozy. My house was small and dim. I liked it that way. A living room, a bar opening onto a galley kitchen, a tiny hallway leading to two bedrooms, and a bathroom. I'd once had paintings—some mine, some done by friends of mine—on every wall. But in the year since Ryan was shot, I'd taken them all down. Mine I threw in the river. The others I gave back. My friends were grateful to remeet old work, and then they were confused, and then irritated, and then impatient—which is why they weren't my friends anymore. Now the walls of my house were empty canvasses of dun. An orange sofa, a tweed armchair, a battered maple coffee table crouched on the wooden floor in front of a big, blank picture window facing the highway and the ocean beyond.

It was pure craziness outside. Leaves and twigs and candy wrappers and torn hibiscus petals cycloned in a kind of devil's dance. The ocean had swallowed the dunes. I fetched us each a pair of dry sweats. I gave him a brown, woolen blanket. He sat huddled on the sofa, watching the storm approach. Warmer, drier, his skin plumped a little at his cheeks and chin, and I recognized him. His photograph had flashed on TV between every storm update. Before the TV cut out. He was the bus driver.

Three days ago a train had hit a school bus. Six kids killed outright, twenty-three hurt. The bus had been stopped at a red light, straddling the tracks, a car in front, a truck behind. When the warning bells rang, the bus had no place to go. The police thought the driver might have been drunk or stoned or homicidal. No one knew for sure because he'd run away. Anyone who saw him was supposed to call a hotline. He might be dangerous.

He didn't look dangerous. He looked smudged. His eyebrows drooped at the corners. His jaw drooped. His mouth drooped. He looked tired. He looked hungry. His eye sockets were shrouded in dark circles.

He looked up at me from inside his blanket. "You know who I am."

"Yes."

"Go ahead," he said. "Call the police." His voice was parched and defiant.

"The phone's out."

"At least you see why."

Asshole, I thought. As if Why were that easy. "Why don't you just turn yourself in?" He didn't like that at all. He threw himself back against the sofa and crossed his arms. Folded in that brown blanket he looked like a sad, angry monk. I waited for him to ask me for my pills. When he didn't, I said, "I know who you are, but I don't know your name."

"Calvin," he said.

"Mine's Kate." Then I asked if he liked chicken noodle soup.

My kitchen window faced the rear. I heated soup over a camp stove and watched the river slosh over my wooden dock, my aluminum fishing boat lashed to the piers. I'd taught Ryan to swim in that river when he was barely three. I'd had to; he was wild for the water and fearless. He'd splashed and played like a river otter. Like a river otter with jug ears and a smart mouth. Shards of grief grated in my heart, thinking of him. He'd have had such a blast in this storm. He'd have thought it one big adventure.

The thing is, I did have quite a stash of pills. But I didn't keep them in the medicine cabinet where Calvin would look first. Or in my nightstand, where he'd look second. This was Florida—hiding drugs here was an art form. They were in Ryan's room. In the box he'd called his memory box. A lethal collection of barbiturate and narcotic nestled in between pictures of him in all the goofy Halloween costumes I'd sewn. Pictures of me and his father scaling a waterfall in Jamaica. Butterfly watercolors and playdough dogs he'd patiently made all those days and nights I painted and smoked and muttered—*in a minute, just a minute, soon, not now, soon.* Bottles of pills and treasured bits of glass and rock and shell, all in a box. If I ever did kill myself, I'd do it in Ryan's room.

Rain spattered the roof in handfuls. The wind hammered the house. The house shuddered in response. I poured soup into two mugs and handed one to Calvin. I settled myself in the tweed armchair. We listened to the storm. Steel needles of rain jabbed the window. Feathers of wind seeped in around the crack.

Calvin tucked the cowl of blanket back on his shoulder. He glanced around at the dry, dun walls, at the beamed ceiling, at the wide, sheet of glass window. "You should have nailed plywood over that. Or at least masking-taped it. How old's your roof?"

I didn't know. Too old.

I sipped my soup and tasted metal. The air smelled of solder. The edge of the storm was very close now. One prickly tail of wind lashed the hair at my neck and promised: *soon*.

Waiting, anxious, I propped my foot on the coffee table. Calvin propped his foot on the coffee table. My foot bobbed. So did his. I was jangled and nervous and so was he. He blurted into the loud hush, "Why'd you kill a dog?"

My foot jerked to a stop. No one had ever asked me about that dog. Not even my husband. I looked quietly at Calvin, and then down at my hands. I'd ground up Percodan and Seconal and gin and milk into one of Ryan's old baby bottles and fed it to the dog. I could still feel that dog's stiff fur, the scratched pads of its paws, the small thump of its heart—slowing, slowing, stop. "It was ugly." My voice ached. I felt like I'd swallowed something too large—a peeled egg. "Part terrier, part hyena, part rat. I couldn't stand to look at it."

"Oh." His foot stilled. "I had a dog like that once. But

he was a nice dog."

Rain slashed sideways now across the window. Every once in a while, a shredded palm frond or a smashed gardenia flung itself at the glass and then peeled away out onto the highway.

But I wasn't seeing the storm. I was seeing Ryan in the car beside me, wriggly and snaggle-toothed, begging for a dog he'd seen in the pet store at the mini-mall where we were going for milk and cigarettes and socks. "He was my son's dog," I whispered. I'd said yes to that dog because it had been easier and quicker than saying no.

"You killed your son's dog? Jesus, I'm glad you're not my mother."

I flinched. My hands flew up to my face. I felt like he'd slapped me. I felt the pink sting in my cheeks. I felt flayed. "My son's dead."

He moaned. He bent over onto his knees and moaned. "Was it…me?"

"No. Oh, God—no." I felt now that I'd slapped him, and I felt sorry. I moved over to the couch. I touched his bent back. "It was a shooting."

The air now was thick and sludgy. I felt like we were suspended in oil, Calvin and me. The storm had crossed the highway, was clanging toward us. But it was a thousand miles away, too. I could hear my heart beating. I could hear his heart beating. Both our hearts, pounding away at the same fast and terrible rate.

He sat up. He covered his eyes with his hands and spoke through anguished lips. "I was scared, that's all. I ran away because I was scared. And then I heard all the reasons they thought…and I couldn't turn back."

He was still scared. He'd be scared forever, I thought. I wanted to give him something. I stroked his arm. I wanted to give him my arms. I wanted to give him my body.

But then my stomach hollowed out. Barometric pressure had suddenly plummeted. I felt it in my knees. An expansion. I felt it in my ears. Any second now I would burst and drain away. I closed my eyes. I lifted my face to the storm: *I'm here.*

Calvin stood. "I'm going to crack open the windows on the lee side."

I opened my eyes. "Why?"

"Letting out some pressure might save the house."

He went into the kitchen and slid the window open a quarter inch. Air squealed through the gap. He moved down the hall, and captive to the coming tide, I let him go. But then I thought: Ryan's room. I shouted, "Calvin, no!" I ran down the short hallway.

He sat on Ryan's rumpled bed. The sight of him, big and bony on that bed, made me furious. "Get out!" *Desecration*—that word screeched in my ears. "Get out of here!"

He sat limp. I tugged at his limp hand. Wind sifted in around the closed window. Ryan's baseball curtains shivered. The memory box sat secret and closed beneath the window, beside the bed. Calvin's face was runneled with pain. "How can you stand me?"

Fury ebbed into fatigue. "Please. Please, I can stand you anywhere but here."

This room—I hadn't changed a thing since the day Ryan died. It was a mess. Plastic superheroes strewn on the floor, Nintendo games scattered about, stained Nikes tossed on the bed, dresser drawers spilling out underwear and T-shirts. A heap of laundry in the corner. Some nights I pulled out Ryan's worn pajamas and slept with them. He used to make me so mad—he would never clean up this room.

"We need to crack open the window," Calvin said.

"Forget about it."

But he was already shoving it open. The baseball curtains slipstreamed out. Air rushed out. My own breath rushed out, so that I had no voice to cry out *stop*. All the last bits swirled past me and out that chink in the window. All the leftover exhalations, all the shed strands of hair, all the last puffs of little boy smell—cherry Popsicles and rubber cement and Bactine. All of it washing up and out and gone. I clutched my stomach and tasted sour vinegar in my mouth. All the mess and all the arguments and all the tears and all the silly frog-in-a-blender jokes that made me laugh even when I was working. Frantic, I tried to catch it all in my hands. Helpless, I begged *please, stop*. And it was already too late.

Calvin touched my hair. He touched my shoulder. He pulled me to him and he smelled of salt and I put my lips to his throat and I whispered into his flesh, but the whisper was a hiss and the hiss streamed out the window too.

The thing is, I'd seen them come in. I hadn't liked the looks of them. Unwashed oily faces, unwashed oily blue jeans. But what kind of assholes rob pet stores? I saw the gun and I wanted to shout: you idiots! There's a liquor store on the corner. There's an ATM across the street. Wait five minutes, some old guy in white shoes will take out a fistful of twenties. I did shout, to Ryan. I shouted: get back! But I'd never raised him to be obedient and I should have. I thought I was raising him to be spunky and questioning but that was a mistake. I should have raised him to do what I said when I said it, or else, and he'd still be alive. I shouted get back, and he ran forward, and the one with the gun turned and shot him in the neck. Bright rainbow blood spurted over me, over the dog, over the shooter. I stuck my finger in that hole in my son, I stuck my hand in that hole, I stuck my whole being in that hole, and it wasn't enough.

Because the heart is stupid and it keeps beating.

Calvin was quiet for a long few moments, and then he said, "I'm sorry."

I wiped my nose, my eyes. "*You're* sorry. Shit."

A giant fist slammed into the house.

We stood in the living room, purely awed. We stood in front of the window with our hands clasped behind our backs. The ocean was gone. The dunes were gone. The highway was gone. There was only green. Green sky, green water, green glass. Lightning crackled, brilliant green. Wind howled, a broken green keening. Wind plucked a crazy green soprano on the tight strings down my spine. Rain fell up. Electricity buzzed green. The hair on my arms stood straight up. Calvin's hair floated around his face, a green seaweed halo. Green water rose beneath us, seeped through the planks of the floor. I heard chiming right in my temples. A green clock striking twelve: *it's time*. The window rippled. It danced and undulated and beckoned. It bowed in to me. I touched it and it was hot. I put my forehead to it and it was soft.

Vaguely, I heard Calvin call my name. Vaguely, I felt him behind me. And then I didn't.

The chiming deepened. A steel green hammer. A bass drum booming just for me. Green water flowed over my feet. The floor floated. The planks arched. The house unmoored. Rain fell up into that green sky. The window arched to me. I spread out my arms to embrace that hot, violent glass.

The storm thrust itself hard into me. Glass exploded all around me. Green slivers struck a thousand steaming cuts. Wind shoved me back by the throat and rain flattened me against the wet, desert walls. The storm rampaged through the house. Things fell, broke, shattered, tore. I was just starting to topple when Calvin scooped me up over his shoulder. He forced his way past the storm into Ryan's room, lay me on the bed, shoved the door closed. The wind pounded at the door, furious.

"You're bleeding all over," Calvin said. He knelt on the floor beside the bed.

"Yes." For the first time since Ryan died I felt alive.

Calvin's busy hand plucked glass from my face, my arms. My sweatshirt was in tatters. "I don't know what to do," he said. "Tell me what to do."

"Don't do anything." I hurt. I felt good.

He touched my cheek. "Kate. There's a big piece sticking out of your chest."

I looked down at myself. So there was. A spear of glass, an inch or so wide, stuck out about three inches from my left breast. Blood seeped around it into the lace of my bra. "That's fine," I said.

The wind clawed at the roof.

Calvin's hand fluttered around that shank of glass. "I don't know if I should pull it out. What if it's in your heart?"

How deep did my heart lie? Wind tapped on the glass and I thought, *yes, a little more, a little further, yes now yes.*

Calvin shook my shoulder. The glass rasped inside me and shivers rippled down my chest into my hips. "Goddammit," he said. "This is not happening to me again."

I licked my lips and tasted blood. "It's not happening to you at all."

"The hell it isn't."

I threw one hand back, down onto the memory box beside the bed. "In here. Thirty of everything. Then you'll be fine too."

He sucked in his breath. He sat back on his heels. "You bitch."

I opened my eyes. "That's right. Finally you get it. Finally you see." The roof began to peel back in a horror of sounds. Rain streamed in along the walls. The sky was a sea of green eels. "I was furious to be pregnant. The only reason I didn't get rid of it was because I was too damn busy working. I had color in my eyes and stars at my fingertips and light—I swam in light. I hated being a mother. Laundry, supper, homework, Cub Scouts. Over and over, I begged one thing: God, give me peace."

Calvin began to cry. His shrouded eyes welled with tears. "Do you think I meant for that bus to be on those tracks? Do you think I don't wish over and over I could rewind the day and stop—just stop? I wasn't paying attention. I made a mistake. I made a bunch of mistakes."

He wrapped a piece of cloth around his hand and fumbled at the glass and shudders coursed from my belly to my knees. *Oh push it in, please push it in.*

"Kate..." He stroked my hair. He leaned over me like a lover. "Please don't do this to me."

I looked up into his sad and scared blue eyes. He wasn't a reason. He would never be reason enough. But what the hell else could I do? I spasmed through one last, long, yielding breath. "Pull it out."

He did. The floor beneath us broke apart and we fell endlessly into black water.

We tumbled, we spun, we floated, we drowned. We breathed and then didn't. We gulped air, greedy, when it was there. We flew apart and then collided together. We grabbed on to what passed by us as long as we could, before it was ripped from our hands. A broken branch, a slice of roof, shards of brick, filaments of straw. A yellow Volkswagen floated by, a rocking chair, a telephone, a frying pan, an apple. A giant, felled live oak, its roots ancient and white and exposed, its branches studded with panicked chickens, crying cats, snakes flushed from their hiding places.

It was as violent as lust, and as senseless as wish, and as loud as birth.

And then, in one fell instant—silence. The eye of the storm. Respite.

Green water, green sky, cracked into light. We floated inside glass.

My wounds burned with salt. But they no longer bled. I couldn't speak. Calvin couldn't speak. We were both stunned by this sudden generosity.

In a small pool of white crystal, my little fishing boat spun and spun, a gentle eddy.

Calvin and I splashed over to it. He hauled himself in, then helped me over the gunwales.

I had no idea where we were. All road signs were washed clean away. We were in another landscape. But the current was pushing us inland. Calvin snagged a plank floating by and I grabbed for another and we began paddling.

A rooster in the oak tree crowed. A cat sang. A pelican winging overhead looked down at us and laughed.

So I laughed. And Calvin laughed. The light was so beautiful. He knew what I knew. We could close our eyes and yet die pierced by such light. The second half of a hurricane is worse than the first. What the hell else could we do but with our makeshift oars pull hard across the river, toward shelter.

War Games

We lived in a community without men. The year was 1972. We were in Florida; the men were in Vietnam. The Air Force allowed us, the families who waited, to wait in this enclave of discarded World War II housing crumbling between swamp and sea. Outside, land crabs skittered in the dark places between house and bush. Inside, damp spots crawled up the walls and multiplied in the corners of the low ceilings. None of our curtains or carpets fit this house, but we jammed them in anyway, pinning up hems, folding in corners. This was the most temporary of all our temporary living spaces. In the sagging kitchen, red *Xs* marched across a calendar hanging from a thumbtack.

Afternoons, I played football. I'd throw the ball the way my father taught me: fingers on the laces, sight down the field, and then BOOM, release the ball. My breath sucked backward for that one second before I could see I'd been on target.

At age fifteen, my being a girl already seemed such a waste.

I played with the boy next door, Buddy. Our passing game was like a dance between us. The slap of leather against flesh was a drumbeat ticking off the days, the weeks, the months. Pass, catch, pass again. Time could elapse without awareness. Time was all that mattered.

Buddy was the same age I was, with soft, sure hands and fast, skinny legs. His forearms were flat, sturdy as two-by-fours, and after a game of catch one blue vein would bulge above his wrist. He hadn't yet begun to shave, but a thickening of the skin at his jaw, a firming of line, hinted at shadows to come. He wore his jeans low on his hips, and his black hair curled low on his forehead. His father out-ranked everyone else's, and was on his second tour of duty in Vietnam. For these reasons, Buddy had promoted him-self to commander of our makeshift air force base. He and I were the only kids around older than eight.

We always broke our games promptly at five o'clock. No bugle ever blew *Retreat*. No unseen hand lowered an unseen flag before headquarters. There was no reason to stop, to pause for a moment and stand at attention. Still we did so. Some atavistic instinct always told us exactly when five o'clock had arrived. After a moment's silence, we'd each troop home. Our mothers would set up trays before the TV sets. They'd heat up frozen dinners or Kraft macaroni-and-cheese. We'd switch on Walter Cronkite, eat supper, and watch the war. Pray that no one we knew appeared on TV.

It was common knowledge in our community that no one survived the evening news.

Fierce fighting in the Central Highlands and northwest of Saigon. Reports that Quang Tri might fall. Two North Vietnamese divisions moving south. U.S. estimates at least eighty portable antiaircraft missile launchers in place. President Nixon ordering around-the-clock tactical air strikes, but for now, low cloud cover keeping most F-4 fighter-bombers on the ground. Cronkite called it the Spring Offensive.

It was early April, and one of the civilian girls at school, Callie Kitchener, invited herself home on the bus with me. I couldn't imagine why. Neither Buddy nor I had made much of an impression on the civilians. There was no rea-son to. We'd both be gone in less than a year.

Meanwhile, we were enough for each other.

Still, Callie's attentions flattered me. Even while I resented the flattery.

She was a big ripe peach of a girl, tan, with gold feathery down on her forearms that caught the light. She had sparkling teeth and big breasts, and she wore bellbottoms and gauzy peasant blouses with elastic that sagged to reveal one round, brown shoulder. Her voice was husky, scratchy, as if she smoked, but the strain wasn't caused by cigarettes, but by laughter. Her chatter entranced all the little kids on the bus.

As we pulled off the highway into the decrepit little housing area, I found myself wishing our sad, old base still had a perimeter, a gatehouse, a guard with an M-16. Someone to let Callie know entry wasn't automatic.

"We play football in the afternoons," I said to her, ungraciously. "Can you throw?"

She just smiled. "You can teach me."

All the cinderblock houses, each identical to the other, sagged in a rank fronted by crabgrass lawns and overgrown beds wild with Florida's jungle vines and shrubs, pink and red petals dripping to the ground. I showed Callie the laces on the ball, explained the aerodynamics of spiral. She cocked back her arm, bounced a few steps forward. Her pass wobbled maybe three yards before nosing into the ground. She tried again, and this time her blouse slipped down her shoulder, constricting her motion—not that it made much difference.

Over and over she tried, with a determination I had to admire. Even if I couldn't quite understand it.

And during all this, Buddy sprawled on the stoop in front of my house, a satisfied smile on his face. Like we were putting on this spectacle for his amusement.

I took the ball from Callie. "Like this," I said. I gunned a bullet right at Buddy's chest. He caught it with a grunt.

"No, like this," he said, standing. He hurled the ball way,

way over my head, into a line of pepper trees.

What a show off, I thought, chugging for the ball. When I returned, Callie and Buddy had each folded themselves down onto the stoop, leaving no room for me.

That evening, after Callie had gone, after supper and the war, Mother pulled her latchhook onto her lap. Smoke spiraled from the cigarette burning in her ashtray. She'd begun a square latchhook panel the day my father left, and then she'd just kept making more and more panels. I couldn't imagine any house we'd live in big enough for the size that rug was going to be.

I scooped up my ball and went to find Buddy. Outside the evening sun shot long, pink spears into the spring clouds. Squadrons of mosquitoes buzzed by. Buddy and I separated into our dance: pass, catch, pass. Closing, separating. Moving down field, and up again. A kind of endless march. But Callie's visit had disturbed our pattern. Every once in a while, a sudden shiver of awareness sizzled down my spine. The blue shadows under Buddy's cheekbones. The taut swivel of his hips. Instead of a nice, tight spiral I'd throw a clumsy, bobbling pass, completely off-target.

I knew Buddy, I told myself. Buddy was not the danger. The danger lay only in breaking the rhythm. The drumbeat that marched us through our days. I threw the ball further and further, backing him away from me.

Then a half-smile slid across his face. He bent to play center and I moved in for the snap. The instant I clasped the ball, he wheeled and came at me. I ran full out, afraid suddenly. I zigzagged, fast, but he snagged my T-shirt and then my waist. I crashed to the ground underneath one of the pepper trees, landing on my back. A knotty root thumped all the air out of my lungs. For one swirly moment I couldn't inhale, couldn't exhale. It was like I was dead. Darkness shattered behind my eyelids; panic skittered in my stomach. Then, in another instant, my body revived itself. I sucked in great chunks of air. Light flooded back into my veins. Relief. A kind of happiness that made me grab hold of Buddy's arm, hang onto him, in gratitude.

"You going to live?" Buddy knelt beside me, his black eyebrows furred and puzzled.

I nodded, still holding onto him. He stared at me. Studying me. Where I'd been drained before, I began to fill with a new, sinking, surging feeling. Inviting. Scary.

"You know, Max, I was thinking. You could be real pretty if you tried."

I sat up, shoved him away, stung. "Just get the damn ball," I said. Pretty was something you were or you weren't, and I wasn't. I told myself pretty wasn't something I cared about.

As Buddy fetched the football, a blue staff car rounded the corner from the highway into the strip of housing area. The setting sun flared up in the car's windshield, its chrome bumper, a sudden explosion of orange. And just as fast, the light died, leaving behind a lavender chill. I could see then the men in the car, in full dress blue, shielded by aviator sunglasses. Buddy and I each stood at attention while the staff car crept past my house, past Buddy's house, past two other houses, and then made its wide deliberate turn into a driveway. A captain's wife and two pigtailed toddlers lived in that house.

The captain had been interviewed on CBS not two weeks ago.

I'd once calculated how long it would take a message to reach us from Vietnam. Say an hour or two for the commanding officer to get the squadron report. Another half day to confirm. (I wasn't sure about this; there was no one to ask.) Time to relay the message stateside, and get a staff car to our house. Surely they wouldn't come in the middle of the night. Add a day for decency's sake. That meant a time lag of forty-eight hours, seventy-two hours at the most. I could be reasonably certain, then, that as of the day before yesterday, my father was still alive.

"Max?" Buddy asked.

"I'm okay. You?"

"Yeah."

At my house, Buddy tossed me an offhand salute, and moved back into the night. Mother still sat on the couch. Another cigarette burned in her ashtray. The window blind behind her was bent where she'd watched the staff car pass by. Now she concentrated on her latchhook, a crimp in her forehead, her fingers tight, white, working.

I didn't look anything like her. She had thin, clear skin that stayed pale against the onslaught of the Florida sun. She'd lost weight—underneath that skin she was all angles and bones and big, waiting eyes. Her body now was spindly and graceful, reminding me of the white wisteria we'd had growing out back of our old house.

I watched the rhythm of her fingers hooking yarn and then I eased down close beside her, so close I could nearly taste the lemony scent of her lotion.

"Teach me how to do that," I said.

"It's not hard." She plucked out a mesh square and some yarn for me. She showed me how to thread the hook and knot the yarn into the mesh. After a few fumbles, I slid into the pattern: hook, knot, hook, knot. I felt the muscles in my back, the ones thumped by the pepper tree root, the ones clenched by the staff car, begin to ease.

But Mother began to grow antsy. I continued to work the latchhook while she sat beside me, crossing and uncrossing her legs, her foot bobbing up and down, her sandal flapping against her heel. Jealously, I guarded the hook, tunneled my vision to the mesh.

I wanted to ask her something. Once or twice I cleared my throat. Then I said, all in a rush, "What if...?"

She jumped up, interrupting. "What if what?" Her voice was bright and brittle as gold leaf paint. She disappeared into the kitchen, opening and closing cabinet doors. "I think I'll bake something," she called out.

Bake something? "Why?" I asked.

She answered me with a crack of eggs against a mixing bowl.

What would it mean to be pretty?

I tugged on my Joe Namath T-shirt for sleeping, examined myself in the mirrored closet door in my bedroom. I pulled the cloth tight around my body. Muscular thighs. Flat curve of hips, small rise of breasts. Mass of spongy dark hair at my shoulders. I took after my father, everyone said. Mud brown eyes. Features—nose, chin, jaw—all squared off and level. And then my unruly eyebrows, just like my father's. I ran into Mother's room and snatched tweezers off her glass-topped vanity table. Leaning close into the mirror, I plucked at the straggly hairs. It hurt in a way that felt good.

When I was done, my eyes stared wide back at me from underneath nearly naked brow bones. I sucked in my cheeks, hollowed out my face: I could see my mother in me. As I thought that, something moved in the mirror. The white moon of a face in the black window behind me. I turned around, and he was gone.

From my bedside radio, Hanoi reported four F-4 Phantoms shot down, but the U.S. command denied that report. Heavy cloud cover still prevented many take-offs. No let up in the fighting northwest of Saigon. I lay with my head on my pillow. When I turned one way, "Peace" glowed pink at me from a poster on one wall. When I twisted the other way, a poster my father had sent glowed blue—"Fly the Friendly Skies of Laos."

Callie was hopeless as a quarterback. For days on end, I stood behind her, showing her how to drop back, how to cock her arm, how to release. But even when she could produce a decent spiral, she had no control. The ball would blunder off stupidly in any direction. It wasn't a question of muscle; she seemed strong enough. And it wasn't a question of will: she wanted this.

I thought I knew why.

"Buddy doesn't care whether or not you can throw," I finally told her.

He was next door, bent under the hood of his mother's peanut-butter-colored station wagon. From the car radio, Country Joe called out the "Fish Cheer." *One, two, three, what are we fighting for? Don't ask me I don't give a damn...*

"What's Buddy got to do with it?" Callie's hair gleamed damp at her shoulders; her cheeks were flushed; her forehead glistened with sweat. Even exhausted, she was beautiful.

"Isn't he why you're here?" My voice was low, dangerous, ready to do battle. It was a Friday, and somehow it had been arranged that Callie would eat supper with us and would spend the night.

She laughed her strained, scratchy laugh. "If I wanted to be with Buddy, I'd be over there."

"Simple as that." I flipped the ball from one hand to the other. I didn't believe her. I didn't believe her presence here was so free of self-interest.

"Come on, Max." She shook her head—in pity? In disgust? "Guys are easy. Hold out your hand, they leap right in. What you do—this," she took the ball from me, "this is hard." She positioned her fingers on the laces, bit her tongue with effort.

I watched her throw, examining her form, thinking. I knew that need to have something to struggle against. It was how I kept my edges honed. But it surprised me that a big soft civilian girl like Callie would need sharp edges of her own. Her pass attempt spun crazily out into the street. Maybe, after all, those ridiculous peasant blouses did hamper her motion. Or maybe their very goofiness communicated down her arm to the ball. "Why don't you try it in one of my jerseys," I told her. "In my dresser. Get Fran Tarkenton's."

Her teeth sparkled in a huge smile. She bounced off into my house.

While she was gone, Buddy retrieved the wayward ball. He and I began to throw, immediately settling into our rhythm. Pass, catch, pass. Slap of leather. Whiff of slipstream. Trickle of sweat. Gradually I became aware of Callie, standing on the stoop, in Minnesota Vikings purple. She rocked back and forth on her heels, waiting. But inertia now held Buddy and me in its grasp.

She must have thought we'd never quit. Buddy misfired, threw one too deep, too high. I ran back for it, hearing breath gasping behind me. Purple flashed in the corner of my sight. I jumped, stretched, reached. I almost had it.

But Callie lay curled up on the grass, hugging the ball to her chest.

At first I couldn't get over the surprise of my own empty hands. And then I had to laugh at her huddled posture, her tight clamp on the ball. I nudged her hip with my foot. "You can get up now. It's yours."

Sheepish, then delighted, she spiked the ball, awkwardly, a little daintily. We'd have to work on that. Buddy came over to congratulate her.

No wonder she couldn't throw worth a damn, I thought.

The girl was born for the backfield. Underneath those bell-bottoms she had the legs of a jack rabbit. Already I was starting to work the expanded permutations of plays the three of us could run.

It had nearly escaped my attention that five o'clock had arrived. But the afternoon clouds shifted and a gray blade of light sliced through my own forgetfulness. Buddy and I paused a moment, facing west, into the setting sun. Somewhere a distant bugle blew *Retreat*. Somewhere the American flag came down.

Suppertime. Cronkite time. As we trooped home, a blue Civil Engineering truck trundled by. The orphaned family down the street had cleared quarters.

Mother had fixed hot dogs and potato chips. She, Callie, and I ate on paper plates, drank milk out of Dixie cups, watched TV. A khaki-clad reporter stood on the flight line at Da Nang. Jetwhine rose beneath him. A shark-toothed Phantom rumbled, cockpit open and waiting on the heat-glossed tarmac. The air around it rippled. Weather had cleared, the reporter said. The North Vietnamese offensive had not halted. The Air Force planned five hundred strikes a day. Heavy American air losses were likely. Such as this one near Dong Ha. And then a film clip ran. A fighter streaked low against green hillside, blue sky, erupted into orange fireball. No survivors likely, the reporter said.

There was no reason for me to feel so suddenly frozen. That wasn't my father. If it had been my father, I'd know. I'd know just by looking. But it was someone's father. Somewhere another girl saw that same clip. I could envision her. She was blonde where I was dark. She was frail where I was strong. She was different from me in every way imaginable. Never played football. Never took after her own father at all. Even if now she choked on a jagged shard of potato chip the way I did. Felt her lungs lock into cold iron the way mine did. Felt her blood slow blue beneath her skin. All this she did with much better reason than I had.

And then a flight-suited pilot with a thick, black mustache walked over to the reporter. The caption identified him as Lieutenant Colonel Robert "Bud" Skinner.

I stood up, aghast. "That's Buddy's father." Swift tears spilled down my face, though I didn't feel I was crying. I wasn't sobbing. The tears seemed to spring from their own source, separate from me.

Over and over, all I could think was *thank God, not my father*.

"It doesn't mean anything," Mother whispered. "It's just superstition."

Callie chattered away, oblivious. "He looks just like him." She said something stupid about the mustache.

I hated her. I had to pinch my own skin white to keep from slapping her. She didn't understand. She would never understand. Muscle thrummed in my arms, my shoulders. I could topple her right over. I could smash her. I could do anything, and she would not be able to resist.

But Colonel Skinner was speaking.

"Shut up, Callie," I said.

"What else can we do? This is our duty." Colonel Skinner ran a hand through his black hair, low on his forehead like Buddy's. "You go up there, do what you have to do, you get home." Helmet under his arm, he strode like a giant in seven-league boots across the tarmac to the impatient Phantom.

The news switched over to commercial.

"I'm going to Buddy's," I said.

Everything inside me was jumbled. Fear and hope. Pain and pride. Excitement and agony. We had to throw the ball. Buddy and I had to play. Only the ball would hypnotize time.

But Mother stopped me. "Leave them alone for now." She busied herself with her latchhook, lit a cigarette.

I stood a moment, jangling, uncertain.

"Come on, Max," Callie said. Her voice was calm, subdued, but firm. Obedient, I followed her into my room, where she rustled through her flowered straw bag for a tissue. "You need to clean up a bit." In the mirror, runnels of dirt streaked my face. Callie pulled out a tiny jar of cream. "Sit down," she said. "I'll do it."

All my fight, all my will, had locked up into that frozen iron weight inside me. I sat stiff and square on the bed.

Callie fluttered around me, dabbing cream on my face, stroking me with tissue. The cream had the pungent, oily smell of dead flowers.

"Close your eyes," she ordered, and I obeyed.

I heard rummaging sounds, popping, snapping. Something tickled my eyelid and I flinched.

"Did you know your eyes have a slight tilt to them? At the edges?"

I shook my head.

"Keep still. I'll show you."

Protest only flickered and died. I felt a slight curiosity. But more than that, I was seduced by simple touch. As she worked, she hummed. A tuneless buzz that meant nothing. I felt myself melting into that nothing noise, into blank dark. Thought evaporated. It was like sleep, without dreams.

Her voice, when she'd finished, startled me. I was ready to view.

At first I nearly shrieked. Who was I? Painted. Disguised. But horror rapidly gave way to amazement. This new person in the mirror, this was still me. Callie had done something, though, to my eyes, to my cheeks. I glowed, dark and golden. I was exotic, elusive. Female.

"Now here," Callie said, holding out her peasant blouse. "Put this on."

She stretched the elastic neckline to bare both my shoulders and then studied me. "I think in your last life you were a gypsy," she finally said.

I completely dissolved. That cold iron in my chest now ran hot and molten.

I had to go find Buddy.

Mother had fallen asleep on the couch, a cigarette burning in her ashtray. I stubbed it out before stepping outside. Black night had fallen. The air smelled of salt and jasmine. Dead fish. A lush whiff of gardenia. A fat, full moon cast odd, eerie shadows around the jungle vines and hibiscus.

Buddy sat on the stoop in front of his house. From somewhere he'd amassed a small heap of pebbles, and one by one, he pitched them into an oleander shrub.

"I thought I saw a snake in there," he said. "Coral snake, maybe. Or moccasin."

"Probably just a garter snake," I said.

Pebble after pebble thwacked into the bush. I had never felt so awkward with him before. The make-up, the blouse, my bare shoulders—all this made me hesitate. Where before I would have sat down beside him, would have thrown pebbles with him, would have known what to say about his father, now I had to wait for him to notice me. Without a football, my hands were nervous. One by one I popped my knuckles.

Callie jumped right into the silence. "We saw your father on TV," she said. She said this with an awestruck, envious tone. Proving that she would never be like us.

"Want to throw some ball, Buddy?" I asked, my voice low and quiet.

But Callie kept on in her eager, chattering tone. "When's he coming home?" she asked.

Buddy sighed. "Supposed to be August." He stood and kicked his pebbles into the dirt. He nodded down the street to the empty house. "C.E. left a light on over there."

The house and lawn in front were dark, except for one square pane of yellow light on the thick Bermuda grass.

"We should turn it off," Buddy said.

"It'll burn itself out eventually," I said, shaking back my hair. He still hadn't noticed this different me. I was acutely conscious of the tickles of a faint sea breeze chilly on my bare shoulders. I felt half-naked. But only half-embarrassed.

Buddy just continued to stare at that yellow glow. His forehead knotted fierce and blue under the thin moonlight. "It's such a waste, though. I think it's our duty to turn it out."

"Can't you just call someone?" Callie asked.

Buddy's expression was flat, impassive. "But we're here now." He set off across the lawns, dismissing Callie, dismissing me.

Whatever he was going to do, I had to do with him. We survived together. "Wait," I called out, following him. I didn't hear Callie behind me, didn't know if she followed or not. Didn't care. Toad song, as we neared the empty house, fell silent.

Buddy rattled the doorknob. "Locked." He moved around to the carport, to the kitchen door. Also locked. He scooped up a rock, winked at me. "Government issue," he said, his voice ironic, bleak. Then he slammed the rock into the kitchen window. He reached through jagged glass to unlock the door.

I knew I shouldn't break into this house with Buddy. I knew there would be costs. There would be penalties. But I couldn't not follow him.

The house was as dark and dank as a cavern. We moved through the kitchen to the empty living room. Bare plaster walls, bare cement floor. Our breathing, our pulses, our nerve endings flickered around the silent room.

Buddy stood faintly silhouetted by ghostly moonlight falling in through the blank picture window. Beyond the glass, I saw shadows of movement, a person, an animal, maybe only the wind-ruffled frond of a palm tree. I couldn't say.

A closed door at the end of the narrow hallway hid the light that had drawn us. But Buddy made no move in that direction. Instead we both stood watching the shadows outside, suddenly comfortable in the dark, in the silence.

Buddy's voice, when he spoke, was so quiet, so tentative, I had to twist my ear toward him to hear clearly. "He didn't have to go, Max."

The faint sound vibrated the air. I could almost see the ripples his words cast dilate out into the beyond.

"He said it was his duty. But he'd already been there once before. He didn't have to go again."

I swallowed hard. I didn't know how to answer him.

Buddy looked at me, then, and in the hurt in his eyes I saw the boy he still partly was. "What about his duty to us?"

"That's not the choice." My voice was sharp, loud. Echoes bounced off the walls. What Buddy was saying— this wasn't to talk about. Some things would always out-rank us. My father had said the same thing. It was his duty to go.

But Buddy kept on talking, with a firmness now, a square line of determination at his jaw. "Part of me, though—a small part, but real—hates him for going. He should just quit and fly home. He should say, it's a stupid, ugly war, and I don't want to play anymore."

I could so easily see it. A full formation of Phantoms, headed north, suddenly veering east, into the sun, light glinting off steel, blue Pacific below.

The hope itself felt like treason.

"Stop it, Buddy."

But he kept talking, saying words I didn't want to hear. "Nothing will ever be the same again, and for what?" He nearly shouted, "For what?"

Echoes clanged and clashed and rioted in my brain. "Shut up," I said, clamping my hands over my ears. "Stop!"

But his mouth kept moving.

"Buddy, stop!"

I grabbed his face. To quiet him, to still that mouth, I kissed him. He made one small sound of surprise and then, silence. Slowly, the room settled back into a comforting dark stillness. He tasted of corn chips and toothpaste. And in the quiet I heard something new, an energy crackling between us. Light. Voltage. Phosphorescence. He pressed the whole length of his body to me. It shouldn't have seemed strange after all the tackles we'd shared, but it did.

His hands traced the fall of hair on my face, the bare flesh at my shoulders. "Max." He whispered my name like a prayer. This time he kissed me. He held onto me as if I could save him.

But I could still hear the faintest echo of his words receding. Nothing would ever be the same again. This new me, with Buddy this new way—we would never be able to play ball quite the same way again. We would never be able to allow inertia alone to hold us. We would be different people, in a different country. I would no longer be the daughter my father had left. I would no longer be the quarterback he coached so well.

And if I wasn't that girl, how would he be able to return? How would things for us ever be the same again?

Would he even be able to find his way home again?

Buddy and I were on the floor. My kissing became biting. I nipped at his cheeks, at his throat. Fierce at his flesh. I would never watch the news again. I would not count the downed fliers listed on the radio. I sat up and smeared my hands over my eyes, my cheeks. I scrubbed away at Callie's makeup. I could not yet let myself be this woman. It was all I could offer up in a prayer for my father: my own childhood. Small, but all I had.

Buddy would have to find his own prayer.

He was making small sounds now, like whimpers.

Callie's voice rang loud and sharp in the empty room. "You're hurting him!" She tugged me away from Buddy, helped him sit, and touched with her soft fingers the places I'd torn.

I left the two of them alone and went back out into the night.

Outside, I was instantly swamped by scent. Wave after wave of lush, florid scent. Callie must have stripped every plant on the block. On the lawn, in front of this dead house, she'd piled a huge mound of blossoms. Geraniums, jasmine, hibiscus, sheaves of bougainvillea, gardenias, oleander. A magnificent jumble of color and scent and life.

Yellow light spilled out around the mound. After everything, Buddy and I had left that one light on, still burning in the window.

I reached into the mass of flowers and plucked up a gardenia. It would be brown by morning, but right now it smelled so rich I wanted to eat it. Instead, I tucked it into the neckline of my blouse.

Behind me, Callie and Buddy appeared, holding hands. She had slid a yellow hibiscus into her golden hair. Buddy reached into the mound and picked up a white rose. He twisted it in his fingers, uncertain, and then tucked it behind his ear, too. "Ouch," he said. "Thorns." He squeezed a tiny slice on his finger and one perfect bead of blood appeared.

Under the streetlight on the way back to my house, Callie stopped me. "You should see yourself, you're a mess." She wiped mascara from under my eyes with her thumb.

Looking at Callie, still wearing Fran Tarkenton's jersey, it occurred to me that I would miss her.

At home, Mother had awakened. She sat in the dark, curled up on the couch under the window, the radio on. All I could see of her was the glow of her cigarette and the long line of moonlight on her shin. "You girls having fun?" she asked.

She turned back to the news without waiting for our answer.

Burning Desire

I have a fondness for silk. Red, royal blue, deep green. Colors that catch fire. But I don't buy silk—I steal it. Macy's, Saks, the Emporium. I visit one or the other on Mondays—my nights out for shopping. Shoplifting. Stealing is my main dishonesty.

Stealing is easy. Glide into Macy's in a Tahari suit and pearl earrings, flash the clerk your best credit card smile. It's eight-thirty and she's tired, she's ready to go home. "Just looking," you say, and she nods. She massages one foot. You slip a blouse off the rack and into the dressing room. The blouse is a little tight, the buttons strain. Motherhood has left you with a certain robustness of figure, but you don't mind. Ripe is how you'd describe yourself. You pull a seam ripper from your shopping bag. Silk is so delicate; they always punch the magnetic security tag through a seam. Rip out three, four inches of sideseam and drop the tag on the floor. Later, in the shop, you can whipstitch the gap. Glide back out the dressing room. The clerk thumbs through dollar bills, counting the take, none of it hers. "No luck," you call out, breaking her concentration. She starts counting all over again. She doesn't even notice the green silk shimmer in your bag.

Afterwards, stop at one of the hotel bars on Union Square. Lean back against black leather and cross your legs. Your stockings make a shushing sound. The Tahari slit skirt drapes. Order a Tanqueray rocks. Just one. Your glass leaves a wet ring on the pink tablecloth. Stir the lime and gin with your finger and then stick your finger in your mouth. The gin brings a flush to your chest. At the next table, gray-suited businessmen busily conduct business. Notice one in particular, in gray glen plaid, his finger tracing his own round, wet stain on the tablecloth. If you were more courageous, or more honest, you'd buy him a drink.

At home, Miles has cooked. The kitchen smells of onion. There is a meatloaf in the oven and a pot of red potatoes on the stove. He has cleaned; the cracked yellow countertop does its best to gleam. I check on the baby and find her asleep in the crib under dim light and the velvet patchwork I stitched for her using remnants left after making thirty cloaks for *Joan of Arc*. It makes me smile to think of the baby sleeping under a saint's cloth.

Miles is proud of his domestic efforts. He brings dinner to the table with a smile and a flourish. Twin dimples wink at either side of his mouth. But lately those dimples irritate me—they seem overdone in a face already too milky clean and eager. He lights two candles before telling me about New York. "That idiot Brookman really screwed up," he says. He cuts his meatloaf into perfect squares and eats the squares one at a time. "The data's so wrecked no one can get a P&L out of there." He chews and swallows and a small roll of fat, of success, bulges above his collar. "They need me in New York on Sunday, I'll be back Friday night."

I think then: New York, the Met, Fifth Avenue. I've never been to New York. The blue heart of the candle flame flickers once, then beats again, steady. Miles says, "But I'll have to leave again the following Sunday, spend maybe four weeks there total to get this thing straightened out."

I wonder then, is he having an affair? Is there a Kimberly or a Jennifer in New York? But no. Our marriage doesn't yet have the cracks that let another inside.

His dimples flash. "If I solve this thing, it'll mean a promotion. We can buy a house."

"I don't want a house."

Miles reminds me why need to move. Schools, crime, rent, taxes, schools. The baby's not even a year old and already he frets about SAT scores. But I love life in the city for all the things that can't be tested: light, color, sound.

"You'll love it," Miles says. "We'll have one bathroom each and a lawn and we'll grow tomatoes."

"I hate tomatoes." I shove my chair back and carry the dishes into the kitchen.

Miles follows me. He leans against my back where I stand at the sink, scraping meatloaf into the disposal. He lifts the hair off my neck and I feel the barest scratch of beard behind my ear. His hands trace my shoulders and then down my rib cage, my hips. A tiny flare of heat shoots from my belly to my knees. "Annie," he says, his voice thick. "You love tomatoes."

And in this he is right. I do.

I love Miles too. I love the baby. I'm just not sure I love myself with them.

Sunday, I help Miles pack. New York would be cool; back East, leaves were already crisping to October red. I lay out a blue pinstripe and a gray flannel, plus assorted white shirts. A maroon and gold rep tie, a bluish paisley, and a black-and-white fleck. White polo shirt and green cotton sweater. Khaki slacks. Black lace-ups, white Nikes. Jockey shorts, T-shirts, black socks, white socks. Toothpaste, deodorant, aftershave.

The taxi honks in the drive and I walk the baby out to wave good-bye. As the taxi pulls away, Miles asks to be sure to get to the cleaners. My fingers clench around the key in the front door. He didn't have to remind me. I visit the cleaners every Monday.

Monday morning is crazy at the shop. Dozens of supers

mill around, waiting to be fitted out as chess pieces for *Rigoletto*. The silver tissue I work slides around the needle. The queen balks at the weight of her crown. Henryk, our lead designer, says he's sure I can reconstruct it. Henryk has a hawkish face and a tan he attributes to good scotch and high blood pressure. He rolls his eyes at the queen. "Can't have any divas toppling over." He winks and moves on. I rip velvet off the crown and prune away at its superstructure. Later, I find that the knight's tail is too long and the hooves are sewn backwards. When Henryk again passes by my table, I rest my needle to wonder if his tan truly seeps from within, or if there is a strip of blue-veined white flesh at his hips. Noon interrupts my imaginings. I throw my apron off, grab up a garment bag I brought specially for today, and change out of my jeans into nylons and a red dress.

The day is gorgeous, the sun hanging low, fat, orange, filling the sky with brittle light like gold leaf paint. I walk with a looseness at my hips, a roll in my gait. Because the day is so beautiful, I feel adventurous and so I pass by Macy's and cross Market Street and move with the noon-time crowd up the escalators to Nordstrom. I shiver a bit on the ride up. The silk supply will be better, but the risk will be greater.

And sure enough, as soon as I step off the escalator, I know I've made a mistake. A black-clad saleswoman sails toward me. Gold half-glasses dangle from a chain out over the prow of her breasts. "May I help you find somezing?"

"Just looking," I say. But she is French and suspicious, or French and eager for her commission. Either way, she steams behind me from rack to rack, plucking out blouses, sweaters, a plum rayon dress, all for my approval.

"I'm not sure what I want," I tell her, and she frowns. I want something mine alone. I want something that when I wear it will transform me. I want trombones and neon lights and nights that never end.

"Is it for somezing special?"

I shake my head. "There's no occasion." She tilts her head as if she doesn't quite comprehend and I find myself waving my hands about, speaking too loud. "There's no reason. Nothing! Nothing at all!"

We have attracted attention. A smaller, blonder saleswoman glides over. "Is there a problem?" I feel the hot eyes of fifty other shoppers on me. The pale wood aisleway is lit too brightly.

"I was just trying to explain that I'm not shopping for any particular occasion." I back away. My skin is too hot under the glare of eyes and lights. I am breathing too fast and stammering. "Does there have to be a reason? Can't I just want something?"

The blonde salesclerk speaks in soothing tones—she's about to call security, I think. "Of course," she says. "Look around. We're only here to help you with whatever you need."

I need to steal something! I need to walk out with a secret shimmer of silk under my arm. I need to buy myself a Tanqueray rocks and feel that flush bloom between my breasts. "I don't need anything," is what I actually say. I ride back down the escalators and out into the burning afternoon. The sidewalks are too white. The orange sun is no longer fat and ripe and promising—the air is just hot and stifling.

That evening, I pick up the baby from day care and stop at the cleaners. Pile the dirty things on the counter. Point out the shirts needing new collar buttons. The sweaty-faced kid in blue jeans flips the receipt across. He and I both know I'll lose it before the next time I come in. I hoist the clean things all on hangers one-handed. I mash the baby in tight against my side with the other hand. The hangers pinch my skin white, then blue.

In the kitchen, the baby smears carrots into her hair. We

play patty-cake games. I wash the carrots out in the bath. I put her to bed. It's only eight-thirty. I pace the apartment. The walls lean inward and squeeze out the oxygen. I open the kitchen window and look out at the diamond city shimmer. Red taillights streak the streets. I hear brakes squeal, laughter. The night is warm. Macy's is still open. Party chatter swirls up toward me from a garden below. I envision myself soaring out the open kitchen window, down into the party, a silk dress on, a glass of gin in my hand. Miles is probably out having a dinner and show in New York on Brookman's expense account.

Then I remember I left the cleaning in the car. I check the baby's snuffling sleep and go down to bring up the clothes. I hang them in the bedroom closet and strip the plastic sheath off Miles' suits, my silk blouses. Just as I wad the plastic into the trash, I catch the warning: Dangerous to Small Children. Instantly, I have a horrifying vision of the baby's head wrapped in plastic, her blue lips drawing clear film into her mouth. Panic stops my own breath. I think, I have to burn this. I carry the sheath into the kitchen and hang it from the rod over the stove, where I hang my pots and pans. I rummage in a drawer for a book of matches.

Plastic melts while it burns. Zzt, zzt, zzt, tiny flaming darts of plastic shoot out. The smell of burning polymer makes you think of napalm. A war in miniature. Fire rains down onto the linoleum. You breathe deep, inhaling oily smoke. After the bag is gone, you want another.

Miles returns on Friday. On Saturday, we drive across the bay to a good school district and look at model houses. They are all decorated in the pale nothing colors I despise. When I point out a particularly banal mauve sofa, Miles becomes irritated. "We aren't buying the sofa, just the house." But I don't want a house that fits a mauve sofa.

We get lost driving through curving streets that meander 'round and 'round and then dead-end into cul-de-sacs. My life, I think. A series of nondecisions that one by one have led me to these bleached out hills that are still and dry, where nothing moves.

We drive back across the bridge. City fog smacks us with a big wet kiss. I touch Miles's knee. "Let's not buy a house," I say. "Let's do something crazy with the money instead. Let's dress up and go to the opera. In Paris. Let's take all the money to Las Vegas and wear sequin everything."

Miles looks over at me, grins, raises one eyebrow. "Everything?" He lifts my hand off his knee, squeezes it, and then grabs hold of the gearshift to downshift off the freeway. He doesn't speak again until he's angled into a parking space near our apartment. "Look, I promise one day I'll take you to Paris. But sequins, I don't know. I think they'd itch."

Upstairs in the apartment, I put the baby down for a nap. Asleep, she is pink and damp and tousled. Charming. Miles stands beside me, watching her. I sigh.

"What?" he asks.

"I'm losing myself," I whisper.

He folds his arms around me and I lean back into him. "I've got you," he says.

Sunday, Miles repacks his suitcase. He dumps last week's dirty shirts into the dry cleaning basket. He asks me to take his gray flannel in also. Monday I visit the cleaners again. All week I'd remembered that napalm smell. I rush the baby through her dinner and her bath and into bed. Then I tear the plastic sheath from the clean clothes.

Plastic burns too fast. Zzt, zzt, the bag is burned, the smoke is fading, the smell drifting away. You wait all week and now again you are dissatisfied. You itch with frustration. You don't have another bag.

A shirt? Could you? The thought makes you giggle. You tiptoe into Miles's closet. You choose one with brand new collar buttons. You hang it from the rod in the kitchen and it twists slowly in the draft sliding in around the window. It looks too white, the perfect white of milk and television. No one is there to watch you, but still you close the kitchen blinds. You strike a match, and still you hesitate. Part of you is horrified. Part of you is thrilled. The horrified part of you trembles, but the thrilled part of you holds the match to the shirttail.

Cotton burns nice and slow, with a woodsy odor. Flames crawl up the white shirt, strangling it. Plastic buttons snap as they melt. You think about forest fires and small animals fleeing. Fire eats all the air in the kitchen. You're sucked into vacuum. Your veins rise electric and spark blue off the surface of your skin. Hot jolts of red desire streak down your belly to your knees. By the time the shirt is gone the ceiling is stained black.

You burn a shirt a night until Friday.

But before Miles comes home, you up-end the mop and scrub the latex ceiling. Don't let him know.

Sunday morning Miles wants only to stretch out on the couch and watch football. I bundle the baby over to the sandbox. Then we stand in line at Safeway for Cheerios and beer. I can't wait for the weekend to end.

When Miles packs, he misses his shirts. "I don't think I'm getting them all back from the cleaners," he says. "I wish you'd keep better track of those receipts." He empties out my purse and then suggests I reserve the inside zippered compartment for his cleaning slips. His fingers probing, rearranging, taking possession of my purse, enrage me. I can barely speak, only nod, when he asks me to stop into Macy's and buy more shirts for him.

Monday at lunch, I buy five white shirts with extra long tails. Then I steal a silver silk blouse for myself. The silk blouse I repair at the shop, and then I slip it on over my jeans. When Henryk stops by my table, he fingers the silk at my shoulder. "Nice," he breathes. His suede jacket gives off a faint steam, like a lathered horse. I look up at him, certain that the flesh at his hips must be pale and tender, and I smile.

After work I stop at the cleaners to pick up Miles's gray flannel suit.

At home, I feed the baby rice cereal and peas. I think about the slide of plastic over that gray flannel. Just the one, I think. I giggle. The baby thinks this is a new game. She giggles back at me. We smile foolish smiles at each other. I bathe her, soaping cereal out of her hair, and still we giggle together. I put her to bed in the crib, covering her in velvet, and then I sit in the rocking chair and hum Brahms until her giggling subsides into snuffling baby snores.

Just one, I think.

I sneak into the closet and lift out the suit. I carry it to the kitchen and hang it from the rod. It hangs heavy, motionless. I press my face into the cloth. I smell the shadow of Miles's musk deodorant in the armpit. I smell a layer of cleaning fluid. I smell Miles' own smell in the crotch. The suit smells like kerosene and sex.

Wool burns slow and smoky. You close the kitchen door so the alarm won't go off. Flames creep along pant leg to coat pocket to sleeve and lapel. The lining doesn't burn; it melts—obviously polyester blend. The suit spins and twists as the flame eats the wool and the lining knots in on itself. It smells like barbecue. Like meat. Like something dead.

When it's all over, oily ash covers the yellow countertops.

The suit lining clots in a bubbling pool on the linoleum. The black ceiling stain spreads smoky arms down the walls. You don't feel lit with fire at all, this time. This time, you feel extinguished. How can he not see? How can you not tell him?

All week I avoid the kitchen. The black oily ooze on the floor shames me. I feed the baby in her bedroom, bathe her, put her to bed. I order take-out to eat in my room. Friday I put on my best red silk blouse. I step into matching red heels. I ask Henryk out for a drink, and then I pick up the baby at day care and drive downtown to the restaurant Henryk picked.

Blonde wood, brass rails, too many ferns. The yellow light accents Henryk's tan. I slide into a booth across from him, the baby in her car seat beside me. He's already ordered me a gin-and-lime and it sits waiting, small drops sliding down the side of the glass. We talk. We talk about opera, we talk about velvet, we talk about Paris. We talk about everything but what we talk about, which is the way my nipples are brushing my red silk blouse, the way one black hair curls at his throat, the way his chest narrows down to warm, white flesh at his hips.

Drink becomes dinner. The waiter is harried, taking our order, whisking away, his quick steps whispering a hundred tasks. Kitchen clatter rings out. The baby pounds her spoon on the table in tune. Henryk and I order rack of lamb, rare. I feed the baby carrots and she spits them out. Henryk orders two glasses of red. Mine has a bit of cork floating in it. I send it back. We eat the lamb slowly. The waiter brings the leather folder with the check. I wink at Henryk. "Meet me outside," I tell him.

Henryk leans across the table, grabs my hands in his. "You're crazy."

"I am. I'm absolutely crazy."

He slides out of the booth while I open the folder, examine the bill, look for the waiter. The waiter is nowhere. I shove the bill away, hoist the baby from the booth, carry her outside, and then Henryk and I dash down the block and around the corner. Under the yellow streetlight, needles of fog rain down on us. I lean back against brick and he kisses me, and then he leaves me breathless from the run.

At home I settle the baby into bed. I hear Miles's key in the door. He throws his suitcase on the bed and begins unpacking, chattering about Brookman and New York and databases. I stare at him, his mouth working, spinning out words upon words upon words He heaps his toothpaste and deodorant and aftershave on the bed, and I watch his arms move, how they are seamed at the shoulders, how his wrists stretch out pale and blue from white cuffs, I see the hairs on the back of his hands weave in and out of the herringbone sleeve, I touch the spidery threads of vein in his palms.

Skin doesn't burn easily. It needs an accelerant. You pick up the aftershave.

Miles pulls something out of the bag. "Look what I found at Bloomingdale's," he says. He lifts up a blue silk chemise by the spaghetti straps. "And these." He holds a matching pair of silk boxers against himself. He does a little jig, and all of a sudden you laugh. You remember why you loved him in the first place. He lays the silk things on the bed, tosses his suitcase off. "I'll get us some wine," he says.

"I'll get it," you say. You feel uneasy about the mess congealing in the kitchen. You have things to tell him. But not yet.

You take the chemise into the bathroom and change into it. Then you uncork a bottle of pinot noir in the kitchen and close the door behind you. When you return to the bedroom the lights are off. Miles lies waiting on the bed. A candle burns on the nightstand behind him. Small illuminations dance in the folds of his blue, silk shorts. You set the wine beside the candle. You climb onto the bed. As you slide the blue silk up your thighs and straddle his hips, the candlelight flickers. A small blue flame of sadness burns low in your heart. You lean over, tracing the bones of his brow, the blue shadow of beard, the blue beating hollow at the base of his throat. You know that, very soon, you will be honest enough, and courageous enough, to hurt him.

Christmas Bombings, 1972

Time hung for that instant Max plummeted from the second story window. She was weightless, without gravity, without mass. She was pure light—a red flare lit by a frozen moon. She wore a red harem costume, veils, bare torso, bare shoulders. Gold coins glinted at her wrists and ankles. She had just turned sixteen. She landed in a thick drift of snow.

It was late. It was November. No one noticed her fall. Wind scraped scattered leaflets from the day's antiwar protests across the icy Berlin square. Slogans screamed up from the sidewalk: U.S. out of Vietnam. Amerika Go Home. Red Army Faction fists, clenched.

Light-footed, barefooted, Max ran along the Eisenhowerstrasse, the broad boulevard at the heart of the American army post, Berlin Brigade. Past the muscular marble HQ building which had once been Hitler's and was now topped by a perpetually lit American flag. Past the low-slung brickwork PX complex, closed now. Toward the three-story dormitory buildings that made up Patton Barracks. Few cars shushed along the black, wet streets. In the armored division lot across from the barracks, tanks rumbled and jumbled and jockeyed for position, an elephantine dance under brilliant, white light. A stone wall topped with razor wire fenced the perimeter of the barracks. Parked in front was a red Porsche. Running past it, Max still had time to appreciate the car. It was exactly what she'd want to drive, if only she knew how. As she approached the tin-roofed guard shack, she slowed to a loose-hipped belly dancer's walk.

Max was thirsty. At least, thirst was a want she could put a name to. Electricity sparked along her nerves, tightened her tendons, lifted the small hairs on her arms and thighs. The open window over the steamy radiator. The tidal pull of the frozen moon. The chill breath of night air on flesh. Max just wanted.

Dress rehearsal for a USO production of *Man of La Mancha*, Max a Moorish dancer. Not truly a dancer and certainly not Moorish, but an air force colonel's daughter with a lithe grace and long, willowy fingers and small, precise feet. A tangle of dark hair down her back. With lots of eyeliner and mascara, Moorish enough.

She moved every other year or so. Every other year or so her father marched into the kitchen with a map. His thick, black flying boots would mark the linoleum, the hundred different zippers on his flight suit would jingle, and his dog tags would clank around his neck as he sat down, pulled the kitchen table to him, and unfolded to Max the place she'd live next. Her friends moved, too. Often. Every other month or so a moving van would lumber up and neighbors would carry out dining chairs and twin beds and drive off to wherever they'd live next. Max had learned to say goodbye as fast as she said hello. Her mother was chipper about this. She assured Max that she was learning a skill; she would always know how to make friends. But even better, Max knew she would lose them.

Already she'd lived in ten different places, been ten different people. She'd been a small bully in Kansas, and a pixie in North Carolina, found Jesus in the California desert then lost him in Texas where she acquired an accent she got rid of in Colorado where she learned to snow ski which did her no good at all in Florida where she'd spent weekends alternately throwing a football and combing the beach for starfish while she combed lemon juice through her hair trying to make herself a blonde. Which hadn't worked.

It had been only three months since the air force had shipped her, the smallest and lightest of household goods permitted an officer, overseas. She had yet to know how this new place would define her.

The barracks guard wore a field jacket over fatigues and bounced up and down, little tenuous forbidden hops to keep warm. He was barely older than Max. Army rather than air force—which meant he wasn't too bright. An E-2 with hillbilly freckles and a pimple on his chin.

But still, the M-16 slung over his shoulder. The .38 at his waist.

As a child, she'd played with old parachutes, empty ammo cans, C-rations, shell casings, discarded helmets, squadron patches, rank insignia. In her father's closet, behind musty smelling flight suits and a jumble of combat boots, she'd found a box he'd brought back from Vietnam containing other things: a shard of blackened, lacy steel; a Colt .45, not loaded; a Khmer-English phrasebook; a cockroach husk the size of her thumb; a copy of Chairman Mao's *Little Red Book*. Power comes from the barrel of a gun. Max believed this to be true.

Ten thousand men, all of them armed. Weaponry, equipment clanking at their belts.

And Max.

Who was she? This unarmed person.

Moving among these ten thousand armed men, she drew eyes like artillery fire. The constant gaze vaporized her. Turned her into pure heat and light. White phosphorus.

Which, she was only beginning to learn, was also a kind of weapon.

She moved to the guard with such slow grace she hardly felt her feet touching the icy asphalt. "Hey, soldier," she said. In broad parody. Yet under the parody, a seriousness of intent. "Got a Coke machine in there?"

"You can't go inside, miss."

Thin, elusive, Max tried to duck around him.

Heavy boots clattered on the pavement. The guard stood in front of her, the M-16 a shield and a challenge between them. They were so close Max could smell cold sweat on him and underneath that, starch and soap and bad coffee. Cold seared her feet, and she willed herself to ignore it.

"If you don't stop, I'll have to call the M.P.s," he said.

Max ran a finger down the barrel of the M-16. "Or you could just shoot me."

He jerked away. "Don't touch the weapon!"

But his voice broke when he said weapon, and Max laughed.

"What's your name, soldier?"

"Holloway, miss."

But Max could see that spelled out across his field jacket. "I mean your first name."

"Willdy."

Max wrapped her whole hand around the barrel of the gun. Wondering if she yanked hard enough, if she were strong enough, she could take it. Knowing at the same time that it was yet too much for her. With her other hand she stroked his cheek. "Please, Willdy. Thirty seconds only. I'm dying of thirst. You don't want me dying, do you?"

She knew that what he didn't want was to be caught fooling around with a girl while standing guard.

He blew out a sigh, exasperated. "Okay. Make it quick, though."

"You're a sweetheart." Max brushed a veil back over her shoulder and scampered down the white sidewalk to the double glass doors leading into Building A.

Inside the barracks, electric guitar blared from a distant

radio. Max followed the sound down a linoleum-tiled corridor to a rec room where a dozen or so G.I.s lounged on
white, plastic chairs in fatigues, in T-shirts and boxers, in
blue jeans playing cards, paging through the *Stars and
Stripes*, or just sitting, laughing, boasting.

Max stopped at the threshold. In one instant, sound,
movement, breathing, gathered force. Fluorescent light
buzzed overhead. Then a tidal surge of noise crested.
Faltering, her veils askew, Max hesitated.

But she moved within the invisible shield of her father's
rank. Within the invisible shield of her own otherness. She
parted her way through sound. "Don't mind me. I just
came for a Coke," she said. At the same time, she felt her
own surge of power as they looked at her and did not move.

Then one man, a four-striper in fatigues, detached himself
from a group playing poker. "Your toes are getting frostbit."

Startled, Max halted six paces from the Coke machine,
looked down at her feet. "I don't feel anything."

He half-smiled. "That's one clue. Also, they look like
radishes."

Before she could truly consider that, he scooped her up,
one arm around her waist, and dropped her onto a couch,
a battered, tweedy thing that scraped her skin.

"What the hell are you doing?" Max cried out.

He knelt in front of her, unbuttoned his shirt. "Skin to
skin contact. The cure for frostbite. It's how we do it in survival school." He was matter-of-fact in his speech, with just
the trace of an accent. From the south, but away from there
a while. Underneath his opened shirt his chest was lean,
muscular, furred with blue-black hair, swooping down into
concavity. Dog tags clanked around his neck. He tucked
Max's feet up under his arms, against the walls of his chest.

Max wriggled. "Do you know who I am?"

His arms locked solid. "Oh, I have a pretty good idea."

The way he said that, as if he might know more about her than she did herself, made Max stop wriggling and study him.

He must have once had the kind of firm, flat face of a recruiting poster. His head was all squared-off corners. Blue-black hair in a buzz cut; the first etchings of horizontal lines across his forehead; slightly protruding brow bone; flat nose; flat, sexless mouth.

But he'd smudged. The outer corners of his eyes drooped downward, a geological shift in the plates of his skull, brought about by heat, by pressure, by gravity. The brown of his eyes was luminescent, velvety, and yet impenetrable, like the tiger's eye gemstone Max wore in a silver ring her father had brought back for her from Vietnam. On the left side of his face, a scar seared a line from temple to jaw.

Tiny jots of voltage began to shoot through Max's toes. "Ouch! That hurts."

"I know."

"Let me go." She tried to wriggle free, feeling trapped as a small animal in a snare. "I don't have frostbite."

"You willing to bet these toes on that?" Max stopped fighting and simply glared. For one moment, she was willing to bet anything, everything, just to best him.

The pain in her toes flamed into orange darts. She arched her back, cried out. His hold on her remained locked solid, frozen as stone. His flat expression never changed. Hot pain flared white. Max crumpled. Betrayed by her own body, she had no choice but to give herself up to the exquisite agony of her flesh coming to life.

That was how she met Hudson.

That was how she decided that what she wanted was Hudson.

Through all the years of moving about, there had always been one constant. The waiting. The waiting, waiting,

waiting for Vietnam. The orders that never came, or came and were changed at the last minute. All the fathers on all the bases received their orders. The fathers left, some returned, some didn't. Then it had happened to Max. Her father had gone. She had waited. They had survived. The war would end, eventually. Now what?

Max sent Hudson tickets to the performance. To watch her dance around Don Quixote and steal from his helmet, his sword, his gold. The play ran four nights. The first three nights, while on stage, she peered into the fuzzy black beyond the footlights, searching for him. On the fourth night, she was certain of him. A deeper blackness in one section of the theater. A place where light flipped inside out. He didn't speak to her, before or after the play. But at the final curtain, a hollow-boned boy in sweater and jeans—Willdy, she recognized—brought her a small bunch of radishes, tied with a red ribbon.

Hudson worked seven days on, three off. His field specialty was demolitions. He was kept busy defusing Red Army Faction bomb threats. Demolitions work was how his face had gotten scarred, he said. A little mishap in Chu Lai. He wasn't any more forthcoming than that.

But Max was used to silence around the war. In her house, Vietnam did not exist. The year, the years, of waiting—no one talked about it. There were things Max wanted to know: what was it like? But she didn't want description; she didn't want a calendar of events. She wanted to know: what was it like in the gut? And in smaller words, she wanted to know: *how could you? Why did you?*

On Hudson's days off, he'd meet Max after school. They'd walk in the Grunewald through the cold, dank forest along ancient snowy paths, and Hudson would tell her about his home. He liked telling her about his home because of the way she listened: with curiosity, with amazement. Hudsonville, Alabama. Named for his family. Everyone related to Hudson lived in Hudsonville—grandparents, great-grandparents, aunts, uncles, cousins, second cousins. It confounded Max to imagine all those people remaining in place. They went to the same church, worked at the cannery or the mill or sold shoes to each other. Hudson was the only one who'd ever left, and all he wanted now was to get back. Back to the world, he said.

Which intrigued Max. For her, *this* was the world.

They'd finish their walks wet to the knees with snow, their fingertips, noses, and cheeks aching with cold. Max would reach up, touch his face. "Getting frostbit yet? Need some skin-to-skin contact?"

He'd gently push her hand away. "You don't get it. I'm already numb." He'd lightly stroke his seared scar. "I'm dead. I don't feel a thing."

But Max would force her way against him and wrap her arms around his waist. He would touch her hair. She would press her ear against the padded down of his parka. She could almost hear the slow beat of his heart. Like the drip, drip, drip of thaw.

Back again on the Eisenhowerstrasse, only four-thirty and already full dark, full moon overhead, he'd give her a chaste kiss on the cheek. Good-bye.

How she hated that word. Good-bye. The first survival skill she'd mastered. The first good-bye she remembered she was four. Her father, leaving for a year's remote duty in Greenland. Midnight. Max and her mother in pajamas. Her father in an orange flight suit, duffel bag at the door. Sitting around the picnic table they used as a dinette. Minot, North Dakota, this would have been then. Eating a midnight breakfast of oatmeal. A clock ticking. Tears streaming while the three of them ate, one spoonful after another.

And all the while that clock tick-tick-ticking like a bomb about to go off.

By December another foot of snow had fallen and temperatures had dropped another ten degrees. It was too cold to walk in the forest. Max and Hudson instead met at the Holiday, a *Gasthaus* along the Eisenhowerstrasse catering to Americans. White-paneled walls, red vinyl booths, a haze of blue smoke in the air. A jukebox and cigarettes that smelled like burning hair. Dark, wooden stairs leading to an upper level with rooms. Periodically, a couple would slide out of a booth and drift up that way.

Christmas was coming. The holiday was strung with tinsel and gold lights. Max wore a red, lambs-wool sweater with a softness that only emphasized her small angularity. She glowed with that Christmas feeling: color and sparkle and anticipation. A sliver of greed. She leaned across the table and kissed Hudson on the mouth. "Merry Christmas."

Hudson wiped his lips with the back of his hand. "Not yet."

The barmaid, all breasts and blonde curls, appeared. Only on government property was Max underage. Everywhere else she could have whatever she wanted. She looked at the cardboard menu of drink specialties and decided she wanted a Blue Moon. She had no idea what it was—she only wanted it because it was blue. So far she'd had red drinks and green ones and pink ones and black ones, but never a blue one.

But Hudson groaned. "That candy-ass shit will rot your teeth. Two Becks," he said to the barmaid, holding up two fingers.

Max made a face. "I hate beer. It tastes like sperm." Color immediately bled from her sweater to her face: she'd never said that word out loud to a man before.

Hudson only sighed. "Where'd you read that?" Then the outer corners of his eyes drooped further downward. "You know, Max, you don't have to seduce me to get me to be your friend." He said this with a tinge of sadness, maybe even of pity, that infuriated her.

Friend! The word appalled her. A friend was nothing. A friend was a name in her address book. She had thousands of friends. She had friends all over the world. She had a blue vinyl address book stuffed with names. All of them had sworn undying love and three months later had stopped answering her letters.

Friend! Max would impress herself much harder than that upon Hudson.

The barmaid brought two glasses of beer, foamy at the top. Max ran a finger around the rim of foam, stuck it in her mouth. Hudson's expression intensified, and Max knew that at that moment, she could do anything, ask for anything, and he would not resist. She took her finger from her mouth, pressed it to his. "See?" she said. "Taste."

He flinched. She exulted.

"One of the guys at school asked me out to a dance," Max said.

They were again at the Holiday. Hudson again refused to buy her a Blue Moon. He again ordered two Becks. He wore his usual fatigues and army parka; Max this time wore pink. A gold locket dangled between her breasts. Her lipstick exactly matched her sweater.

"You should go," Hudson told her.

"I can't," Max said. "I told him I already have a boyfriend." Her fingers plucked at the gold locket, stuck it in her mouth.

"I'm not a boy," Hudson said.

But today he looked more like one. He was happy. The

outer corners of his eyes had perked up. His flat mouth curved in a smile. The creases at his forehead, the seared scar on his face, seemed to have receded into smooth flesh. He'd gotten a MARS line out to his family in Alabama. He'd spoken with Miss Lila, his grandmother. He'd spoken with his cousin Joe, who was taking care of his hunting dogs, two English setters. And he'd crossed the one hundred-day mark in this last hitch—he was officially ninety-nine days short. Ninety-nine days and he'd be back to the world.

"Would they call me Miss Max if I went there?"

"It's the way they do," Hudson said.

Max licked at the foam on her beer. She imagined Hudson taking her home, Miss Max in Hudsonville, all his relatives spilling out onto wood-frame porches, the setters racing out ahead, tails wagging, Miss Lila pressing a glass of sweet iced tea into her hand. It would never happen.

Moving so much, she was like a ghost—always hovering at the periphery of the party. No one ever truly knew she was there, and then Poof. She was gone.

Max wondered about Hudson's return to Hudsonville. She wondered if the town would be any more real than the glass reflection he constantly polished. Would he find that he had grown too heavy for the place? Or would he be the insubstantial one? She could see him at the edge of Miss Lila's dining table, a ghost fading to shade. And then to one frozen splinter of light. Poof. Gone.

As they walked back toward the barracks, toward the street corner where Max would turn into the housing area, they passed that red Porsche, parked again in front of the low, stone wall, a heap of snow on its hood. Max stopped to trace her name in the snow on the car. M-A-X. She carved the letters deep. If she were lucky, if no more snow fell, if no one started the car, her name might stay there until spring.

Max's family gathered early Christmas morning in the living room, atop the Oriental rug, beside the green, woolly sofa, across from the baby grand piano, beneath the framed oil portraits—all of which had come with the house. A fire flickered in the fireplace. Max's mother had given her small things: a purse-size vial of gardenia perfume, the scent half-enticing, half-nauseating. A satin case containing a manicure set. A single pearl on a gold chain. Her father gave her large things: a telescope, a football, one of the new heavy Texas Instruments calculators. Then he changed into fatigues and left to stand guard somewhere, relieving some poor grunt for Christmas morning, while Max's mother busied herself in the kitchen with her long-practiced Christmas dinner S.O.P. Max went back to bed, and dreamed that she was warm, that it was summer, the sky yellow with heat, and that she was swimming in the ocean with Hudson, her wet skin as soft and slippery as a seal's. When she woke, she wrapped up one of her starfish to give to him as a Christmas gift.

In the afternoon, Max's father returned with four airmen he'd invited for a home-cooked dinner. The airmen all wore full dress blue. Max's father remained in camouflage fatigues. The airmen were wispy, one and two-stripers, their blue uniforms bare of decoration. One of them had the faint fuzz of a mustache starting. Max's father was tall, clean-shaven, barrel-chested, shoulders weighted with American eagles. Max's mother wore a winter-white dress that made her pale ethereal body seem to shimmer, made her Nordic blonde hair look silver under the light of the dining room chandelier. Max wore her red sweater and blue jeans, and had sprayed herself lavishly with the gardenia perfume her mother had given her.

Silver clattered against china. Crystal hummed. Max's mother flirted with the airmen in a genteel manner. Max's father bragged about Max. About her studies—chemistry, physics, calculus. About the paper she'd written comparing the effects of a mid-air nuclear detonation to a ground hit. About the way she could loft a football, and how fast she could run. About her eyesight.

"Look," he said, standing behind her, holding his index fingers at either side of her head, slowly moving them forward. "Tell me when you can see them," he instructed, and when she did, he tousled her hair, dark like his. "Outstanding peripheral vision."

The pride in his voice made Max duck her head, made her pick at her food with her fork. She did try to be what he thought she was. Later, after dinner, as in years past, her father would tell Max to get out her football. He'd suggest a game of three-on-three, two-hand touch. Max would quarterback, and when she cocked back her arm to release the ball, she'd smell of gardenias. The airmen, as usual, would grin sheepishly as the passes she threw slapped their fingers.

But in the meantime, Max's mother had a sweet, indulgent smile on her face. She sipped at her champagne. "Honey, let these boys tell us about their families." A gentle reproof.

The day after Christmas, Hudson agreed to take Max to Morpheus. She carried along in her coat pocket the starfish. Hudson had misgivings; Morpheus was a freak joint off the Ku'damm. But better that he go with her than she go alone.

They heard the shouting as soon as they surfaced from the U-bahn station at Wittenbergplatz. Fake corpses and red paint and bits of plastic bone lay strewn everywhere. Placards screamed at the U.S. in English and German, protesting the renewed bombing attacks on Hanoi. What the press called the Christmas Bombings. Clusters of people merged and swelled into a crowd at the stops of the

Kaiser Wilhelm *Gedächtniskirche*, the bombed-out church. Spotlights glared up into the black night, washing a dummy Richard Nixon white as he twisted from the noose around his neck.

With her jeans and sheepskin coat, Max had worn a pair of goofy yellow snowboots: she thought she could pass for Canadian or Dutch or something. But Hudson, even if he wasn't wearing an army parka and combat boots, had a rawness to him that was unmistakably American.

"We're not going this way," Hudson said.

He led Max off the Ku-damm onto a side street. They wound along cobblestones and high brick walls. Audis, Mercedes, and the occasional tin-can Deux Chevaux stood canted two wheels up on the sidewalks.

A fat moon hung in the sky. Even blocks away, Max could still hear shouts and whistles. Gradually, they made their way toward a small, blue arrow on a pocked brick building, pointing down to Morpheus. They descended a slush-covered staircase to a black, leather-padded door. Inside, swirls of smoke clouded the air. Smelly European cigarettes. Dope. Music hammered the blood-red walls. Scarlet neon wires looped everywhere. People huddled at small tables, on fat, red velvet pillows. A few people stood dancing in the middle of a parquet floor.

"One drink only," Hudson said. He elbowed his way through the crowd and secured two barstools. The bartender looked to Max like Dracula: bony, white face, oily hair, yellow teeth. Hudson started to order two beers, but Max interrupted. "I want a Blue Moon."

Hudson's flat lips tightened. "He won't know what that is."

But the bartender's fangs poked out in an accommodating smile. "Yes I do." He set up the glass.

Max could tell Hudson hated it here. He'd turned on his

barstool, his back to the bar, arms folded across his chest. On the dance floor, one woman stood staring at a red light overhead, her neck bent back, her body tilted at an improbable angle. Her blouse hung open. Pink breasts jutted upward. Hudson's left knee continually bobbed up and down: tension; impatience; excitement? Max wondered. A man in leather approached the woman and knelt before her, rubbing circles over her breasts. Was this how they danced? Was it a show? Max didn't know.

She touched Hudson's bobbing knee, ran a finger along the ridge of quadriceps. "Does that interest you?" She nodded toward the dancing couple.

Hudson jerked away from her as if scalded. "No."

Another woman, all in black, oozed by, holding a syringe aloft. "Jesus Christ," Hudson said. He wrapped an arm around Max and she shrank in toward him, hiding from the needle. Scared, all of a sudden, that she was in over her head.

On the dance floor, the leather man and the leaning woman changed positions. The man stared up at the light while she knelt in front of him.

"Shit, you can't see this." Hudson threw some Deutschmarks on the bar. He dragged Max off her barstool.

"But I haven't got my drink yet."

"Tough." Hudson forged their way to the exit while Max tried to see through the crowd what she was missing.

Outside on the street, though, she was suddenly glad of the cold fresh snowy air. She felt she and Hudson had survived something together. She felt exhilarated. She wanted to run, to leap, to dance. She cracked a joke about the Dracula bartender, about the Bride of Frankenstein with the syringe. Hudson began to smile. He still held her hand, icy now without gloves, as they made their way back toward the U-bahn station. It was still early. They could go back to the Holiday for a beer and a song on the jukebox before Max's curfew.

On the sidewalk, a woman with goopy red hair approached, and as she passed by, she craned her neck and hissed up at Hudson, "Babykiller." Then she swirled away into the snow.

Hudson stopped, as if he had to catch his breath. "Babykiller? Fuck." His voice sounded ratchety. Like something had broken inside his chest. He moved as if to go after the woman, but Max grabbed his arm, held onto him.

"Forget about her."

But Hudson still stood, shaking his head. "Babykiller, Jesus. This from a country that goddamn perfected the art of babykilling. What gives her the fucking right?"

Deep inside Max thought, in words she could never say to him or to anyone at that moment: maybe just that.

But Hudson seemed to read her mind. He clamped his jaw. Stuck out his chin. Mulish. "You want to know how to kill babies, Max? I'll tell you how to kill babies. Find a school, a big one."

"Stop it." Max pulled at his arm. Her fingers were raw now, tingling. "Let's go."

"No, Max, now you're the one who always wants to know everything. You have to hear this. You find a school, see, and you squeeze off a round, right at the school bell. It dings and all the little kiddies think it's recess. They all come running out, right into your gun sights. Then you've got them. Then they're sitting ducks."

"Hudson!" Max screamed. She pressed her hands to her ears. She couldn't feel her fingers at all. They were completely numb.

"You can spray them a little with the M-16. You can light them up with white phosphorus. You can call in the F-4s, and have them walk napalm up and down the play yard.

Killing babies is the easiest damn thing in the world. Not killing babies—now that's another story."

Tears spilled down Max's face, burned her cold cheeks. He hadn't done any of that. That wasn't the kind of guy he was. (*But maybe he had. Maybe he was.*) He set off without her down the street in a resolute march.

"Hudson, wait," Max pleaded. She ran to catch up with him. Cold stabbed her lungs. She grabbed at his arm and he shook her off. She hesitated only a second, and then launched herself directly at the backs of his knees. They tumbled down together in a heap on the icy cobblestones.

"Just what do you want from me?" Hudson's voice was furious.

"I want..." Max couldn't finish. She swallowed hard. She was a jumble of wants. She wanted a Blue Moon. She wanted Hudson to say her name. She wanted him to love her and never leave her. She wanted him, after he'd gone, to remember her name.

Hudson grabbed her chin. His other hand tugged her hair off her face. The back of her head thunked against the curb. "Is this what you want?" He pinned her wrists to the ground. He stared down at her and she stared right back, holding her breath, unafraid. Willing herself to be unafraid. He breathed out a shuddering, frosty plume. Then he kissed her, at first not touching her anywhere but wrists and lips. Her blood stopped. The snow stopped. Then he pressed the whole weight of his body onto hers and everything in her surged forward.

She opened her eyes and found his open too. His expression flat, curious. That glacial slide at his eyes unchanged.

Back in front of the barracks, Hudson began to jog in place. "I'm going for a run," he said.

"Now?"

"Yes." His boots clomped on the pavement. His breath

hung in sheets in front of his face.

All around them, bright white light blanketed the street, the sidewalks, the stone walls. But just beyond the tank lot, the black emptiness of the Grunewald forest shrank from the light. Ice on the trees made faint popping sounds as the branches shivered.

There were wild boar in the night forest, Max knew. Bear maybe. Goblins. It was a place where she couldn't follow him. The dark absorbed Hudson in seconds. Max waited a long time, but he never came out.

At home, Max's father sat on the woolly sofa before the fireplace, a scotch-and-soda on the table beside him. He was busy with a notepad and sharp pencil, sketching aircraft under the faint glow of lamplight. He had on his uniform still, but the blue blouse hung unbuttoned over his T-shirt and dog tags. *Lohengrin* played on the stereo. Max's mother had taken a bubble bath and then had gone to bed. The scent of lemons still wafted faintly down the hall into the living room from her mother's bathroom.

Max sat beside her father the way she had when she was younger, her feet tucked up and warming against his legs. He was telling her about a trip that he'd have to take to Washington. He was telling her something about sidewinder missiles. But she wasn't listening. She was looking into the red snap and crackle of fire and thinking of Hudson. Of the searing scar on his face just before he'd disappeared into the forest.

She'd waited and waited and he hadn't come back out. What if he never came out? Underneath the crashing rise and fall of Wagner on the stereo, her father's murmuring voice, she became convinced, became scared. She envisioned Hudson bunched up in his army parka like a forest gnome, slowly turning to ice beneath a frozen tree.

The phone rang, the gentle buzz-buzz of the German telephone. Max jumped to answer, hoping it was Hudson.

But it was Tempelhof Airport, asking for her father. He hung up, did up the buttons of his uniform. Security had caught one of the Red Army Faction, he said, trying to stuff a bomb on a fully loaded C-5 transport plane. If the bomb had gone off, flaming chunks of tank would have fallen all over the city. He had to go.

Max waited until he left, then grabbed her coat and a flashlight.

The dark was absolute. Max held the flashlight in front of her. She stepped carefully into the small circle of yellow light. First one foot. Then the other. She pushed at the air hanging frozen in front of her. It was so cold it didn't feel like cold. It felt like heat, like a burn. She could feel herself sweating in the cold heat beneath her sheepskin coat. From the trees, small sounds emanated. Sounds she could not decipher. Chittering sounds and creaking sounds and low cooing sounds. Haunting sounds. She knew she should turn back, but she couldn't. She knew she should call out for Hudson, but she was afraid. She could only move, step by cautious step, further into the forest. Her breath rasped; her heart scurried. Don't panic, don't panic, don't panic, she told herself. It was what her father had taught her about fear: feel the fear, but never give in. Fear, and not panic, propelled her. Fear made her step faster and faster, until she wasn't placing her feet so carefully, until she thundered along, more and more frightened. She bumped into low branches. She slipped on patches of ice.

An arm snatched at her out of the forest and she screamed.

"Remind me never to take you hunting," Hudson said.

Max's breath heaved in and out. She punched at him.

"You scared me." But what she felt was relief. What she felt, all of a sudden, was safe.

"Shh. Come here." Hudson backed into a small space between the trees and sat on the ground. He pulled Max onto his lap, the two of them facing the path. He cupped a hand and whispered in her ear. "If we're quiet, they'll come back."

"Who?"

"The ones who live here."

They sat like that a long time, listening. Far off there was a crashing clamor in the woods that might have been a boar. One lone rabbit hopped by, a pale whisper in the dark.

But Max was far more aware of the weight of Hudson's arm holding her, just under her breasts. His breath on her ear. She twisted around, bent her face into his neck, where the artery pulsed. She tasted salt. He lifted her, turned her, so that she faced him. She kept her face buried in his neck, unsure. Underneath her, he began a rocking motion. Like they were on a swing, but different. She felt chafing, she felt friction, she felt heat and gravity. She felt light flaring deep in her hips. She felt him knot his hands in her hair, felt his mouth shudder against her ear: *Max.*

Later, walking with Hudson out of the forest and along the Eisenhowerstrasse, Max saw a blue-uniformed, square-shouldered silhouette marching toward them. She recognized that walk. "Shit," she said. "It's my father." Instantly she and Hudson separated. But her father had a pilot's quick eyes. Max ducked behind the red Porsche, still heaped with snow, still engraved with her name. She knelt there, shielded by the car, knowing the shield was already useless, as her father marched past and was saluted into Berlin Brigade HQ.

The morning of New Year's Eve broke even colder. Heavy clouds pressed down from the sky. Max's mother stayed in the kitchen all day baking ham, biscuits, simmering black-eyed peas. The New Year's good-luck dinner they'd have the next day, watching the football games on Armed Forces Network.

But Max didn't care about football. She hummed with anticipation. She had a million things to do: wash her hair, paint her nails. She hadn't been able to see Hudson since the night of the forest—he'd been on duty. A party, she'd told her mother, purposefully vague.

She'd bought a new dress—red, shiny, with spaghetti straps.

She was not afraid.

As the dark afternoon deepened into blacker night, fireworks began to burst. The German New Year celebration. Red and white blooms popped overhead, blue and green petals shimmered, falling. Max still carried the starfish for Hudson in her pocket. She carried a pair of red dancing shoes in a bag. She made her way through slushy piles of snow toward the Holiday. The long whistles and cracking booms of firecrackers exploded all around her.

As she neared the *Gasthaus* she saw a half dozen German police cars blocking the Eisenhowerstrasse. Ambulances; a clot of M.P.s in silver helmets; a couple K9s on leashes, at attention. The pavement was roped off. Broken glass sparkled in the snow. The air was filled with a pungent chemical smell.

A crowd of partygoers, G.I.s in fatigues, women in vivid color and makeup, stood huddled, watching. A bomb, someone explained. Two guys dead for sure. It was then that Max saw that the partygoers, the women in rosy color, were bloodied. The men in camouflage were spattered with ashes.

"Hudson!" Max screamed.

She pulled at each of the G.I.s. Was Hudson inside. Had anyone seen him. He was supposed to meet her there.

Maybe she'd been early. Or maybe he was late. She set off running toward Patton Barracks. She'd see him coming; they could go somewhere else for New Year's.

But she passed all the way along the Berlin Brigade perimeter, past the armored division lot opposite, tanks rumbling and ready, past the path leading into the blank, black hole of the Grunewald, all the way to the tin-roofed guard shack at the entrance to the barracks—without seeing Hudson.

It was Willdy again, on duty. This time he didn't confront Max with his M-16. This time he wished her Happy New Year.

"Hudson still inside?" Max asked.

"Hudson's gone, Max," Willdy said. "Orders came through late last night. Fort McClellan, Alabama, first available transport."

Gone.

Max leaned against the flimsy guard shack wall, looked up at the fireworks still exploding over the Berlin sky.

Poof.

It began to snow, huge flakes, flat and white as chrysanthemums.

"He left you something," Willdy said. He handed her a small box and a note. Max read the note first. *Happy New Year. Love, Hudson.* Inside the box was a pair of tigers-eye earrings to match her ring.

Love, Hudson, she read again. He loved her. In a small way, at least. She leaned back, let snow fall on her face, and then saw, overhead, that the moon had risen, fat and blue in the flaring light of the firecrackers. She would not cry. No matter what, she would not cry. Good-bye was her best survival skill. And she was happy for him, she was. All he'd wanted was to get back home. She imagined Miss Lila and all his cousins and his dogs surrounding him. She imagined him, at one point, telling Miss Lila of a girl who'd walked with him in the forest.

It wouldn't be long before her father, too, got orders. She'd be another person, in a new place. She had no idea who that person would be. But she would glue Hudson's note into her address book. She would carry to her new home the starfish she hadn't been able to give Hudson. And dimly she understood, by the colliding pain and pleasure she felt she right now in her chest, that if in that new place she found a man who'd swear to love and never leave her, she would be wearing Hudson's earrings and she would hear, ever so faintly, his voice breathing her name.

Angels in White Dresses

Ivy Wade dreamt of Marlon with an urgency that left her pulsing from her belly to her knees and sent her straight to prayer in atonement. Pastor Brooks had taught her that the Lord saw into her dreams. But more than apologetic, she felt embarrassed: thinking of Him having to watch her and Marlon as she'd dreamed them.

All that day, Marlon didn't come into the store. The heat inside fretted him.

Instead, he sat out on the porch with the men and the beer bottles while Ivy stayed in the store's heated gloom and popped open a Coca-Cola for sweetness. She leaned her elbows on the windowsill and listened to the men.

"Anyone hear about that spaceship out by Allapattah?" Marlon asked.

No one but Marlon believed that spaceship story. A farmer out by Allapattah had taken a fit and woke up talking of white light and little green men. But Marlon was convinced spaceships were out there. He wanted spaceships to be out there. He wanted to believe that out beyond the black sky a superior Martian wisdom looked down on the earth and pondered the strange ways of humans. Marlon believed in science. He believed in progress. He believed one day humans would fly to the moon.

Ivy drank deep from her Coca-Cola, unimpressed. It was 1938, and she knew better than Marlon. Out beyond the hot ochre sky was a pale blue Heaven and Jesus Christ.

She could picture Him: He was tall. He had velvety brown eyes and long, sturdy limbs and the kind of taut, muscular frame that made His body hum with invisible power. She'd been sixteen, two years ago, just after her mother left, when Pastor Brooks first told her about His love.

Now she waited for Him with a loose, liquid expectancy. The signs of Him were all around. It was October, the dead time. For weeks the air had had a weight to it, pressing flesh toward earth. The sun burned close, threatening to drop fire to the tops of the pine trees and sweep across the saw-grass straight to the sea. Steam seeped out of the ground into the sky, streaking into pale yellow wisps that refused to boil into thunderclouds. Men talked about fishing but did-n't stir. Women put off ironing and just sprayed a little water on the ragged marigolds. Only the children, fast as little chameleons, moved through the dusty streets to the Booth's big white house to listen to the grand excitement of the new radio.

"Tell you what," Hoot Patterson said, slapping his knee. "We get any Martians here, we'll let you do the talking. You're the one with the big Yankee words."

Marlon laughed right along with Hoot.

The men all liked Marlon. They didn't even mind that he was one of Roosevelt's New Dealers sent to string elec-tricity into town. He had a funny, pinch-nosed northern speech and didn't know beans about fishing or farming. But he was good with machines and could always get the jalop-ies to turn over and the outboards to fire up, and he was quick to do a man a favor without keeping tally.

Wilson Booth stood, the heavy weight of coins jingling in his pockets. "I'll listen for spaceship news on the radio," he said, laughing, clapping Marlon on the shoulder, boast-ing only slightly of his new possession.

Hoot Patterson coughed and spat and switched the con-versation over to Eleanor Roosevelt's oddities. "If any space-ship does land, we can count on her to go right inside and shake those Martian hands. Green skin won't make a whit of difference."

A few of the men snorted at that.

Marlon looked up at Ivy with that quiet gaze of his. A gaze that made her want to stand still for him and just be looked at. He had thick, dark eyebrows, a long, sharp nose, a sweet, sweet mouth. And since he'd come into town, just four months ago—maybe it was the summer heat, the heavy, humid air, the long, sticky afternoons and golden evenings—it was like Ivy lived her life in slow motion. In a thick, yellow haze. Sometimes, like now, listening to the creak of floorboard, the spurt and murmur of conversation, the faint clink of beer bottles, and then feeling herself held in place by Marlon's quiet eyes—Ivy couldn't be sure if she was awake or asleep.

Marlon wanted to marry Ivy. That is, he wanted to make her his wife. He couldn't care less about the ceremony part of it all.

It was just three weeks ago she and Marlon had been sitting outside on the steps of this very porch. Ivy had on a peach-colored blouse with buttons on the shoulder. A lock of her hair had gotten tangled on a button. Marlon unwound the strands and then stuck them in his mouth. Her hair was spun out so fine and long, he said he just had to taste it. Then he took hold of her left hand like it was a small bird. His fingers grazed her palm and slowly her fingers unfurled. She began to feel the quick uneven beat of her pulse beneath his touch, a kind of shivering. "Ivy, marry me," he said, sighing through the words. Holding her with those velvety brown eyes. Sitting so close she could smell him—limes and fresh hay and the barest whiff of engine oil.

The sinking feeling she felt in her belly as he touched her knee. Ivy had to swallow hard, had to force herself to remember Pastor Brooks and the pledge she'd made. "I can't," she told Marlon. "Not until Pastor Brooks comes back around and you can go down to the pond and get saved." Sorrow dampening her voice as she told him she could never promise her life to a man when death would mean eternal separation.

But Marlon laughed right out loud, a happy, joyous laugh. "Is that all?" He got up, excited, pulled Ivy off the porch and swung her around into the middle of the dusty street. "I can do that. What do I do—dunk my head in the water? Can I pinch my nose?"

He held her by the waist and pulled her close to him. His hands traced small circles on the small of her back and her hips lifted to his touch. Even while she pushed him away. His very foolishness betrayed him. He didn't truly plan to welcome the Holy Spirit into his body. Pastor Brooks was going to have to work Marlon a while.

But once he was saved...once they could marry...it would be just like Matthew promised: *seek first His kingdom and all things shall be added to you.* After she'd gotten saved, business at the store had picked right up. She'd gotten saved and Marlon had come into town, into the store for a tin of salt crackers and a can of soup. She'd gotten saved and Marlon had settled his quiet gaze on her.

Just thinking of Him made her close her eyes, made her sway a little with a drowsy, sinking feeling. She put her empty Coca-Cola bottle back in the crate and circled through the gloomy store to her room at the back. She curled up in her grandmother's old flowered armchair. The chintz still smelled of her, a sweet-sour smell of rosewater and a slow, coughing death. Outside the back window the yellow afternoon deepened to dusky orange evening. Ivy felt a change in the air. A lick of breeze. A taste of salt. She settled in the chair, expectant, dreamy, half awake, half asleep, imagining Marlon touching her again on the knee. Imagining Jesus holding out His arms to her.

Fully asleep, she fell into other dreams. Her grandmother, slapping biscuit dough on the counter—biscuits for supper again. Good farmland all plowed under—hogs slaughtered and milk dumped into the road, not worth selling at six cents a gallon—and nothing but biscuits and watery gravy to eat. Hunger like a cold fist in the belly. Her crazy mother, all pink and wild-eyed, scrabbling through the dresser for the dimes that were the only cash money in the house, smashing her glass teacup, a souvenir of St. Augustine, onto the floor. The slap of dough, the crash of glass.

Whoops and hollers penetrated her dream. Ivy sat straight up, blinking. Her first thought was that the men had better pay for all that beer. She shoved herself up out of the armchair and onto the porch to demand her money.

But the porch was empty.

The evening light was hazy and brown. Little Charlie Booth, chocolate smearing his mouth, ran down the street, ahead of a pack of boys. Wilson Booth ran behind, his mouth working. "Martians!" Charlie shouted out. Wilson gasped out, holding his stout chest, "It's true, we heard it on the radio! Martians have landed!" Even Mrs. Booth, in her sateen lounging gown and feathered mules, ran along, begging for Charlie, her precious, to stay close to Mama.

In pairs and in small knots, people piled into the streets. Hoot Patterson fetched his shotgun. Someone forgot to latch a gate and chickens fluttered through the gathering crowd. Dogs bayed. Ivy looked for Marlon but couldn't find him in the shadowy movement. The wind had picked up. Her hair twisted around her face. Marlon's electrical wires danced between their poles. Other guns appeared and Hoot shouted orders, trying to assemble an army.

"They've got the President!" someone shouted. And despite everyone's harsh words for Roosevelt, this news caused the crowd to stop its swirling and sag in place.

"Maybe that farmer out by Allapattah told the truth!" Hoot said. "Maybe what he saw was a scouting unit."

Flurries of panic rippled through the crowd.

"My candlesticks!" Hoot's wife cried. She left to bury them in the same flowerbed her granny had used to hide the silver from Union soldiers.

"Well, I for one intend to drink myself a tall glass of gin right now," Mrs. Booth announced. She clutched her sateen gown and flounced off in her mules. The crowd, seeming not to know where to go, followed. Everyone knew the Booths stocked the best liquor in town.

And all the while, Ivy stood trembling on the porch. The faintest lightning bug of hope darted 'round her mind and then that swarmed into a fierce blaze of light. Jubilation buzzed right through her. There wasn't any Martians coming! The Bible never talked of Martians. It was Him! It was Him and His angels, coming for the ones who loved Him.

Her fingers shook and then her arms shook and then her very blood shook. She stared up into the deepening sky and the black pine trees at the horizon. *Here I am*. The words, in her mind, sounded husky. She pressed her hips against the porch rail. *Come to me*.

But she wasn't ready! All she had on was her old housedress, and her hair was a mess. She whirled back into the store, into her room. She snatched from her grandmother's walnut chifforobe her best dress. A white lace gown she'd stitched from a tablecloth—she'd planned to marry Marlon in that gown.

Fingers fumbling, clumsy, Ivy did up the small buttons. She breathed through a shuddering pang for Marlon. The Lord was here and he wasn't yet saved.

There might still be time. She'd get him to the pond. She smoothed down her skirt, wished she had daintier shoes than her clumpy old oxfords. She piled her hair into a knot on top of her head.

She felt beautiful: Jesus was coming for her, and she was beautiful. In the mirror, her reflection was pure. She looked like something carved from shell or pearl. Collarbones like swan's wings, long bare neck.

Though just as she turned from the mirror, out of the corner of her eye she caught sight of her own mother in her: a pink wildness in her cheek, a hunger in her blue, blue eyes. Her mother was south of here, Ivy guessed, if she was still with that rum-runner she'd rode off with, and with pain and love combined, Ivy crossed her fingers for her mother. If anyone could charm an escape from Hell, it was her mother.

Full night had descended. Stars rose from the horizon and then disappeared into a blank black squall line. Wind tossed the tops of the pine trees. The panicky crowd had turned wild, tossing bottles and shooting pistols into the sky. The barbershop's plate glass window had smashed, and wind riffled the girlie magazines strewn about the street. Piano music tinkled out from the Booth place. A smoky barbecue smell floated from that direction. Hoot Patterson marched up and down, wearing his old doughboy cap, his shotgun tucked under one arm. "No wonder this town's always been such a sorry place," he said. "They've all given up already."

"Have you seen Marlon?" Ivy asked.

Hoot shook his head and spat at the ground. "He's probably at Booth's. Everyone else is. They've decided to die drunk."

Over at the Booth house, the parlor drapes were open. Yellow light spilled out. Women danced to the piano and men passed bottles between them. The men still wore their work clothes but the women had changed into fancy wear—rose-printed chiffon, purple dancing dresses, paste jewelry of all colors. Mrs. Booth pranced into the parlor with a plate of pickles and cheese. "Eat up!" she cried, her voice shrill and quivery as a lap dog's. "Can't let the Martians get good pickles." A pair of man's hands—not Wilson Booth's—wrapped around Mrs. Booth's waist, spinning her around. She dropped the pickles on the floor and leaned into the man's kiss. Ivy turned away from the window, sickened by the Devil's work here, and when she looked down the street toward the store, she saw Marlon's jalopy rumbling toward her.

"Thank God I found you," he said. "Come on." He tugged her toward the car. "I want to get over to Allapattah to see the Martians."

"Allapattah? You can't go there." Ivy shook her arm free.

But Marlon had a look of rapture on him. He scanned the sky, peered up toward the black tree line and the squall moving in. He urged her toward the car. Behind him, the jalopy rumbled, impatient.

"Ivy, I've been waiting for this all my life. Ever since I first learned about the planets and the galaxies, I've known there's more out there. What do you want me to do? Hide from them? Get drunk like the rest of them?" He waved a disgusted hand toward the Booth place.

"But Marlon, there aren't any Martians." A sudden, sharp gust of wind rushed in, swamping the party sounds. And then just as suddenly, the wind fell away and the piano music bobbed up again.

"Marlon, think! I read to you from Revelations. *Stars will fall from Heaven*—that's what people are seeing. It's not any Martians coming. It's Jesus Christ and His angels."

"That's all just story. I'm talking about science. I'm talking about cold, hard fact. Think about this: if the Martians already have space travel, their whole civilization must be more advanced than ours. Think what we could learn from them. What if they could cure all disease? What if they could control the rain and the sun so that the crops always grew?"

He looked so certain, so eager, his furry eyebrows rumpled, his brown eyes luminous—but stubborn, so stubborn it made her sad for him. "No hunger, no sickness." Her voice was gentle. She reached up to him, stroked his cheek. "That's what Heaven promises: whosoever believeth in Him shall not perish but have everlasting life. How can you be so smart about some things and not see that truth?"

She began tugging him toward the sandy path that snaked behind the Booth house toward the pond. "But we have to get you saved before He gets here." It made her so happy, thinking of her and Marlon, saved in Heaven. Her feet felt so light, she was practically skipping. They could get married there. Maybe one of His angels would marry them. Or even—she could hardly think it—maybe He Himself would do the honors. "Oh, Marlon, I hope there's white cake in Heaven. I used to love white cake."

Wind howled by. Overhead one of Marlon's electrical wires hummed.

Marlon grabbed her by the shoulders. "Do you know how stupid you sound? Prattling on about white cake and Jesus? The radio people said Martians. Don't you think they'd know the difference? And it makes perfect sense: our scientists have dreamed up rockets; why wouldn't theirs?"

A loud crack burst above. Sparks cascaded from the sky. In a flash, Marlon shoved her off the street, away from a bolt of fire. She landed on the sandy path and jumped back up, instantly furious. "You messed up my dress."

But Marlon leaped around and over something on the

street.

"What is it? A snake?" Ivy asked.

"Stay back. It's an electric wire. It's live."

The yellow light in Booth's house had died. One by one lantern lights bloomed in the window. The piano music faltered only a moment.

"Just leave it," Ivy said. "If we don't get you to the pond and get you saved before He gets here, you'll roast in Hell." Her voice escalated into a plea.

"Someone will roast right here if I don't see to this wire. You just go on without me. If Jesus comes, you're welcome to Him."

He was so mulish. His chin out, his dark eyebrows gathered, a blue knot of stubbornness in his forehead. He was going to die a horrible death. "Marlon, please," Ivy wailed.

But he'd already started shinnying up the electrical pole. The loose wire dangled like a limp and broken wing.

She watched his long legs working up that pole, the ridge of muscle in his thighs, the roll and shift of his shoulders. He was so strong and yet so gentle. He was so smart and so misguided. Maybe Jesus would understand that. Maybe she could pray hard and convince Him to spare Marlon. Or maybe Marlon with his smarts could hide himself somewhere and escape the wrath.

But even as she hoped that, she knew the hope itself was blasphemy.

Her heart split wide open. Rain began to fall, huge drops, fat as pigeon's eggs. She wanted to stay with Marlon and she just couldn't. Jesus was coming for her, and she was certain He'd be looking for her at the pond, His sanctified place, where she'd pledged herself to Him.

Marlon, good-bye. She thought the words but could not say them. Tears spilled down her face and mixed with the rain, steadily falling now, as she thought of the life they weren't going to have together—the trip up the coast in the jalopy he'd talked about, the children they'd have, one girl and one boy each, the orange tree she was going to plant in the yard when they married, and the electrical things she was going to start to sell in the store. But she didn't have a choice. She turned from him, from the pole where he grunted and struggled with something up there, and walked slowly down the sandy path through the tomato field. She wiped tears and rain from her face, felt her hair slipping from its pins. Beyond the tomato field stretched the flat, black emptiness that was the pond. Lit up now by car headlights: Pastor Brooks' truck. A giant tin cross rose from the truck bed. As Ivy neared the truck, wind rattled the tin and made a powerful drumming. In cages beneath the cross, Pastor Brooks' water moccasins writhed. Ivy hated snakes. She scooted past those cages, quick.

Pastor Brooks stood beside a stand of cattails at the pond's edge. Rain dripped off his black-brimmed hat. In the thin light his face looked burned blue.

Ivy ran to him, clutched at his black suit coat. "Is Jesus here?"

"Not yet." Pastor Brooks' hand shielded his face from the rain as he looked out at the sky. Then he turned to look at Ivy. "Daughter," he said, "you look beautiful." He touched the lace at her sleeve. "He'll be so proud of you."

Ivy looked down at her feet, shy suddenly. A flush bloomed its way up her throat to her face. She couldn't wait to see Him. Or for Him to see her.

A huge gust of wind roared in. The giant tin cross rattled. Pastor Brooks' next words were swept away. The wind sharpened itself and whined against the tin.

"There's not much time." Pastor Brooks shouted above the wind. "We should rededicate ourselves."

Wind tore the air and metal shrieked. From the bed of

the truck, the giant tin cross began to rise. For a moment it held steady against the wind. Then slowly it cartwheeled off the truck. One arm swept the snake cages to the ground. Then the cross smashed down onto the tomato field. For one split second, the truck's taillights cast a red glare on a writhing mass of moccasins. And then the snakes slithered away into the cattails edging the pond.

"Come," Pastor Brooks said, holding his arm out to her to escort her. A raw, dank smell rose off the water in front of them. Wind lapped small waves on the surface.

"But my dress," Ivy said.

Pastor Brooks turned to her with a fierce look. "Are you wearing that dress for Him?" She nodded. "All right, then," he said. He held out his arm to her and she hesitated, thinking of the beautiful white lace but then thinking of Him waiting for her at His altar; she took Pastor Brooks's arm and waded into the water.

The water felt neither cold nor wet. It simply was. In the middle of the pond, Pastor Brooks asked, "Do you accept the Lord Jesus Christ now and forever into your heart?"

"I do." Her voice was husky. She felt heat in the water now — her own self, liquid, melting.

"Then I give you to Him." Pastor Brooks bent her back over his arm into the water.

Tiny currents tugged at the pins in her hair as she sank beneath the surface. Submerged, she heard the muffled voice of Pastor Brooks praying. She heard the flickering hiss of snakes in the water. She heard her own blood drum in her head. She sank down and down, dissolving into the pond. There was no longer any boundary between her and the water. She was the water, she was the earth, she was all the universe of His creation, stars, planets, galaxies. She was the light, shattering into a thousand pieces. And in the midst of the light, Jesus approached. His figure was shadowy. He had broad shoulders, long arms, sure, square hands rimmed with gold fire. Sparks spun from His hair. He reached for her. She heard His ruby heart beating. She felt His gold fire on her flesh. He looked at her with calm quiet eyes: Marlon.

She shoved herself up out of the water and sucked great chunks of air into her lungs.

"I held you under extra long to wash away every last sin," Pastor Brooks said.

But even here, in this sanctified water, she'd dreamed of Marlon. She could only hope the Lord had been too busy scourging the earth to see her dreams. Water streamed down her face, her hair, her back. It pearled up on her eyelashes, on the points of lace at her neckline. It hurt to breathe. Her lungs felt burned hollow, like a coal had dropped down into her chest and charred its way through from the inside out. She was just a papery shell now, awaiting revelation.

She splashed toward the shore. Off in the distance, lightning split the sky. Thunder cracked. Pastor Brooks stayed in the water, craning his neck toward the sky. "Any minute now."

Lightning spears shot down. The ground vibrated. Ivy felt a buzzing shoot from her feet to her fingertips. The black sky had the weight of iron. The air smelled of metal filings. Over the tomato field, something floated down from the clouds. A blue mass, quivering. It hovered, and then began to drift toward the pond. Ivy pointed and shouted, "He's there. I feel Him." Her heart thudded with dread and hope.

A crashing noise burst from the cattails. "Ivy! Ivy Wade," a voice called out, "where are you?"

Everything in Ivy surged toward those cattails. "Here I am, Lord! Take me now, I'm ready!"

Marlon leaped in front of the cattails, yanked Ivy away from the water. "We have to get out of here. There's lightning everywhere!"

Behind him, the blue jellied mass floated and sparked. "No, look," Ivy said. Her voice was tight, aching toward that light. Marlon clamped his arms around her. "He's here." Small darts of blue shot out and she stretched her arms toward them.

"Ball lightning," Marlon breathed. "I've heard about it, but I've never seen it before." Ivy struggled in his grip but he would not release her. "Pastor Brooks," he shouted, "get out of that water."

Ivy's hair rose from her shoulders. Marlon's hair floated in a halo above his head. But Pastor Brooks remained stone still in the pond, his mouth open. "I've waited my whole life for this." A sob broke from him. *The hour cometh and now is!*"

The blue mass rippled, floating, inexorable, toward the pond. It hummed with the sound of a thousand insects. Ivy struggled against Marlon. "Let me go, I want to go too."

"Angels!" Pastor Brooks said. "I see them." The blue light hovered directly over his head. He was bathed in blue. He lifted his face, his arms, as if to embrace that flickering blue light. "Take me now, Lord," he moaned.

Ivy writhed in Marlon's grip. "Me too, Lord. It's me, Ivy Wade!"

Pastor Brooks rose from the water, his face contorted. He floated in the air, surrounded by light. His mouth worked, his eyes grew huge, his fingers clenched and released, clenched and released. "It is beautiful, so beautiful," he moaned. Then one sharp spear of light shot straight into his chest and he cried out, in terror, in awe.

Instantly, the blue mass evaporated. Pastor Brooks fell back into the pond. Steam hissed off his body. Snakes slithered around his corpse. He floated face up, and then slowly he rolled over and sank.

The stand of cattails burst into flame.

"What about me?" Ivy wailed.

"We have to get inside somewhere," Marlon said. He half dragged, half carried her up the sandy path toward town. She sobbed as lightning struck the tomato field, cracked over the tin cross, the pine trees. How could He not have taken her?

As they passed the Booth place, Ivy caught a fleeting glimpse in the lantern-lit windows of bodies sprawled everywhere. "He took them too and not me?" How could He have come for that Mrs. Booth and not her? She felt so cheated. "All of them, they're all dead and in Heaven."

"Huh," Marlon said. "If they're not, they'll wish they were in the morning." Lightning slashed the sky. Marlon hurried Ivy along, down the street, muddy and puddled with rain, toward the store.

Inside, he lit a kerosene lantern and yellow light warmed the walls.

"You were right about one thing," he told her, disappointment in his voice. "There never were any Martians. All my big ideas about rockets and going to the moon—I feel so stupid."

"*You* feel stupid," Ivy said. She moved close to him and put her forehead against his. Her beautiful white dress was limp and ruined. She was so cold. She was shivering. Her hair hung limp and sodden down her back.

Then Marlon's eyebrows furred together, puzzled. "What's that on your cheek? Stand over there, by the light." His hands turned her face this way and that. He looked at her neck, her arms. "These are snake bites. Are there snakes in that pond?"

"The moccasins escaped."

"My God. I'll go find the doctor."

"Stop," Ivy said. "I'm fine." And truly, though she could see the snake bites on her arms, she didn't feel any poison inside her at all.

She was only cold. She was cold everywhere but where Marlon's body heat warmed her. She moved closer to him and he looked straight at her, with that calm quiet gaze that made her stand still, that made her look straight back at him, that made her ready to say right then to him, *here I am*.

Defying Gravity

Every day nobody buys Jim and Linda Wilson's house.
Linda keeps it fiercely scrubbed and waxed, just in case. But
after six months, they still have no takers. Every day after
work and supper and storytime and bedtime, after Becky,
age four, and Sara, age two, tuck under matching unicorn
bedspreads (Sara with her thumb in her mouth, no matter
what Linda says about braces), Linda swoops through the
house, scraping Spaghettios off plates, rinsing milk rings
out of cups, throwing toys into boxes she's stashed in each
room, wringing out wet towels, and wiping toothpaste crud
out of the sink. All this in the hope that while she's at work
typing into her terminal, and Becky and Sara are mashing
playdough at daycare, and Jim's rehearsing dogfights at
twelve thousand feet, some nice young couple with kids of
their own and no sense for numbers will buy the house.

Fat chance.

Jim tells her not to worry, but for Linda worry is constant temptation. He seeks rationale: maybe their real estate
agent smiles too much, or maybe they painted the front
door the wrong shade of yellow. Linda thinks these reasons
blame her. She chose the real estate agent; yellow is her
favorite color. Am I responsible for the savings and loans?
she asks. Am I the one who built so much gimcrack housing where there are no jobs? Her hair flies crazily around
her head when she asks these questions. It's the one part of
her with any real mass; she's eroding as surely as the limestone land the house sits on. She's down to angles and
bones.

But Jim believes both in fate and in trying harder—an inconsistency Linda has given up on pointing out.

The plain fact is the house down the street just sold for thirty thousand less than Jim and Linda need. For Linda, their mortgage balance is the number that tells their story.

Jim's tour of duty in this jungle corner of Florida is almost up. Linda pictures the Air Force scratching its chin and spinning the globe, seeking out just the right far-flung hellhole to send them to next. Minot, North Dakota; Izmir, Turkey; Del Rio, Texas. The where doesn't matter since they can't pack the house along.

They have a VA loan. Walk away from the mortgage and Uncle Sam will take his bit out of Jim's paycheck. And Jim will lose his security clearance, so he refuses to even think the word "default."

But Linda thinks it. At night her mind races through a maze with no exits. But one. She could walk away. There wouldn't be much to leave. An old couch, a TV on a cart, the stereo Jim brought back from Korea. Twin beds for the girls and the double bed she bought used from a hotel redecorating itself.

Sunday evening. Tony and BettyJean D'Angelo are over. The kids are asleep. The boys aren't flying tomorrow, so the grownups are all sitting around the picnic table that serves as a kitchen dinette, eating take-out pizza and playing Dirty Words Scrabble, a variation Jim invented. Quadruple points for dirty words and a fifty-point bonus for one of seven true obscenities. Between turns Jim and Tony tell Linda and BettyJean about another captain in their squadron, a guy named Matson. Jim chomps into some pizza. "Matson's damn lucky," he says.

"He hit a bird," Tony tells them. "What kind?" he asks Jim. "Buzzard, osprey, what?"

"Shit, who could tell? He said he was going two hundred

fifty knots when the windscreen temp heated up. That bird slammed through the glass like a shotgun blast of blood and feathers."

"Oh, please," BettyJean says, holding her stomach.

"He's lucky that bird didn't hit him in the head." Tony says, laughing. He pops open the last beer and foam spits out.

"Birdbrain," Jim says, and Tony finds this hysterical. He laughs so hard beer dribbles down his chin. When the laughing dies down, Jim says "Birdbrain" again, and sets them both laughing again. Linda doesn't find any of this funny at all. She's thinking about Matson's wife. She's wondering how Matson managed to land the damn plane. She clears away the pizza-crusted paper plates while Jim and Tony get through laughing.

The two men battled flight school together. Coincidence reunited them at the same base and in the same squadron two years ago. Tony is dark and big-toothed where Jim is fair and freckled, with four small moles flying in formation under one eye. But they're both built the same: neither too tall nor too short nor too fat. Just the right height and weight to squeeze into a fighter's tight cockpit. Both are still wearing flight suits, though Jim's unzipped his down to his waist, exposing his once white T-shirt. They've been sitting alert the past twenty-four hours and they smell a little whiffy. Linda notices their boots are leaving black marks on the linoleum. Better that than blood and feathers, she thinks.

Jim is pretty well shitfaced by now. Linda sits back down at the table and checks her Scrabble tiles to see if she can add "faced" to where Tony spelled out "shit" on his last turn. No *C*. The two men had hit the O Club and damaged the Beefeater supply before landing here. They cruised through the Budweiser in the fridge, leaving a heap of crumpled cans in their wake, and now Jim's attacking the Johnny Walker the C.O. gave him for Christmas. The boys finish trashing Matson and the game resumes. It's BettyJean's turn. She sets down an *M*, *E*, and *S* to add to the *S* in Tony's "shit." The others just look at her. BettyJean went to Catholic school. She shrugs and says, "Well, a mess is dirty if you think about it."

Jim and Tony bust up again. Jim pulls the bottle to him, still laughing, and sucks at its neck. Their laughs climb into high drunken snorts, and BettyJean and Linda roll their eyes at each other. BettyJean's got these big, black-lashed eyes and a sweetheart face. Linda thinks she looks a lot like Elizabeth Taylor, though now she's pregnant she looks more like a fat Elizabeth Taylor. Linda gets up to go pee. She's worked out her own streamlined route to the bathroom; she's had a Bud or two herself. She and BettyJean collide outside the bathroom. "Oh," BettyJean says, her face bubbling up into a cherrypie smile, "the baby's kicking."

Linda's had babies twice already, so she can't get all worked up. "That's nice," she says.

In the kitchen, Jim and Tony have quieted down some. Jim's still hanging onto that bottle. The fluorescent light flickers overhead and Linda swats it. It's Jim's turn now and he stares at the board, his face suddenly tight. He lifts out three tiles and adds r, e, and f to BettyJean's m. REMF. "That's not a word," Linda says.

"Sure it is," Jim tells her. "Rear Echelon Mother Fuckers." Jim and Tony are laughing again. BettyJean's eyebrows arch at Linda, and Linda feels the tiny hairs on her arms rise. The fluorescent light buzzes.

Tony wags one finger at Jim. "Abbreviations don't count."

"Okay, then, I'll spell the whole damn thing." Jim's not laughing anymore. He roots through the turned-down tiles in the box and the tiles on Linda's stand, stealing the *K* she'd been saving. He shoves aside the words on the board to make room for the letters he needs. The skin at the edge of his nose pinches white and his eyes flare up. The moles under his eyes stand out.

"Hon, I think it's time to go," BettyJean says, pulling Tony's arm.

"In a minute," he says. Jim's spelled echelon with an *S*, and Tony fixes it for him. "Take it easy, buddy," he says to Jim. Then he slings his arm around BettyJean and lean-walks with her through the kitchen door and the carport to the rusting VW squareback BettyJean parked on the street behind Jim and Linda's Hyundai.

After they wave the VW off, Jim and Linda stand a minute outside. Linda smells gardenias blooming. She picks one and fingers its fragile petals. It'll be brown by morning. No cats cry. No toads croak. No jetwhine rises from the base. The quiet is rare, and nice. Then she hears a scrabbling sound.

"What was that?"

"I'll find out," Jim says. He bends into a crouch and creeps through the carport toward the utility room at the back. The way he moves gives Linda the shivers. His boots don't make a sound on the concrete. He inches over to the washing machine. "Flashlight," he whispers.

Linda fetches the one hanging on the refrigerator door and hands it to him, stretching so she doesn't have to leave the safety of the kitchen step. Jim aims the beam behind the washing machine. The scuttling starts up again. Jim switches off the light. Silence.

"It's a rat," he says.

The Budweiser's back in Linda's mouth, sour tasting. Jim pushes past her down the hall into the bedroom and Linda follows. "I'm going to kill that little sonofabitch," he says.

He opens the glass-front gun cabinet and lifts out a rifle. He sorts through the cigar box on his dresser and loads the gun. "Airgun," he says. "This way we won't have rat brains all over the wall." He pumps the gun, filling the chamber with air, the muscles in his forearms pumping under the skin as he works the bolt, back and forth. He slips another pellet into his pocket.

Linda watches him through the cracked-open jalousie windows in the kitchen door. He lays a trail of peanut butter from the utility room into the empty carport. "Turn off the light," he whispers. The kitchen and the carport fall into instant shadow. Jim takes up position on top of the dryer. Linda sees him in silhouette, holding the rifle low, ready. She reminds herself to breathe.

She can't see the rat come out of the utility room; the angle from the jalousies is too steep. Instead, she sees Jim slowly pull the rifle up to this chest then to his face to sight down the barrel. He pivots on the dryer as he follows the rat with the gun. The shot is oddly quiet. A muted thump travels from the ground up Linda's shins and then settles in her knees.

Jim reloads and pumps the bolt again, filling the chamber with more air. Then he jumps down from the dryer and creeps into the carport, inching toward the rat, holding the rifle ready. This time he shoots from close in. This time the thumping sound doesn't weaken Linda's knees. Jim raises his eyes to look at her. He grins. Thumbs up. "Confirmed kill," he says.

Back in the house, Jim picks up the Johnny Walker. The beer and the tension have given Linda a headache. Yellow light stabs behind her forehead. "I'm going to bed," she says, and she lies down in the dark. Later, the bed shaking when Jim falls into it wakes her. She can't read the blue numbers on the clock by his side, but she feels sated with sleep. Anyway, the smell on him chases her out. She wraps up in the afghan on the couch and flips through TV channels, staring at gray reruns while the air thins into morning. The news shows come on. Bryant Gumbel is dressed in khakis and interviewing some white-robed Arab sheik. The sand kingdoms are fighting. Linda hears the girls murmuring awake and she flicks over to the cartoon channel. Then she sets into clearing up last night's remains.

Becky and Sara eat their Cheerios without much fuss while Linda gets dressed. Jim's snoring in bed, but the girls don't ask. Linda loads everybody into the car and then has to scoot back into the house because Sara forgot her FunnyBunny. As she roots through toys, she hears Jim trudge into the bathroom and slam the door. She calls out a good morning good-bye and takes off.

At the insurance office, Linda's boss hands her a stack of yellow premium notices to check in and file. His fat face smiles an apology like he knows it's shitwork, but it's her job, after all. Linda doesn't mind. Her brain doesn't feel much like thinking after last night. Her boss once said if she was going to stick around the area he'd recommend her for the company's agent training program. But right after that, he asked her out for a drink, so she's not sure what he meant. She alphabetizes the flimsy pages and passes the day in front of the file cabinets.

BettyJean calls during Linda's lunch hour and chats while Linda eats a tuna sandwich. "Sorry about last night," BettyJean says, and Linda tells her she doesn't know why BettyJean's the one apologizing. "Anyhow," BettyJean says, her voice bright, "I was thinking we could get together after the boys take off for TDY."

"What TDY?"

"Didn't Jim tell you?" BettyJean asks. But Jim hasn't had much chance to tell her anything, between getting drunk and passing out. "They're off to Nellis for a couple of weeks." Great, Linda thinks. Nellis. Las Vegas. Jim will have himself a time. Still, her breath comes easier. She realizes she's been holding herself against whatever stayed unsaid last night.

"When?" she asks.

"Tomorrow night. Dennis Quaid's playing at the base theater. How does that sound?"

"Sounds good." Linda agrees to meet BettyJean at her place before the movie.

After work, she picks up Becky and Sara from daycare. They're frantic and whiny from the long day and she tosses them the baggie of graham crackers she keeps in her purse. As soon as she opens the door to the house she's knocked over by smell. The afternoon sun has baked the garbage bag in the kitchen into a sharp, dead stink. Linda holds her breath and carries the trash to the can in the carport. She leaves the kitchen door open to air things out.

Jim's not home. The bedcovers slouch half on the floor. His underwear is wadded up on the towel bar in the bathroom, and the towel lies curled up next to the toilet. Newspapers are scattered in the living room, headlines thick and black. Linda plugs Becky and Sara into *Sesame Street*, changes her clothes, and sets some chicken noodle soup on the stove to simmer.

She hears Jim's long stride before she sees him. "Where the hell have you been?" she asks. She grabs a wooden spoon off the counter.

"Golf," he says.

"Golf!" He's deranged, she decides. "Look at this place! How the hell is this house going to sell when it smells like death in here?"

He grunts, rummages through the refrigerator. There's no beer left. "You smell it too?" He closes the refrigerator and fills a glass of water at the faucet.

"How could I miss it? Why didn't you take the garbage out?"

"It's not the garbage," he says. "I still smell it."

"So what is it?"

"Death."

"You're drunk." Linda turns to stir the soup.

"Nope," he says. "Can't you smell it? It's like that liver my mom fries up for turkey stuffing. Stinks."

"Oh, God." Memory churns Linda's stomach.

She broils cheese toast, microwaves peas, ladles out soup. Jim's at the picnic table, his head on his arms, so she puts everything on a tray and carries the tray into the living room. She tells the girls they can eat on the floor. *Sesame Street* is over and *McNeil-Lehrer* is on, both their long faces droning serious tones. "Can we watch a movie?" Becky asks, and when Linda says yes the kids bounce up and down, narrowly missing the soup, while she loads a Mickey Mouse video into the VCR.

In the kitchen, Jim's head is still down. Linda brews coffee. The sound of water bubbling rumbles under the tension in the room. Linda fills Jim's squadron mug and shoves it in front of him. "486th T.F.S.—We Get Ours At Dawn," the mug says. "I'm not drunk, I'm just tired," he says, his voice muffled by his arms.

"Good. So what's with this TDY?" Linda asks.

"Nellis."

"Right. I heard from BettyJean."

Jim lifts his head. His eyes narrow. "Sit down," he says. Linda pours a cup of coffee for herself and joins him. The look in his face scares her. He reminds her of a condor, doomed and knowing it, proud. "I've got orders. After I get back from Nellis, I'm going to Saudi."

In the silence that follows, Linda hears from the living

room the cartoon voice of Mickey Mouse tussling with Pluto over an armchair. Mickey wants to sit there and Pluto won't give up the chair for his dog bed. The girls are giggling even though they've seen this one a hundred times already.

"So we don't have to sell the house," Jim says.

"Yet," Linda adds. "We don't have to sell the house yet."

"Right."

"This whole Persian Gulf thing could resolve itself in a couple of months and then what?" Linda sips her coffee and eases it over the stone in her throat. "I'd better keep it listed."

Jim folds his arms over his chest and stares out the window over the sink. The light is fading into gloom. "I don't think I'm coming back," he says, not looking at her.

"Stop it." Linda's voice is a hiss. She looks over to the hallway and the living room beyond, but the girls are safely entranced.

Jim starts pacing to the door and back. "I just know it. I told you. I smell it."

"That's ridiculous," Linda says.

He stares down at the floor a while and then back at Linda. His face loses some years. "Let's be honest," he says. "I know you've been thinking about divorce. I have too." At this Linda bites her lip and tears nudge into her eyes. "It's not you or me or anything, it's just"—he waves his hand, encompassing the house, the kids, her—"all this. I figured it'd be just you and me roaring around a while. But one thing leads to another and before you know it, here we are. Bogged down in all kinds of complications." He wipes his eyes with the backs of his hands. "Anyhow, maybe all that's solved now."

Linda stands and puts her arms around him. "Hush," she says. She wants to stop the words. She wants to not come to any answers. She senses there are all kinds of possible outcomes and meanings to explore, given time, given no grave decision arrived at too soon.

Jim pulls away and sits down. He runs his arms across the table as if he's clearing away workspace. He clears his throat and ticks items off his fingers. "My will's in the top left desk drawer. Everything's to you and the kids except for my daddy's watch. I want that to pass to my brother." Linda's heard all this many times before. "Be sure to keep the life insurance paid up." She nods. "Your allotment will go directly to the bank. If something happens," he says, his voice faltering only once, "be sure you get all your benefits. There's a brochure in the desk."

He tells her he wants to walk outside some. Linda sits with the girls while their show finishes. She keeps kissing their hair and Becky gets annoyed. She bathes them and then sits cross-legged on the floor between their beds, listening to their breathing subside into snuffling snores.

She finds Jim on the couch in the living room. The stereo's on, softly, so as not to wake the kids. Sinatra's singing. "You should see the stars," Jim says. "It's a night for flying." Something in his face has calmed. Linda sits down next to him and rests her head against the couch. He reaches over and cups his hand lightly over hers, as if it were a fragile piece of china. "I still love you," he says.

"I know."

He strokes her fingers, twisting her wedding band where it hangs loose over the weight she's lost. He turns her head and grazes his fingers over her palm. Gradually her fingers unfurl and stretch open. He stands and pulls her to her feet. "Come here," he says. He begins a dance for her, a slow graceful hula, his freckled forearms waving gently, beckoning her. She feels a stirring in her abdomen. She wonders where he learned to dance like that. She follows him into the bedroom. "Let's have another honeymoon," he says, unbuttoning her blouse. His dog tags are the last thing he takes off before they make love. James D. Nichols; AB Negative; Protestant.

The next morning Jim wakes Linda before dawn. "I've got to go now," he says. "Paperwork; then Nellis."

"What time is it?" Linda's mouth feels cottony.

"Early." He kisses her hair, tangled from the good-bye they started last night, and then says, "Listen, Sgt. Kramer from Civil Engineering's going to call you. He's coming by, as a favor, to check out the rat situation, okay?"

Linda sits up in bed and pulls the sheet around her. Jim's in his flight suit, his eyes clear, his chin smelling of after-shave. The predawn dark dims his captain's bars, but Linda feels their glow. They've had this scene before: the warrior's farewell.

She sits unmoving, her shoulders slowly chilling in the air-conditioned room, while his absence fills the house. Then she goes into the kitchen to drink the coffee he left.

Later that day, Sgt. Kramer calls her at work. He asks if she can meet him at the house at three. Linda fingers the stack of yellow carbons on her desk and says yes. She conjures a dentist appointment for her boss and drives out to daycare for the girls. On the way, the Kmart sign snags her eye and she wheels into the parking lot to surprise the girls with a new My Little Pony for each.

Sgt. Kramer tours the house with a flashlight. He has a glass eye and as Linda talks with him her focus keeps shifting back and forth from the good eye to the glass one. "Your basic rat is nocturnal," he says. "But we can tell his presence by the droppings. About the size of watermelon seeds." His good eye squints at his thumb and finger, spread a smidgen apart to demonstrate size.

He inspects the entire house, Linda following cautiously behind him, looking for the telltale signs. "Looks like you're secure," he says. "The one your husband got must have been the point man."

"Where'd he come from?" Linda asks.

"Oh, they're everywhere. They burrow in the dirt like little moles, or they set up camp in the palm trees or in the thick bushes, your hibiscus or your oleander." Linda looks outside at the flowering beds she's been so proud of and feels sick.

"The main thing," the sergeant continues, "is to make sure your perimeter is secure. You're all right as long as they can't get in."

Linda thinks of the girls now on the floor in the living room playing with their ponies. She resolves the keep the doors closed and just open the jalousies for air.

"Now if you see one again, you call me," the sergeant says. "Don't try to trap it yourself."

"Don't worry, I won't."

That evening, Linda makes sure the baby-sitter knows not to leave the kitchen door open. Just in case.

Linda flashes her ID card at the gate and the guard waves her on base. BettyJean's house is in a row of identical others—two-bedroom duplexes earned by captains. The house is furnished with a strange mix of strange items BettyJean and Tony have picked up in their series of moves: a sonorous German grandfather clock, two leering Japanese foo dogs on the bookcase, a cowhide from San Antonio hanging above the couch. Linda and BettyJean both decide not to go to the movies after all. Linda feels too distracted to sit in the dark, and BettyJean wants to keep her feet up. Tony told her about Jim's orders, and she is worried about Jim but also worried Tony will be next. Linda fixes herself a screwdriver and BettyJean a plain orange juice. They just sit, sometimes talking, sometimes not.

"Have you thought of names yet?" Linda asks, after she pours herself a second drink.

"Boys' names," BettyJean says. "We've got it narrowed down to Tony Jr. or Anthony." She grins. "Which would you pick?"

"I guess Tony's pretty sure it's a boy."

"If it's not, number two won't be far behind," BettyJean says, patting the bulge on her lap.

Linda leans back into the couch, appalled by this remark. She remembers how crazy it made her, having two kids in diapers, both toddling into trouble together. But she can't think of a thing to say in the face of BettyJean's blithe innocence.

She picks up the *TV Guide* to see what's on. Just then noise rumbles. The ground shakes and the bits of wedding china on the buffet rattle. One foo dog tips over. "Oh my God," Linda says. BettyJean's eyes show panic and her head wavers on her neck. Linda reaches over and shoves BettyJean's head down between her knees. "Breathe slow." BettyJean gulps air and then waves Linda off.

"I'm okay," she says.

The roar in the air dies down and they rush to stand outside and listen. Mockingbirds chatter a minute and then sirens clamor all over the base, drowning out the birds.

"Fire-rescue," Linda says, and BettyJean nods. They both know the danger of spilled fuel, the slim chance of survival.

BettyJean goes back into the living room. Linda shuts the door and follows her. Her arms and legs feel heavier, as if the pull of gravity has suddenly become much stronger than before. A vision of palm trees toppling flashes before her eyes. Something furry scurries out from under the felled fronds.

"How long do you think it'll be before we know?" Linda asks.

"Not long. Look, I need a drink."

Linda doesn't comment on BettyJean's pregnancy. She refills BettyJean's orange juice and splashes it with vodka. She pours herself a stronger drink and struggles to set it down gently, without smashing the glass. They wait for the phone to ring. The sirens quiet and the birds settle back into sleep. Outside the windows, gray cloud shapes drift across the night sky at their usual height, as if no fundamental change in physics has occurred.

Finally, a long blue staff car pulls into BettyJean's driveway, and a major in dress uniform steps out. The driver stays in the car, shielded by mirrored aviator glasses. Linda looks at BettyJean. "You or me?"

"Mrs. D'Angelo?" The major asks.

"That's it then," BettyJean says. She turns to Linda. "Do you mind coming back later?" She looks smaller. Even her belly seems to have caved in.

"Are you sure?" Linda asks. "I can stay."

BettyJean shakes her head.

Linda's fingers tremble against the steering wheel as she drives home. She asks the baby-sitter to wait. An hour later, when she calls BettyJean, the major is still there. Linda wonders what there is for him to talk about, but she is glad he stays. Later, she'll hold BettyJean, make calls for her, fix weak drinks for her, whatever. But not yet.

The phone rings: Jim calling to tell her he's okay. "It was a fluke," he says. "The canopy blew open just after Tony took off. All his charts sucked into the intake. He was too low to eject."

Jim is coming back home. Nellis is off. They'll have more time together before he leaves. His voice thickens. "God, what a stupid thing to happen. A one in a million accident." Linda thinks of all the nuts and bolts and screws and rivets that hold a plane together.

She goes into the kitchen to make a fresh pot of coffee. It'll be a long night. She looks out the window at the empty sky beyond. The palm trees sway in the breeze blowing in from the Caribbean. The hibiscus rustles gently. Something out there is moving.

The Beatification of Beth

"Consider my servant Beth," God says. He and Satan are at the bar, playing liar's dice. The game is going nowhere. Satan may be the king of lies, but God is omniscient.

"Are you proposing a tiebreaker?" Satan asks. The two of them have been at stalemate for millennia. It's getting boring. They both look over at Beth, seated at the other end of the bar. Satan lifts one arched eyebrow. As far as he knows, she's no one's servant.

Beth averts her face. God with his blue light, Satan in red—these two have been shadowing her all her life. There was a time when she was perfectly willing to climb up on a stake and be lit on fire. Searching for grace; transcendence; her old wish to be so small she could curl up inside a man's pocket, so large she could swallow the world in one swift bite.

But she's twenty-six now and has finally found a point of precarious balance: the scars on her wrists have begun to tan over. She has moved into a tiny cottage all her own on the wrong side of Nob Hill. She has decided to buckle down at work, even if it is only telephone customer service. She is trying to taste happiness in thin-blooded sips. She has known ecstasy. She has known despair. But mere happiness… This March evening, the cusp of winter and spring, the air unusually sultry, the exact temperature of her flesh. Walking home from work, halfway up the hill, one arc of setting sun had caught her eye. On a wrought-iron balcony, yellow light haloed three nodding daffodils. For one moment, the random touch of goodwill had touched her. So she'd decided to treat herself to one glass of a really good cabernet. Not realizing that God and Satan were waiting at the bar.

This bar is a sedate place. Indirect lighting; discreet piano. The bartender—a thin, reedy guy with rusty hair and gold eyeglasses—polishes the long slab of pink granite and makes small talk. There is no smoking allowed, which doesn't stop Satan from lighting up. The bartender only frowns; he's not a cop—he's not up to challenging a guy carrying a pitchfork.

Tiny blue flames outline God. Actually, he and Satan don't look so different. Except that Satan has those cloven hooves and those horns sticking up out of his hair.

"Body and soul," God says. "She's mine."

"Stakes?"

"What do you suggest?"

"Let me come home," Satan answers. "One weekend only—I couldn't stand it longer than that. But for one long weekend let me be the prodigal returned. Roast a fatted calf or two, break out a dozen or so of your best bottles, gather round the other angels. I want to hear them sing 'For He's a Jolly Good Fellow.'"

"Ha. You wish." But God realizes the advantages are all his: he's not just omniscient. He's omnipotent too.

"Okay, it's a deal. But if I win you have to kneel at my feet. You have to put your forehead to the ground and your ass in the air and say five times out loud: God is great."

"You just can't get enough, can you?"

They shake on it, Satan's cloven hoof in God's large palm.

Beth, as God sidles up to her, tries to convey disinterest in the slight turn of her shoulders, in her studied concentration on her half-empty glass. The fact is, she knows what's going on. It's not the first time she's been the subject of a bar bet. Men, she's found, can be pretty damn easy. She's got young breasts; she's got gold streaks in her hair; she knows lipstick. It doesn't take much more than that.

But God has his ways. As he nears, she's warmed by the flames illuminating him. As he seats himself at the barstool next to hers, his kneecap brushes hers. Her slit skirt drapes open and color blooms up her thigh where he touched. He smells of spice, of ginger and cardamom. He says hello, he introduces himself—as if he needed to. At the other end of the bar, Satan lifts his glass, another unnecessary greeting. God's voice is rippling and soft as chiffon at her earlobe. When she finally turns to look at him, she is speared by an instant shaft of lust: he is exactly what she has always fallen for. Those Semitic looks, deep-set, dark brown eyes, strong regular features, a distance in his gaze even as he looks so unflinchingly at her. His throat is taut, delineating tendon, vein, Adam's apple.

But she's been here before. She's been here a thousand times before. She's about to tell him to take a hike when he whispers into her hair, "I can take you to Paradise."

Beth bursts out laughing—the line is so lame. But then she stops. She closes her mouth. She closes her slit skirt. Because she senses it might be true. That it might be true, she thinks, is the last thing she needs. She has spent three years learning perfect balance in one position—absolute zero. It is the still point from which she cannot fall. And yet. She runs a finger around the rim of her glass and the crystal hums an exact, shattering note. She looks at the blue hollow base of his throat, where one tiny, dark hair curls, and temptation rises in a narrow pink surge up her own neck and settles onto her angular cheekbones.

She lifts her glass, sips, demurs. Knowing herself well enough to know the answer is already yes. Even so, she has every intention of making him work for it. She looks up at him from the corner of her eye, partly teasing, partly afraid. "Don't you buy a lady dinner first?"

Amused by her resistance—which he knows is feeble, which he knows is only delay and not denial—God says, "Sure. We can have dinner. What do you feel like?"

She feels like glass. As friable as glass. Like glass that has been smashed and then carefully reglued—so that only in certain light do the cracks appear. But she wants to feel like steel. As ringingly sure as steel. She can remember a time when she would have been unafraid to say yes to anything. She says to him, "I thought you were into seafood. The whole loaves and fishes thing."

As it turns out, he is. He knows a good place in South Beach.

She was thirteen years old when she first sensed there was something she needed to find. She looked into the mirror first. A stormy August night alone in her bedroom, up on the second floor of a white, wooden, empty house in Florida, in a small murky town sinking between swamp and sea. The squall blowing in had dimmed the power, and the light oozed thick and brown and silent. She saw the muddy isolation of her body—her arms, her rib cage, her long-muscled thighs—waver and dissolve. Uneasy, she leaned in close, so close her short, sharp nose touched the glass. She looked hard into her opaque dark eyes, trying to find something beyond the mirror. But she couldn't see and she wasn't sure and she wasn't breathing, couldn't breathe at all. Scared, she placed her hands to the glass, to squeeze her reflection into her palms. Then electricity cut out completely and she fell into blank, black nothing.

Outside, lightning flickered. White flare backlit the beckoning grace of a camphor tree rising out of a bed of red mud. She climbed up over the windowsill and dropped lightly down to the ground. The scent of camphor scourged the night. Quick and agile and trusting, she climbed up into the tree. The bark was rough and jagged under her bare feet. She climbed up high, to where the branches thinned and stretched.

She could see everything. She could see the jungle of mangroves at the end of the road. She could see the ocean and whitecapped waves and phosphorescence like tumbled stars in the water. She could see the black-breasted sky and its neckline of squall spitting lightning, and she wanted it— she wanted it all. She was hungry. She hadn't eaten. She looked down and she could see her house, its ragged gray shingles, its ragged gray eaves. Electricity had returned. Gray television light glimmered from the living room window.

She crumpled a fistful of camphor leaves under her nose. The scent washed like white glass into her head. Vertigo tunneled up from the red mud and tugged at her hands. If she jumped, would she fall up or down? Something moved in her—not yet desire and far, far from faith—only the first grace notes of a prayer to heaven or hell. It didn't matter which. *If you love me, catch me.* She swanned out her arms, lifted her chest, closed her eyes, and leaped.

For one long moment, the sky held her. Then she landed hard on solid ground and broke her leg.

At the hospital, Beth's father tugged his few strands of gray hair and said he'd never in a million years understand his daughter. Beth's mother touched up her pink lipstick and told the doctor Beth didn't take after anyone in her side of the family. She blamed music. She blamed books. She blamed the men and the boys who were already beginning to glance sideways at Beth when she walked by tan and lanky in cutoffs and Keds.

Beth didn't blame anyone. She didn't think there was anything to blame anyone for. She was what she was. She would have pain. But she'd have miracles, too; she was certain.

When she was fifteen, her chemistry teacher gave her a string of pearls that matched perfectly the milky shade of her breasts. He kissed her throat and murmured breathlessly over and over that she would get him fired. When he told her they had to stop, she dropped the pearls into a beaker of hydrochloric acid.

When she was seventeen, she fell madly in love with the wildest boy in town and burnt his initials onto her jutting hipbone with the head of a dead match. Immolation, she told him, is the truest love. In return, he offered her a beer. She smashed his beer bottle against a pepper tree. She'd seen enough Hollywood to believe she'd find transcendence in California.

At the seafood place God favors, there's a small crowd of anorexic men and women in black—black silk, black leather, black denim—standing outside under yellow light, smoking cigarettes, waiting for tables. God elbows his way through to the restaurant's etched-glass doors, pulling Beth behind him. Inside, she is buffeted by clatter and aroma. God gives his name and asks for a table. A tuxedoed waiter with oiled hair offers to seat them right away. Votive candles flicker on white tablecloths and rosy sconces splash sheer red light over the walls. Beth and God sit down at a table for two beside another table for two, where a man and woman in tight-fitting gray argue intensely. Beth hears the word "betrayal." She hears the word "heartbreak." The word "divorce" smashes like a gavel down onto the table. The waiter presents menus, a wine list. "Drink?" God asks, his tone pleasantly light. He seems oblivious to the rage surrounding them.

Beth hesitates. She's already had her one permitted glass of wine. Then she decides, what the hell. She orders a champagne cocktail. God orders a Heineken. The waiter brings their drinks and Beth stirs hers with the straw. Then she sticks the straw in her mouth, sucks the sugar off, slides the straw between her lips. Watches God watching her. She notes the slight slackening at his mouth, the faint flattening of his eyelids. She thinks: he's not so all-powerful. He's not nearly so all-powerful as he thinks he is. She takes a long, slow sip from her drink. The bitters bite her tongue. The alcohol slithers down to coil up inside her belly.

"So. Why me?" she asks.

"Why not you?"

Beth makes a face. He sounds like a lawyer. Or like a shrink.

He asks, "Haven't you been looking for me?"

"What makes you think that?"

God drinks his beer straight from the bottle, tilting his head back, not taking his eyes off Beth's face for a second. "All along, all those men—I think it was me you wanted."

The ego of this guy! Beth thinks. And then, appalled, she sits back wondering if he was right. Unsettled, she drinks again. Reminds herself she doesn't want anyone. She has taught herself not to want. Not wanting, she has found, is the secret of balance.

The alcohol in her belly rustles, stirs. God sets his beer down and one tiny drop lingers at the corner of his mouth. She has a momentary impulse to put her finger there, to take that drop and touch it to her own mouth. Instead, beneath the table, she crosses her legs. Her stockings make a shushing sound. She feels her nipples tighten beneath her lace bra, sees God's gaze graze her chest. Leaning forward, onto the table, she says, "Maybe you've got it vice-versa."

God reaches across, takes her hand, turns it palm up. His fingers brush the ragged remnants of her scars. He wraps two fingers around her wrist. "This is not a contest of wills,

Beth." Which is good, she thinks, because her will is the last thing she trusts. "Nonetheless, I am that I am." Beth tries to pull her wrist free and finds that she can't. His two fingers have her locked in a deathgrip. "And you are that you are, the one who seeks surrender."

She pulls with all her strength and yanks free of him. Or does he merely release her? She can hardly breathe—she feels like she's been kicked. That he knows so much about her—how?

God shrugs. "Omniscience, what can I say."

The waiter arrives to take their order. Beth is not a bit hungry. She is pissed off. She ought to leave, she thinks.

But she can't leave. That rustling slithering movement in her belly isn't alcohol at all. It's desire, awakening. It's need. It's as dangerous as hell.

She decides that if she can't eat, she will at least cost him something. Even if the cost is of no account to him. She orders a huge amount of food: carrot soup, baby greens, swordfish, pasta, zucchini. God orders crab and shrimp and crayfish and another champagne cocktail for Beth.

Eighteen years old, Beth plunged into the Los Angeles basin with a greed that stunned even herself. She would have everything. She enrolled in school. She couldn't choose; she couldn't leave anything out; she read everything. Philosophy, physics, literature, voice. She read until her eyes seared into slits. She danced until she fell down. She wore ribboned sandals and no underwear, her hair fierce as a lion's mane. She took up smoking. She took up men. She fed them hash brownies and swallowed them whole. She never slept. She took to climbing out onto her fire escape and staring down into the reaching whirl of vertigo. She was only on the second floor and she knew by now how to land. She let the grassy shock travel through the balls of her feet, up her knees, into her loose hips. She traveled up the coast. She walked along jagged cliffs and the siren span of Golden Gate. She took up religion, briefly. She took up a woman, briefly. Exhausted, cynical, dark, she took up celibacy. Then she took up a medical student who fed her tablets of Ecstasy and she curled up inside his furred chest and finally relaxed. Marcus: milky, dimpled, with big hands and slow speech. She told him he was never what she'd love. She was straddling his hips, her wild hair hanging in his mouth—he wasn't going anywhere. But he was smart, like she was, and patient. Which she was not and never would be. In his studies, he'd already learned this about the human heart: it is as heliotropic as a sunflower.

Beth's soup and salad have been cleared, uneaten, and she has finished her second drink, when a charcoal smell drifts under her nose. Satan pulls up a chair. He hails the waiter, orders a Manhattan and another drink for Beth.

"What the hell are you doing here?" God asks. The silver on the table rattles. The arguing couple at the next table flinches, startled. They look over at God with identical pale fear. A glass of red wine on their table topples and the wine drips heedlessly onto the woman's lap.

"Easy, big guy. Just thought I'd check how things are going. Since I do have an interest."

The waiter oozes over with another champagne cocktail and Satan's Manhattan. Satan plucks up the cherry, pops it into his mouth, and speaks around it to the waiter. "Let me have some lamb chops, rare. And an ashtray." From nowhere a Marlboro appears between his lips. The waiter practically clicks his heels together as he nods his head, hurries away to fulfill Satan's order.

"You want a cigarette, Beth?" Satan asks. He leans his head back, blows smoke rings up to the ceiling.

"I don't smoke."

"Oh, that's right. You quit. Good for you." He lifts his glass to her and she drinks from hers. He leans over to God, confidential. "You remember the bet, right? Body *and* soul?"

God shrugs. He's busy eating. Dismembered shellfish litter his plate. His fingers are shiny with butter. "Beth, you really should try your swordfish. This crab is excellent." To Satan, he says, "Have faith."

Satan snorts. Beth is into her third drink now. He places one cloven hoof on her shoulder. "Sweetheart, you ought to know, this guy plays winner take all."

Beth feels the slight spin of vertigo—or perhaps, of champagne.

At the table beside them, the woman notices the wine on her lap; the man comes to her side. He brushes at her with his napkin. His hand touches her hair, her head tilts toward his hand. His expression moves rapidly through anger to sorrow to concern, and Beth senses an infinity of possible outcomes opening between these two people. When Satan's lamb chops arrive, God says to Beth, "Shall we go?"

Beth hesitates. God sighs. He puts his lips to her ear. "Beth, don't think so damn much. Just close your eyes and feel what you feel."

So she does. And what she feels is, ripe. Knees weak, she stands. Unsure, she says, "Yes. Let's go."

As they are leaving, the waiter presents the leather folder with the bill to Satan.

In the cab on the way to her house, God kisses her fingertips. She asks if they should stop at a drugstore. He tells her not to worry, it's not time for that yet.

Beth's cottage is itself a kind of city miracle. Tumbling halfway down a hill, weather-beaten gray shingles, leaded windows rippled with age, and a tiny yard with sandy soil that, if she wanted, she could enrich with clay to start a garden. A small front porch where, if she wanted, she could fit a dog. If she wanted a dog, she'd want a bloodhound.

God has to duck his head to fit through the doorway. In her living room, her best piece of furniture, a long camel-back sofa draped with gold damask cloth, sits angled in front of a small stone fireplace stacked with kindling. God breathes into the hearth, and flames ignite. Beth pours two glasses of club soda. She doesn't keep alcohol in her house—it's another of those small rules she has inscribed around herself to maintain balance. But when she sits down next to God the soda fizzes, thickens, and turns gold. She sips carefully and tastes sweet, sweet wine. An *auslese* or a *spätlese*. She pictures a single grape, high on a mountain, inside a shell of ice, its sugars crystallizing.

God lifts her hand to his mouth to kiss her scars.

That old sorrow. It is still so close tears singe her eye-lashes. "Why are you here now," she asks, "and not then?"

God sighs. It's a question he's asked a lot. He wants to answer: people don't understand he can't do everything. He is, after all, only one god. But he's too politic for that; he keeps his complaints to himself. Instead he tells her what he thinks she needs to hear. "Maybe I was there. Maybe that's why you can be here now."

Was he? Beth tries to remember any hint of sanctification in that night. But what she remembers most is being supremely alone. Marcus had said she was crazy. She made him crazy. They had lived together for two years in a tiny, over-the-garage apartment, two desks in the living room and a cramped brass bed in the bedroom. He had given her everything. Everything. He had taken her to mountains and deserts. He had bought her necklaces and flowers and had cooked eggs and bacon for her. He had massaged her tense shoulders, had rubbed oil into her feet, had half-carried her to the hospital when her fever spiked to a hundred-and-four and her breath stank of dreams. He had finally made her love him. Now he wanted his own place. He wanted to sit in a black recliner and watch a baseball game and drink a beer. He had exams. He had work. He had someone else. He'd gone into the bedroom to pack his things.

She'd sat down at her desk and looked at herself in a mirror propped against a stack of books. She pulled her wild hair over her face, peered through the veil of hair. She couldn't see herself. What could she give him to make him stay? She picked up a pair of scissors. She cut off all her hair. She cut it close to her scalp. She piled the snakes of hair into a ceramic bowl, stuck a match to them. They sizzled and curled and disappeared in a stink of smoke.

Marcus came running into the room. Shorn, her head was innocent and vulnerable as a duckling's. He stared at her, aghast. "I did it for you," she said. She rose from her desk and wrapped her arms around him.

"I don't want that," he said.

"Yes you do. You always did. Immolation—the truest love."

For a few minutes he could not stop touching that odd soft stubble of her sacrificial skull. But then he pulled himself away. After he left, she picked up her empty mirror and smashed it. She poured herself a glass of wine. She leaned against the kitchen counter, drinking it fast. She poured herself another. Anger whipped like a hurricane through her. She dashed the wineglass to the ground. Then a tidal surge of grief buckled her knees. She fell into the scattered shards of glass. Grief and anger rippled through her in clashing waves, pulling her apart. She had wanted so much, it was impossible. She had wanted so little, it was pathetic, just to be held in the hand of something that would not let go. She plucked up one jagged piece of glass and savaged her wrists, first one and then the other. Now, she thought. Now she would know.

She stood alone in that kitchen watching her blood drip down onto the blue linoleum. The red and blue, merging and separating, merging and separating. It was like looking down through a kaleidoscope at the whole sad pattern of her life.

But she is certain now that there had been no one else with her that night. She'd stood alone, staring deep down. Remembering that night in the camphor tree so long ago when she had been young and yet untouched. How certain she'd been of miracles. Her body, slamming into dirt. No one, nothing, had caught her. No one, nothing, would catch her this time either. She could fall forever. Or she could climb back down to Earth and try very hard to keep her feet on the ground. She'd held tight to the phone to keep from toppling over. She didn't call Marcus. She'd called 911 and told a disembodied voice what she'd done.

That phone call. It may have been the only true miracle in her life. Ever since, it's been a silver ring around her finger as she's tentatively put one foot in front of the other. She would rather live than die.

"What matters," God says, cradling both her hands in his, "is that I'm here now." He nuzzles her neck, her ears. He kisses her eyes, he licks her eyelids, his tongue traces the invisible line tears have etched down her face.

She can't help but be warmed by all the tiny blue flames surrounding him. She still feels like glass. But now she feels like heated glass, translucent and pliable.

And then there is heat on the other side of her. Satan, perched on the sofa.

"I was there, dollface," he says. "I'd have caught you."

God breaks away from Beth, outraged. "You? With those mitts of yours you couldn't catch a bus."

Satan stretches out his arms, examines his furred hocks, his clumsy black hooves. "Okay, you've got me there. But if I had been there I'd have at least thrown her a bon voyage party. I'd have said: enjoy the ride."

Which makes Beth laugh, a sudden, deep bubbling sound. Satan laughs too, and his eyes, the same deep-set, dark eyes that God has, are surprisingly gentle and wise. A quick vision flashes in front of Beth. Satan's cloven hoof on her left thigh, God's hand on her right, the both of them stroking her, her legs parting for them both. Her bed, she knows, is big enough.

Omniscient, pissed, God says to Satan, "Do you mind? We're kind of busy here."

"Fine. I'll go. I can come back, whenever," Satan says. "Just wanted to let you know I didn't appreciate getting stuck with the tab back there. But you know me, I stiffed them. Sweetheart, one word of advice," he says to Beth. "If this guy offers you the stars, get it in writing. Believe me, it's a long way down."

Satan disappears. God touches her breast. "Now, where were we?" he asks.

They were in her bedroom. The room is done in shades of pale yellow. The blue fire outlining God makes it seem as if dawn is breaking right there beside her bed. He murmurs something, and in an instant their clothes fall away. He kisses her shoulder. He kisses her scarred hip. He kisses her wrists. Petals of heat shimmer from his lips to her skin. Beneath her sternum, beneath her belly, she is lit with a white chrysanthemum heat all her own. She feels her ligaments loosen. She can barely stand. It is more than she can stand. She is afraid. She is terrified. She tries to reassure herself. This is only what it is. This is only something she's done a thousand times before. He smells of sandalwood and rain. They are on her bed. His knees part her legs. He enters her and her breath rushes out of her throat. She can't breathe, can't breathe at all, it doesn't matter. He breathes for her. They move in a rhythm as ancient as he is. For as long as it takes, they are two wings beating together, rising up toward that hot sun hanging over her bed.

Afterward, she lies with her cheek nestled in the dark hair on his chest. Relieved, content, Beth's fingers skip lightly down to toy with his sated penis. Annoyed, he brushes her hand away. Absently, he strokes her back. The bet was body and soul. A thousand years ago, the soul would have been the easy part, but this is the twenty-first century and even he's had to adjust. Deliberately, he cradles her head, whispers into her hair, "Give yourself to me."

Beth laughs. "I just did."

"No. I mean—believe in me." He runs a finger down her temple, her cheek, to her breastbone. "Let me inside."

Beth shivers. That one leap, desire to faith—she's never made it yet without falling short. She gets up, belts her old scruffy robe around her waist. "Look, you were right. It was Paradise and more. But I think it's time for you to go."

God frowns, and a tremor shudders underneath the warped oak floorboards. Beth braces herself in the doorway while a few small chunks of plaster fall from her ceiling. But then God rearranges his face into an open expression, and the ground quiets. "I can make you happy," he says.

He's wrong, she thinks. She has never learned to be merely happy.

"What do you want most in the world?" he asks.

Everything. "I don't want anything."

But she does. From nowhere a bloodhound lopes into the room, leaps up onto the bed. Charmed, Beth falls down onto the sheet beside the dog. It lays looking up at her, jowls splayed, brown eyes sad with love.

"You see?" God says. Instantly a whole garden blooms in

her bedroom. Red hollyhocks tower over her, white daisies flutter, pink tulips quiver. Sunlight filters down through the flowers and warms Beth's face.

"What else?" God asks. They are both sitting up now, against the headboard. God smiles down on her and she can't help feeling the first blush of love. She pets the dog; it wags its tail. God reaches over, plucks a gardenia, tucks it into her hair.

What else could she want? She could want emeralds. She could want a winning lottery ticket and a Saab convertible. But she doesn't, not really. She could want world peace and a cure for cancer and ten years of clear sky....

"Well, let's not get carried away," God says.

But he knows what she wants. What she's always wanted. Immolation—that truest love.

"Who better than me for that?" God says. "It's what I'm famous for."

He pushes the dog off the bed. She slides down to lie beside him. He opens her robe. He places his hand on the hollow between her flattened breasts. There is a stillness in the room. The flowers no longer flutter and quiver. There is a hush. Her pulse slows. Her breathing slows. The room, the flowers, the dog, the sun, all of it falls away and there is only him and her, in a white and quiet space all their own. He strokes, over and over, just that one bare strip of flesh. Her skin warms and softens. She can only look at his hand. She can't look at his face. To look into his eyes now would be death itself. Her skin thins to a membrane of oil and salt. Underneath, Beth can see the red beating muscle that is her heart. Carefully he presses her fine transparent skin with one finger. There is resistance. He presses harder. There is the slightest give. An opening. He pushes on. One finger becomes two becomes his whole hand sliding down into her. There is heat. Nearly unbearable heat. He takes the whole weight of her heart in his hand.

Beth throws her head back. Her body lies inert. But inside her skull, she shatters into hot shards of glass. Behind the glass is velvet dark. Hours pass, or maybe minutes. Then, rising from the dark, she hears music. All the shards of glass whirl together into one bright mirror and she sees straight through her own face. She sees waves of music cohering into one vibration. One absolute note plucked on one silken string. Her own name, sung in ancient song. *Beth*. She shudders at the sight. She smolders. She flares into color. She bursts into flames.

"There," God says, withdrawing his hand. "You see? That wasn't so terrible." The smile on his face has only partially to do with her.

Tears spill sideways from her eyes to pool onto the sheet beneath her. Her mouth is burned sand. She can only whisper, "Please don't leave."

But he's up, off the bed. He pulls on his trousers, he checks his watch. "Oh, jeez, look at the time." He's got a million simultaneous places to be.

He leans over the bed. He kisses her forehead. She can't even manage to lift an arm to him. "I'll call you," he says. "Or you can call me. Leave a message; I'll get back to you."

When she wakes in the morning, she can't find any trace of him. No pawprints of the dog, no seedlings cast by the hollyhocks, not even the brown husk of the gardenia he'd stuck behind her ear. She looks at herself in the mirror on her closet door and her eyes are as opaque as ever. But she knows now...something. Ghostly wisps of revelation tease her. Miracles, yes. But pain—oh, God. She has never in her life felt so bereft. She goes back to the bar where he and Satan played dice, but he is not there. She asks the bartender if he's seen God, and he tells her to get lost.

The day is hot, the sun white and searing. The sidewalks glare up at her as she climbs the city hill. She is thirsty. She is exhausted. Her hands hurt. Her feet hurt. Ahead, at the top of the hill, is the cathedral. It rises from the earth, massive as a granite cliff, gargoyles leering, emaciated saints twisting gaunt necks to stare at her with stone dry eyes. Teresa. Agatha, her breasts on a platter. Joan.

Outside, Satan sits on a bench in the plaza. "Crash and burn, sweetheart," he says. "I could have told you. Here, have a cigarette."

Beth sits down on the bench beside him, takes the Marlboro. She smokes, and the nicotine kicks right into her veins. The palest imitation of what she seeks.

Satan lights up one of his own. He's seen all this before. He's seen all this a thousand times before. Maybe God will call her, who knows? So the big guy won this round, that doesn't mean he'll collect. Satan smirks. Now's his chance to play his own hand. "Come dance with me," he says, offering her a hoof.

It's been forever since she last went dancing. Desire uncoils in her belly, slithers up her throat, bites her tongue. She hears music, the song she heard last night, and remembers how she once loved to dance. She takes Satan's arm. She'll need a new dress. Red, silk. And while she's out she can get herself a dog. She can plant hollyhocks in the sand. Her hands itch; she scratches them; blood beads up on her palms. Stigmata: she can't help but laugh, excited by this game. Body and soul, it'll never be over til it's over.

The Hands of the Evangelist

Grandpa didn't eat with us that morning. Instead, he stood in his pajamas, arms hanging limp, watching some invisible scene through the louvered front room windows. His absence sped us through breakfast since Mama's prayers weren't near as long as his. I spent a few extra minutes shaving my recent whiskers, which were coming in blond and sparse, and then I sideparted my hair with a little Brylcreem to smooth its tendency to rebel. I waited outside for Daddy and watched Timmy Rogers, the three-year-old boy next door, romp with his new cocker spaniel puppy. The puppy tumbled around the boy, tripping over its own ears. Timmy asked if didn't I think his puppy was the greatest ever, and I agreed he sure was. Then Daddy came out to drive me to school in the '65 Ford Fairlane, its red vinyl seats still smelling new. We got to school before the buses did and I stood kicking a few pebbles outside the green portable classroom where Mrs. Shiffield struggled to teach French rolled *R*'s. I had just stubbed the toe of my boot on the sidewalk when I heard a raspy voice mention Heidi Muller.

I edged my head around the corner. Sammy Watts and Junior Barnes leaned against one end of the classroom. Sammy's hand poked down deep in his pockets and Junior sucked on a cigarette. They both wore the kind of blue jeans Reverend Tyler called worldly. Junior bent one leg and rested the sole of his boot against the tin siding. "Soft and easy as pudding," he sighed, blowing a stream of smoke in front of his sharp chin.

Hurricane season was on us, and the air was hot and

heavy. The smoke hung limp and Junior fanned it away.

"Vanilla pudding," Sammy said, reaching for the cigarette. My mouth filled up.

"Taste like it, too," Junior said.

"No." Sammy coughed and grabbed at his chicken neck. "She didn't. You lie like a hound dog."

I swallowed the spit in my mouth. Sammy turned and hawked out a bubbly goo at my feet. "Look who's here," he said, nudging Junior. "Why, it's the Angel Gabriel. Who's blowing your horn, Gabriel?"

I clutched my Bible and told them to go smoke in Hell. Then I climbed the two cinderblock steps into the portable and slouched down in my seat. Mrs. Shiffield's breasts jiggled like pig bladders as her arm scratched verbs on the board. "*Bonjour*, Gabriel," she said. I sat through the whole hour thinking about Heidi. The bell rang and I determined to find her that afternoon.

She and a gaggle of girls chattered inside the glass doors at the seniors' end of the one-halled school building. Voices chased all around the metal lockers. Heidi wore a short-sleeved sweater made out of some fuzzy, pink wool. A gold heart-shaped locket dangled off the ridge made by her breasts. Just as I said hello, she lifted that locket and stuck it in her mouth. Her lipstick matched her sweater and the ribbon around her ponytail and the polish on her fingernails. Oh, she was worldly, all right.

I straightened my shoulders and strolled past her to my own locker, where I kept a whole tower of Grandpa's pamphlets. I found the one I wanted: a green foldover with stories of the Holy Spirit entering a body and flooding it with rapture.

At that moment, Sammy and Junior tugged the glass doors open. Sammy tossed another cigarette onto the floor and squashed it under his boot. They were each almost a

foot taller than Heidi, and they circled her, their arms darting around like gulls swooping. Sammy chucked her under
the chin and then somehow both boys culled Janice Peters
out and leaned her against the wall, one snake-veined male
arm on either side of her. Heidi bit her lip and color bled
from her sweater to her face. I thrust my pamphlet at her
and walked on, pulling the glass doors open and moving
out into the dank air to wait.

The other girls streamed out the doors in pairs. School
buses rumbled out front, waiting to carry us in either direction, north to Florida Springs, or three miles south to
Kingdom. An uncomfortable pressure had built up in me.
I nearly missed Heidi coming out of the building. She'd
pulled out her ponytail, and her ducked-down face was
almost obscured by her thin, blonde hair. I touched her
shoulder and she jumped. "Oh, it's only you," she said.

"I'm walking," I told her. "Want to come along?"

She looked over at the kids climbing onto the buses.
Sammy and Junior already leaned against the back windows, and Janice sat one seat forward, her face turned
toward the rear. "Sure, why not," Heidi said.

We tramped along the asphalt road between the fields
lying outside Kingdom, not saying much. Dragonflies hovered over the drainage canal that tagged alongside the road.
We passed the field where in summer yellow corn shot up.
When I was little, those cornstalks terrified me; I was certain snakes slithered inside the husks.

We warmed with the walking, and Heidi pulled her
sweater away from where it had started to stick to her skin.
At one point, she lifted her hair off her neck and held it up
a while. I struggled to keep my eyes forward and not watch
how her breasts rose. I could smell the soap she used and
some other scent, like lemons, steaming off her. Out on the
horizon, a hawk circled against the low sky. Somewhere

below a mouse trembled.

"Why'd you give me that pamphlet?" Her voice sounded very loud in the quiet.

I coughed and stuck my hands in my pockets. "I guess I thought you'd be interested. You looked unhappy there for a minute."

"Did you hear something about me?"

"Hear what?"

"Nothing."

We were getting close to town. Ray Mundy's Esso station lay just ahead, and Ray was busy pumping gas into what looked like the new model Lincoln. I sped up my pace and Heidi fell a little behind. "Want a Nehi?" I asked her, leading her toward the station. I stepped around the pumps, peering at the car. It was about half an acre long, white with blue interior, and all kinds of needles and dials on the dash. The man driving the car paid Ray with bills peeled from a wad he stuffed back into his front pocket. I watched him maneuver the car out onto the road, then turned back to Heidi. "Grape okay?" She nodded and I dug out some coins.

We walked along into town sipping the Nehis. Four blocks on and we'd reach the place we had to separate. "Did you read it?" I asked.

"Some," she said. "You think all that's some kind of cure for unhappiness?"

I shook my head and stopped her walking. The rims of her ears peeked through her hair, making her look young and awkward. I looked down full into her face. "Happy's got nothing to do with it," I said. I looked off in the distance, like I was gathering my words, and then turned back to her. "You know that field south of my daddy's car lot— the one mostly gone to clover?" She nodded, squinting up at me. The sun was right at my back and making her teary.

"Once, when I was maybe five years old, my grandpa took me out to the middle of that field while a storm watch was on. We stood there and watched four tornadoes march across that field—great big twisters reaching down and sucking up everything. We planted our feet in that clover and Grandpa held my hand and tilted up his head, shouting out glory, and I shouted along too, even though my voice wasn't near as strong as his. Those twisters passed right by us, not even lifting one hair on our heads."

She had finished her Nehi while I was talking. "Here, I'll take that," I said, reaching for the bottle. "I go by Ray's all the time."

We started walking again, passing Bach's jewelry store and a bakery next door. A lady and two kids stepped out of the bakery, each kid with a chocolate grin and clutching a cookie. I could tell Heidi was thinking. "Come to church sometime with me," I told her. "You'll see. Happiness isn't the issue—what you have instead is peace."

"Peace," she said, sighing through the word. "I like that." We'd reached the corner where she turned left. Her folks kept an old cinderblock house swelled near to bust by the number of people living inside. Catholics. Mr. Muller ran the five and dime in town.

I kept on heading straight through town to the new house I'd convinced Daddy to buy. Normally, I slowed as I got near to take in the scalloped shingles and the crisp yellow paint and the wrought iron balcony. But today, I practically leaped inside. Bringing over a Catholic, wouldn't that turn some heads! And maybe Heidi would give me something finally to repent around the bonfire at Bible Camp.

Mama was inside the house churning noodles in a pot on the white, electric stove. The kitchen smelled like mustard. Daddy and Grandpa sat at the kitchen table not speaking.

Grandpa pulled his dentures out and spat onto the teeth, then began polishing them with the corner of his pajama top. Without teeth to structure his face, his head looked like some ancient fruit, a peach maybe, long forgotten in the bowl. Mama's face had a worrisome crimp in it and the skin around her nose was white, even in the heat of the steam rising from the noodle pot. Daddy leaned back in his seat and drummed his manicured nails on the table. "I've been waiting for you, sport," he said.

I dropped my Bible on the table and Grandpa's spoon clattered from the edge of his teacup. "What's wrong?" I asked.

"I need your help with a customer," Daddy said.

Grandpa chomped his dentures back in and said, "Nevermind that, we got serious problems."

Mama turned from the stove, her wooden spoon dripping hot water onto the linoleum. "Grandpa had a vision today," she said.

"Grandma Rose," Daddy said. "Again."

I turned one of the green, vinyl chairs and straddled it, leaning my arms against the back. "Really? Where?" Grandpa pressed his dentures up with his thumb and ran his tongue across them. "She was sitting on top of the car," he said.

"The Fairlane," Daddy said. He chuckled. "Tell him what she was wearing, Pop."

Grandpa's face fired up. "Go ahead and laugh. She was warning us about the worldliness in this house." He turned to me. "Son, you should have seen. She was all tarted up in lipstick and earrings, wearing this low-cut mini-dress and plastic boots." Daddy's chuckling turned into a full barrel laugh, his head tipped back to let it out. "Stop, you," Grandpa said.

"I can't help it," Daddy said, wiping his eyes. "You got to

admit Rose in a mini-dress would be a sight. She was built like a tractor tire."

"Oh, honey," Mama said. She turned back to the noodles.

Daddy turned and put his arms around her from behind. "I'm sorry, sweetie; she was your Mama." He kissed her neck where the hair fell down from its pins. "But thank the Good Lord you took after his side of the family." His hands smoothed over Mama's body, and her back arched ever so slightly. He pulled away. "Even if he is a scrawny old turkey vulture now," Daddy said, looking at Grandpa.

"Oh stop, you two," Mama said. She turned to me and smiled. "Gabriel, what do you think?"

I looked at Daddy and my brain raced. Then I stood up, frowning, and ran my fingers over the Bible. Grandpa's face was eager. "Go-go boots, huh? Maybe Grandma was warning us about that dance place just opened up in Florida Springs." I thought a minute. "Which way was she facing?"

"North."

"Well, there you are." Daddy winked at me as I spoke. "She's telling us God wants us to shut that place down. Best tell Reverend Tyler."

"And what about the car?" Grandpa asked.

"Will you stop fretting about that car," Daddy said. "There's nothing wrong with new things."

"I don't like them red seats," Grandpa said. "They're worldly."

"Come on, Gramps." I moved behind him and rubbed his thin shoulders. "The Bible says God wants us to prosper as our souls prosper. So what's wrong with being comfortable?"

Daddy and I left for the car lot to meet his customer. The guy wanted to test-drive the '63 wagon. Daddy needed me to sit in the back seat and chatter so the customer wouldn't hear the rattle in the differential.

The guy was short and round and he scooted the bench seat up as far as it could go, crunching Daddy's legs but leaving me room to sprawl. He must have thought I had a river of words in me. After we'd tooled around town a bit and then turned onto the highway, he said to Daddy, "Don't your kid ever shut up?" and Daddy said, "Quiet down," but his fingers hanging behind the front seat were crossed. I flicked my hair up and tried to look younger and nattered on about homework and lunchroom and Reverend Tyler and the president.

The customer was all over grins when he drove that wagon off the lot. He'd paid Daddy in cash and Daddy folded a twenty into my hand. At home after supper, Mama cut into a pecan pie and served each of us a hefty piece. Then I went upstairs to pray for an *A* on my French test and to think about Heidi Muller.

For weeks, I softened her. We walked home together often, stopping at Ray Mundy's for Nehis, sitting on the washroom steps and talking. I asked her what she planned on doing after graduation and she told me she dreamed of moving to New York. Her one ambition was to work at Macy's. I held her chin in my hand and studied her. "Well, you couldn't sell makeup because you don't wear any." She'd given up the lipstick. "And you don't look foreign enough to sell French perfume. Actually," I told her, "you look like the kind of girl who could sell men's things—you know, ties and stuff."

She held her face steady in my hand and when I moved my hand she moved her face, just a little, leaning into the touch. I brought my hand slightly closer to me and her face stayed with it. When I did drop my hand entirely, she had to scoot back on the steps to keep from tilting over.

"It's all beans anyway," she said. "I'll never be able to leave." She sighed. "I'll end up marrying someone around here and have kids of my own and help my dad at the store."

Then Heidi gave me a soft look and asked about my plans. I spread my fingers and looked at them. "Whatever God's plan is for me, that's what I'll do."

She wrapped her hand around my arm. "You're so good," she said. "I've never known anyone like you."

I pulled out my Bible. "Let's look at some Scripture," I said. I read to her verses from John. I pointed out the errors in her Catholic church. We talked of grace without confession. We're all sinners, I told her. I stroked her fingers. God understands.

A storm was blowing in from the Atlantic. Breezes lifted her hair and she shivered. She hugged herself and I caught a glimpse of her lace bra as her blouse shifted.

I asked her if I could take her for a drive that evening after supper.

Rain gusted in that afternoon and at home the lights dimmed. Mrs. Rogers and Timmy stepped over to borrow some candles just in case. Timmy wrapped his arms around my leg and told me how scared his puppy was. Mama couldn't cook supper on the electric stove; she laid out cold fixings for us. Power wasn't knocked out completely, just weakened by the storm. The brown light thickened the shadows and made the rolled-armed sofa and chairs in the front room look like beasts hunkered down and waiting, for what I didn't know. I watched the sheetmetal skies rippling outside the louvered windows. Mama suddenly remembered wash on the line and ran outside. She came back in with wild hair and a flushed face. Daddy took the clothes basket from her and led her by the hand upstairs, leaving Grandpa and me in the living room. I was jangled by all my thoughts of Heidi, and I paced while Grandpa fiddled with his dentures.

Noise built up all around me—the rain spattering the window, the wind, the creak and roll upstairs, all of it deafening. I lay down on the carpet, pressed my hands to my ears, and heard my blood flooding in my head. I closed my eyes and then I must have slept.

I woke up under the burden of one rumbling sound. The storm had passed. The sky was black with lighter gray patches of clouds, but the air was dry. Grandpa still sat in the same chair, in his pajamas, his hands planted on his spread knees, his dentures in place. He was groaning through "Amazing Grace," which must have been what woke me. I told him I was off to work a conversion, pulled on my raincoat, snatched up the Fairlane keys, and stepped outside.

The heavy rain had flooded the street with an inch or two of water, which was now percolating down through limestone and trickling into the drainage canals that wove through town. The streetlight at the end of the driveway cast a yellow glow on creatures washed from their hiding places: slugs spotted the lawn, a snake oozed from my path, a blue-bodied landcrab stared at me with tiny mica eyes. I picked up the crab by one claw and hurled it out into the asphalt and its shell split open.

The ground under the gravel driveway had softened with the rain. A ridge of silt and muck had washed up at the edge where the driveway met the street. But the new Fairlane fired right up. I switched on the heater and the defrost and let the interior warm a bit.

I could see how events would unfold. I'd take her down the highway and then turn into a side road. We'd stop someplace quiet, in a mango grove maybe. Someplace with no one nearby.

I put the car in reverse, but when I backed up, the wheels churned against that ridge between the driveway and the street. I climbed out and surveyed the situation, thinking I should lay some boards down, but I was too distracted to bother. It seemed only a small ridge. I could rock the car over it. I got back in and let the engine run a while longer, thinking.

The heater would roar at our legs and we'd shed our rain things. I'd talk a while and Heidi would listen and then she would bow her head. She'd finally accept the Holy Spirit's blessing and be saved. She'd cry. In joy, I'd kiss her.

I shoved the gearshift into reverse and rocked up against that pile of mud. I put the car in neutral, revved the engine to get her going, and then shifted back and forth, from drive to reverse, the car heaving first one way and then the next, building up momentum.

She'd kiss me back. My hands would seek the buttons of her blouse. Her eyes might open in surprise but then they'd close again. I'd push her further. My mouth at her breast, one hand stroking her knee, her thigh, slowly, slowly. She'd be warm to the touch. Her hand might stop mine, might try to push it away, but my hand would be stronger. Insistent.

I worked the car back and forth, rocking it forward and reverse, wondering why there was so much resistance, until finally with one more heave forward and a great lunge back I was up and over that ridge and off.

Afterwards I'd pray with her.

I could think of nothing but Heidi as I plowed the car down the street to the corner. I signaled left and checked the rearview mirror, not even registering what I saw. The brown spill seemed just a part of mud and sand. But as my vision spun with the turning car, under the yellow streetlight that huddled, brown shape took on features.

I wheeled around and drove back to the driveway just to be sure, but I knew even before I knew. I pulled the car to the side, not bothering to shut off the engine, and sprawled out the door. Air wheezed out of my lungs and I struggled for my voice as I ran, finally able to shout for help, to the boy stretched across the gravel.

Mrs. Rogers flew out of her house, the puppy at her heels, her hair foamy with shampoo, her pink bathrobe clutched tight with the sash trailing wet behind her. She stumbled down beside Timmy and placed both hands on his cheeks, and by sheer will, it seemed, forced his eyes to open. She didn't seem to notice or care how her robe gaped. He squirmed a minute, tried to rise, and then twisted his head at the sound of the ambulance. He closed his eyes again.

Mrs. Rogers rode with Timmy, and Daddy followed in the Fairlane, all the time muttering that this was "a hell of a thing." Grandpa had pulled boots and a yellow slicker over his pajamas and he held my hand in the back seat. At the hospital, doctors and nurses surrounded Timmy and took him away, Mrs. Rogers hanging on to Timmy's hand beside the cart. The rest of us waited on tweedy orange chairs in the lounge. Gradually, the room filled up with neighbors and members of our church. Grandpa's prayers rumbled under their voices. Someone pushed a carton of juice onto the scarred plastic table next to me but I wasn't interested. I tried to pray for Timmy but mostly all I could pray was *please God don't let me go to jail*. Over and over I prayed this, my hands folded under my chin.

Slowly, though, people began to question how I'd come to run over Timmy. My own mother's eyes cast worried looks at me. Daddy was talking to someone on the phone. Then Grandpa stood tall and crusty as a tree and said, "I'll tell you how this happened." He pointed a finger at me.

"Satan!" he cried, and a stone swelled in my throat. "This boy was on his way to save a soul—a little Catholic girl lost in her papism. What's a child's body to Satan measured against a soul lost to him forever?"

I swallowed hard and the pressure in my throat eased. Voices in the room picked up, wondering. My mother stroked the hair at the back of my neck. Daddy hung up the phone and sat beside Mama, his hand on her knee.

Finally, Mrs. Rogers stepped into the room and told us Timmy had two broken thighs and a concussion. He was asleep.

"You know what that means," Grandpa said. "Angels are still battling for him."

"Oh, Jesus, save our poor Timmy," someone wailed.

"Go to him, boy," Grandpa prodded.

Mama squeezed my hand. "Honey, you've got to pray for him."

I stood up and reeled. Blood washed from my brain. My vision began to shrink and the people in the room seemed separated from me by some fold in the air. Mama's face bobbed in front of me and then was gone. I heard a piano playing. My skin felt damp, but not uncomfortable. And then bright shards of color broke before my eyes, dazzling. I began singing, but not in any language I knew, and the words pulsed with joy. I looked down at my body, fallen on the floor, and then pale hands carried me off into a sea of warm cotton.

As soon as I opened my eyes again I spoke. "I've been to see Jesus."

Mama patted my forehead. "I know." Her face was flushed with sweetness.

I lay resting. The light overhead flickered and Grandpa held his finger to his lips. "Something holy is near," he said. We all waited. "Everyone, take off your shoes."

Women stepped out of pumps; men unlaced boots. We formed a ring between the furniture, holding hands, and we prayed. Tears ran down my face and dripped onto the linoleum where I'd lain. Grandpa told me to speak and so I did, calling over and over to Him to cast the demons from poor Timmy. And when my throat finally closed and no more words could come, I whispered, "Amen."

I shut my eyes. I could see Timmy asleep and dreaming in his hospital bed. Slowly the warring images would fade from his child's mind and his eyes would peel open. I opened my own eyes. "He's healed," I told the crowd. Mrs. Rogers came to the lounge to tell us Timmy had awakened.

Grandpa and Mama, our neighbors and church members, even Daddy, stared at me. And then one by one, they came to where I stood in the middle of the room and knelt. Mrs. Waters told me of her trick knee and how it hampered her gardening. She mourned her prize azaleas. I touched her knee and called on the angels to firm the joint.

Bob Johnson said his back spasmed up after extra hours in his truck. He'd just made a run in from Biloxi and was clenched now. I pressed the muscles with my fists and then touched his forehead, where tension also knotted. I prayed for Jesus to ease his muscles and relax his spirit.

Bessie Millhouse had a glass eye, and the right side of her world was blocked from her. I grazed my palms across her eyelids. The lashes fluttered against my skin. I called on all the power in Heaven to grant her vision. I moved to her right to welcome her as she opened her eyes. She pulled her grandmother's ruby ring from her knotted old finger and thrust it into my hand. "For your good works," she said.

And then Heidi Muller was there. "I came as soon as I heard," she said. She looked down, shy, and the fine strands of hair veiled the sides of her face. "I've been praying all the way over." I grabbed her hand and led her down the corridor, turning one corner and then another, moving away from the crowd, to where the hospital hummed with silence. We came finally to a long hallway lined with closed doors and lit with flickering light. She leaned back against the wall and I grasped her other hand as well, holding both of them together in mine.

Looking at her I felt power surge up through my legs, my stomach, my chest. Her anklets were wet with rain. The corduroy skirt she wore flared out over the curve of her hips. Her locket flattened her blouse between her breasts, and underneath the white cotton I could see the patterns of lace in her bra. A pulse leaped in the hollow at her throat. Her face was naked with trust. But I knew that deep inside, where her heart lay beating, some sliver of doubt caused her pain. I would lift my hands to stroke it away.

Flamingo

The night before her fiftieth birthday, Dottie Jean Denham's husband Jarvis died of a heart attack.

After supper, Dottie had excused herself to visit the downstairs bathroom, all the while thinking about turning fifty. She still felt the same as she had when she was twenty and just starting out. By now she was supposed to have already made her choices, so that from here on in she could just keep on down the road she'd been traveling. But it seemed as if it were time that kept hold of the wheel, not her. She just couldn't wrestle it into her own hands.

She looked at her fifty-year-old face in the mirror. Some gray hair, a few wrinkles, the skin around the neck a little crumpled. Not bad, but not the face she thought of herself in. She would wait another minute before flushing. As soon as he heard her finish with the toilet, Jarvis would be hollering for his coffee. Jarvis insisted on coffee after supper. Without it, he'd doze off before the news came on. Let him think she needed time. She did. She needed time to think about turning fifty.

Jarvis now, he was different. Ten years older than she, he'd grown into his age as if he'd been waiting for it all his life. Wrinkled skin fit him as comfortably as old cotton. He talked about retiring as if it were him going up on blocks instead of his truck. She could just picture him lying around all day in the recliner, flipping channels with the remote, grousing joyfully about the Democrats. Sundays would be their only break, when they'd both strangle into their good clothes and drive out the graveled road into

Wonder to hear Reverend Tull preach. Dottie figured Jarvis was paving his way with God for a Barcalounger in Heaven.

Sighing, she flushed the toilet. Sure enough, Jarvis's voice hammered through the walls of the clapboard farmhouse. "Dottie! Coffee!"

Dottie found Jarvis sitting at the blue Formica table, chewing on a toothpick. The supper dishes were still on the table, waiting for Dottie to clear. A half-filled pitcher of iced tea sat rain-streaked in the middle of the table, next to a small, cracked jug holding a full-blown yellow rose. Dottie had plucked that rose from her garden just yesterday.

She brewed the coffee then handed Jarvis's to him in his Peterbilt mug. He took one sip, then set it down with a thud. His face washed a sudden bone white and his hands scrabbled at his chest. Dottie's heart rattled at the sight, and she knocked over the pitcher of tea in her rush to him. Half-melted ice cubes skated across the worn linoleum. Dottie tried to loosen the buttons on Jarvis's work shirt, but he shoved her away with one oaken forearm and gasped at her to call an ambulance. Dottie slipped and slid through the iced tea to the telephone hanging on the wall.

Just then a hot flash seized her. She could feel the color blooming on her face. Her hands were damp and trembling. She stabbed at the tiny buttons on the phone, hitting several numbers at once. The phone clashed a series of tones. "It's nine-one-one, damnit," Jarvis wheezed. Then he pitched forward onto the kitchen table, sending the dirty plates clattering to the floor. He was stone dead by the time the ambulance got there. Bits of leftover chicken-fried steak floated in the pool of spilled tea.

The paramedics, two reedy kids, carried Jarvis out the door. Afterward, Dottie thought about how easily they had scooped him up, as if death had released some weight in him. Jarvis had always seemed solid, a fixture in her life, as substantial as her old walnut sideboard, and then he'd been carried out the door as easily as a broom.

"Lord, welcome your child Jarvis to the Kingdom of Angels," Reverend Tull cried out at the funeral. Dottie looked up at the baked November sky and sighed. This Thursday was Thanksgiving and she could feel a storm cooking. No clouds in sight, but the pressure was dropping, seeming to pull the sky right down on top of them. Moisture beaded up on Reverend Tull's broad, fleshy face, and dripped onto his shoulders. The sun glared off his black robes. He droned on, and she focused on a tribe of fire ants swarming in and out of a dirt mound.

Finally, Reverend Tull said the amen and everyone echoed. Jarvis was lowered into the ground. Everglades Life had paid out ten thousand dollars insurance money and Dottie had spent a lot of that on a brass-trimmed, mahogany casket lined with blue satin pillows she knew wouldn't last more than three months in the damp and teeming soil. She thought she owed it to Jarvis in return for outliving him. "He wasn't a blue-ribbon husband, I know," she told Reba when she settled on the casket. "Honorable mention, maybe. He did love me, deep down."

Dottie had been surprised to find out that Jarvis had already bought two cemetery plots. He'd even paid for the headstone and left word with Reverend Tull not to let the choir sing. Jarvis had always been tone deaf. The stone wasn't there yet; the dates still had to be carved—Dottie and Reverend Tull would see the stone set in later.

After the burial, Reverend Tull's green Oldsmobile led a procession to Dottie's house. The town of Wonder faded out in a string of rusty gas stations and abandoned drive-ins until there was only the narrow blacktop road leading away, and then it too died out into a long stretch of gravel. Years ago, the land all around had been farmed: sweet corn, tomatoes, pole beans. But acre by acre, the land had been sold to giant nurseries growing hothouse plants in the dank Florida outdoors. Dottie's old farmhouse was nestled in a jungle of orchids, giant elephant ear, kentia palms, diffenbachia, gardenia—plants designed for grace. The congregation all parked where they could and stomped into Dottie's house for refreshment. The church ladies all brought casseroles. Dottie had fixed up her famous bacon, peas, and mayonnaise salad. Reba brought her tofu muck over from her house, next one down the road about a half-mile.

"Turn to the Lord for comfort, Dottie," Reverend Tull said, as he dished himself some salad. He looked pointedly at Reba in her paisley printed pantsuit, what Dottie called her guru get-up. Reba always wore colors more fanciful than anything growing naturally. Reverend Tull told Dottie to come to him after Sunday service. Being busy would keep her from grief.

"You know what that means," Reba said, making a face at his back. "Choir robes to hand wash, starch, and iron." Reverend Tull had a whole army of widows working in service to the Lord, polishing the pews, tending the babies in the nursery, washing up after the potlucks. Dottie was never one to mind work, though. Hand washing was no trouble; it was only the ironing that got to her, in this heat.

That night, Dottie stretched out on her side of the bed under the white chenille spread and propped herself up on both pillows. Jarvis was really gone. She could still smell his presence in the room. His Old Spice aftershave. The sweat on his workshirt still in the hamper behind the door. The leather of his tooled belts hanging in the closet. She could smell the engine oil on the rag he always kept in one pocket. She could smell his breath still on his pillow.

Dottie stretched her legs across the wide bed. She was

used to falling asleep while Jarvis watched the sports news on TV. She was used to hearing his rumbling breath in her sleep and the creak and roll of the bedsprings as he turned, his knee edging her in the hip. Sometimes, he'd wake her and they'd come together in the night, a quick, gasping pairing that startled them both. But mostly they just slept, together and apart in their dreams.

Sleeping alone was lonely. Dottie couldn't settle into it. She kept the bedside lamp on for comfort and looked down at her hands. Overnight she'd become old. And a widow. An old widow. Her skin seemed drier, almost crisp, like a dead, dried marigold. The bones in her fingers seemed impossibly sharp. She felt the chill of age on her. Sighing, she trudged downstairs and snatched up the pink afghan from the living room couch. She wrapped it around her like a shawl, settled back into bed, and lay still until she finally fell asleep.

Thanksgiving dawned and the weather hadn't broken yet. Each day the sun boiled the air into a thick soup. Steam seeped out of the ground, out of the thick, green plants, out of Dottie's own skin, and rose up to the sky. But the clouds just streaked into pale, weak wisps.

Reba and Dottie drove into Wonder in Reba's old Galaxie to have Thanksgiving dinner at Morrison's Cafeteria. Reba was wearing some kind of orange kimono thing, and Dottie wore her blue polka-dot dress with the white lace handkerchief sewn into the pocket. Dottie had told Reba that this year she wanted to look at all the food someone else had cooked and pick and choose just what she wanted. But the truth was the thought of doing any cooking, any at all, made Dottie tired. She'd been living on the leftover funeral casseroles. "We don't have to go to Morrison's," Reba had said. "I'll cook." Dottie could read Reba's exasperation in the way she threw out her hands as she spoke. But Dottie was stubborn. If Reba cooked, Dottie would feel obliged to bake a few pies at least.

A ragged line of people stood waiting to pass their red plastic trays along the counter. Mostly old folks, thought Dottie. She shuffled her feet along in line behind Reba. She looked at the selection of foods and suddenly felt her teeth loose in her head. Reba frowned at her as she chose applesauce, macaroni and cheese, custard. "I thought we were having turkey," Reba said, a little sharply. Dottie just smiled a closed-mouth, careful smile.

After they finished eating, Reba excused herself from the table. She came back carrying a box wrapped in plain white paper covered with "50" written everywhere in pink dayglo marker. "We missed your birthday," she said.

Dottie glared at her. "I know I'm old. You don't have to announce it to the world."

"I didn't say one word." Reba leaned back and folded her arms into her long, orange, butterfly sleeves.

Dottie cautiously pried the tape off the paper and then eased the box out of its wrapper. Out of habit, she set the paper aside to fold and reuse. She looked down at the box and sucked in her breath. For one brief blue flash she wanted to smack Reba. Her jaw muscles worked. She read the curlicue lettering on the box over and over. And then finally she relented. She laughed. "Good Lord, Reba. Only you would give a Ouija board to a widow."

"You never know," Reba said. "Now, are you going to eat some real food, or should I just drop you at the rest home?"

"I wouldn't say no to some pecan pie," Dottie answered. She turned the box over to read the directions.

Dottie and Reba sat across from each other at the card table set up in Reba's living room. It was the only clear surface in the room. The side tables were cluttered with yellowed romance novels from the paperback exchange at the library, bits of rock Reba actually paid money for and swore by, and tiny snips of plants she cut from the nursery acreage and rooted for her own garden.

Reba opened the Ouija board between them. Dottie rested her fingers lightly on the white plastic triangular pointer that came with the board. "I can't believe I'm doing this," she said.

"Shhh!" Reba lit some sandalwood incense and a small red pyramid-shaped candle. "You have to concentrate. Now see if you can call Jarvis."

Dottie started speaking, her voice low and doubtful. "This is Dottie calling Jarvis, come in Jarvis. Can you hear me? Come in, Jarvis."

"Give me that." Reba took the pointer from Dottie. "This isn't CB radio. You have to be spiritual about it." Reba set her fingers on the pointer. "We are calling the spirit of Jarvis Denham. Speak to us, O spirit," she intoned. The pointer swung under her fingers to the letter D. "See, he answered! He wants to talk to you." Reba passed the pointer back to Dottie. "Ask him a question."

"What question?"

"I don't know; ask him what you should do now he's gone."

"What should I do now you're gone?" Dottie asked, trying to match Reba's spiritual tones.

She felt a tiny vibration in her fingers. Nothing really. Just a quivering of nerves. The pointer began to shake under her hand. It began to inch across the board. Dottie could swear she wasn't steering it.

S-E-L-L-T-H-E-H-O-U-S-E, the pointer spelled out.

"Sell the house!" Dottie yelped. "Do you take me for a fool?" As if in answer the flame flickered atop the pyramid candle, but Dottie couldn't tell if that meant yes or no.

She kept her fingers on the pointer, her whole hand trembling now. What was moving this thing? The pointer worked slowly, spelling out: L-E-A-V-E-W-O-N-D-E-R. Dottie looked up at Reba. In the candlelight, Reba's eyes were bright as pennies. "Is this some kind of trick?" Dottie asked. "Just where am I supposed to go?"

The pointer swerved across the board, spelling rapidly now, bouncing from one letter to the next. L-A-S-V-E-G-A-S-C-R-A-P-S-T-A-B-L-E-S. Dottie exploded out of her chair. "I never in all my life heard such foolishness. Sell a paid-up house to play craps in Las Vegas! I don't know how to play that game and I even hate saying it. It sounds like a bad word."

"Too bad he didn't say Atlantic City," Reba answered, studying the board. "It'd be a whole lot easier to get to."

"You know good and well Jarvis never sent me that message. This is all just more of your mumbo-jumbo."

"If Jarvis didn't send it, someone did."

"Reba Mae Jenkins, I should have smacked you like I wanted when you gave me this fool thing. I've had enough harum-scarum for tonight." The candle blew out in the gust as Dottie slammed the door behind her and set out for home.

The sky was low and flat-black, no moon, no stars. Clouds had finally gathered. Dottie tramped along the road, occasionally swatting gnats and mosquitoes from her arms. The waxy green leaves of the jungle plants on either side of the road stirred in a faint breeze. The air was filled with night noise. Crickets chirped one continuous drone in the heat, frogs croaked, and now and then a cat cried out. The gravel crunched under Dottie's feet, flying from her tread to land like tiny hailstones behind her. She walked fast, propelled by anger.

Suddenly, as if it had materialized out of the dank air, a pink flamingo stood in the middle of the road. Dottie stopped in midstride and shrieked before she realized it was just a bird. It must have come from one of the tourist shows up the highway. The flamingo stood staring at her, unwaveringly still on its slim legs. The pink head bobbed as the long neck undulated. Dottie tried to remember if she'd ever heard of a flamingo biting anyone. She edged closer to the bird. It didn't move. She reached out a hand to stroke its sleek feathers. It quivered under her touch. She was surprised by how warm it felt. Its marble eyes blinked at her once, twice. And then the bird slowly picked its way across the road into the thick growth. Dottie watched it disappear into the green. And then she went home.

"Dottie Jean Denham, you can't tell me you're not dying to go to Las Vegas. I remember you singing and dancing at the Senior Class Talent Festival. I remember all the sequins you stitched onto your outfit."

"That was more than thirty years ago. What's that got to do with anything?" Dottie asked.

Reba's voice boomed through the phone. "It shows your liking for bright lights."

Dottie snorted.

"You've always wanted to travel," Reba continued. "And the furthest you've got so far is DisneyWorld with Reverend Tull and his flock of geese."

That much was true. Dottie was always itching to go places, saving up cruise brochures and pictures of Indian cliff dwellings and Austrian glaciers and slow-moving South American rivers. But truck driving had spoiled Jarvis of any taste for travel and oddity.

"Even if I did want to go, I don't have to sell my house to do it," Dottie said.

"You do if you want to do it in style. Besides, you can't ignore the message you got."

"Yes I can. I've got to go meet Reverend Tull out at the

cemetery to see Jarvis's stone." Dottie hung up the phone and rinsed out her coffee mug. Jarvis hadn't sent her any message. He'd die all over again to see her sell their house.

Dottie parked her Ford Fairlane next to Reverend Tull's Oldsmobile. He bundled the choir robes into the front seat of the Fairlane for Dottie and then the two of them walked out to look at the stone the graveyard workers had set in early that morning. Dottie carried a small bouquet of yellow roses she'd snipped from her garden.

She had to hurry to keep up with Reverend Tull's long stride. Her high heels kept sinking into the sprinklered cemetery lawn. She was breathing heavily and concentrating on not tripping, so she was startled when she reached Jarvis's grave and saw the size of the headstone. It seemed immodestly huge to her, chiseled gray granite stretched out four feet wide.

Then she saw the need for the size. Her own name was carved beside Jarvis's, with the date underneath left blank. A double-decker stone, she thought crazily, two graves in one. How like Jarvis to find that economy. She stared at each of the letters of her full name: D-O-R-O-T-H-Y-J-E-A-N-D-E-N-H-A-M. The murky air pressed down on her, battling her will to breathe. A pulse hammered in her temple: she could feel her heart beating, still beating. She thought about that clump of muscle keeping her alive. It could stop at any moment, just up and quit, and here was the place she'd lay, already marked for her. How many beats was she allotted, Dottie wondered, before the final one and then nothing?

"I'm not ready to die," she said, aloud.

She'd forgotten Reverend Tull was there. He placed a hand on her elbow. "Of course you're not. But you've prepared your soul for salvation, that's what counts. Until then, Jarvis will be waiting for you."

And that was it, Dottie realized. Her place was marked in life, too. She was to sit and wait, drying and curling up under the solitude of widowhood. All her life she'd done what was expected of her. She'd married the man who asked her and lived in the house he bought. She cooked the foods he liked and washed up afterward. She'd cleaved to him and him alone and sorrowed at the lack of children. She'd yearned for distant sights and had never so much as left the state. She'd bowed her head in church and sung the hymns and put her quarters in the offering plate and never once said what she truly thought.

"I don't believe..." she started, and then she stopped. Her eye had caught a small flutter of pink against the far stone wall separating the cemetery from a field of kentia palms. She scanned the wall, looking for the pink to flurry again.

Reverend Tull was speaking to her, his voice spinning words like thick cotton wool. Faith, hope, charity. Faith in what? Hope for what? Charity for whom?

A brief sheen of pink rustled again, like someone shaking out a piece of satin cloth. Something about the movement, how small it was, how quickly it died down, tugged at Dottie. She felt something like a small, round egg in her throat.

"There's something over there," she said, interrupting Reverend Tull's flow of words.

She started to move, but Reverend Tull held her arm. "Dottie, wait, this is important."

She shook her arm free, suddenly furious at the arrogance around her. How sure of her Jarvis must have been to have her plot already bought, her name carved and waiting. And Reverend Tull, with all his talk of the Lord's work, had a list of chores a mile long for her, starting with those choir robes in the front seat of her car. Meanwhile, something against that wall needed her help. She ran with sinking heels toward the cemetery wall, leaving small holes in the lawn with each step.

The huddled pink form lay on the ground like spilled laundry. It was the flamingo. She'd known it would be. She approached it slowly, trying to see what was the matter, afraid it might suddenly spring up and fly in her face. Up close, she could see the bird's problem: its long legs were snared in barbwire, the coils binding so that the bird couldn't raise itself. The wire must have come from the field next door, but how had the flamingo made it over the wall? Dottie watched as the bird struggled again, its wings and neck stretching out to her, its marble eyes gazing at her without expression. Reverend Tull came up behind her, sweating. "Oh, Lord, look at that," he said. "We'll have to put it down. I've got my .32 in the car, under the seat."

"No, wait," Dottie said. She knelt on the grass near the bird. "It's not hurt. It's just tangled up. If we can get the wire off, the bird will be fine."

"Dottie, it's a wild bird. Soon as you try to touch it, it'll be all over you. Heaven only knows what diseases you could get from that thing."

But Dottie inched her hand toward the bird. The feathers rustled. The flamingo stretched its legs against the wire, trying to right itself. Its eyes looked at her, not blinking. Slowly Dottie veered her hand toward the wire and the bird seemed to sigh. "I wish I'd brought my gardening gloves," she said quietly to Reverend Tull. She grasped the wire between two barbs and tried to open the coil so that the legs could slip out, but then she could see that wouldn't work. The pale, pink skin on the legs, so naked without feathers, would snag on the barbs. She sat back on her heels. The wet grass had left small circles of damp on her dress where her knees had pressed. "Reverend Tull, if you don't mind, Jarvis always had a pile of tools in the trunk. Could you see if there's a pair of wire cutters there?"

Dottie stayed with the flamingo. She rested her hand on the flamingo's body, trying to offer it comfort. She could feel the flamingo's heartbeat underneath its chest as it lay on the cool ground. The pulse thrummed much faster than she expected, and for some reason, she waited for it to stop. Now, she'd think, after a beat, now it will stop. Or now. But it didn't. The feel of movement deep within was like the feel of hard-packed earth when somewhere off in the distance horses are galloping, and the horses kept on and on and on until Dottie realized they weren't going to stop. Not today, anyway. Maybe not for a long time.

Dottie heard Reverend Tull return before she saw him. He was breathing hard. Concern for her alone with a wild creature had made him hurry. He held the wirecutters in one hand and waggled his .32 in the other. "Just in case," he said. "It may be the kindest thing to do."

Dottie took the wirecutters and bent toward the coils around the legs. She snipped one wire and pried each end away from the bird, bending the wire toward the ground. She worked one coil and then the next and then the next, until finally the bird lay on the ground, unmoving but free. Dottie and Reverend Tull backed away from the bird. Slowly it began struggling to right itself. Carefully, it levered itself up onto its long, slim legs and stretched its wings as if it had just wakened from a long sleep.

"You're lucky you're not at the hospital right now getting stitches and some kind of shot," Reverend Tull said. His voice had a note of petulance in it that Dottie ignored. She bent to sweep slivers of grass off her knees. She'd put a run in her stocking. She pried herself up again, her hands grabbing a sudden pinch in the small of her back and looked again at the flamingo.

But the bird was already gone. Dottie couldn't believe how fast it disappeared. She scanned the wall running flat against the grass, the field behind. The pink should be easy to spot against such lavish green. She looked up at the sky and the sun stabbed down at her, hurting her eyes. Far off, between churning clouds, she thought she saw a speck of pink sailing near the sun, but surely that was just the light dazzling her. A flamingo couldn't possibly soar so high or so quickly.

Back in the parking lot, Reverend Tull held Dottie's car door open for her. "Let me buy you a cup of coffee at Morrison's on the way home," Reverend Tull said.

Dottie licked her lips. She got in behind the wheel and then looked full at Reverend Tull, looming over her. She hadn't noticed before how tired he was looking these days. His fleshy face seemed to sag and his shoulders rounded down from his neck as if they were worn out with holding him up.

"Thanks, but I'm going someplace," Dottie said. She backed her car out of its space, leaving Reverend Tull to watch her drive off.

Maybe she'd stay here and maybe she wouldn't. She was fifty. She had half the time left that young folks had; she'd have to make her decisions twice as fast.

She drove straight into town. First, she stopped at the dry cleaners to drop off the choir robes. "You can bill Reverend Tull," she told the clerk. Then she headed out past the old gas stations toward home.

The clouds had finally boiled up into thick gray turrets, blackening at the edges. A few heavy drops of rain splattered down. Dottie drove fast, racing away from the storm. She wanted to go back to Reba's. She wanted another go at that Ouija board. She thought she knew now who was sending her those messages.

Her speed smudged her view of the plants and trees on the side of the road into a green blur. Ahead of her, the black asphalt road shimmered and disappeared from view behind a veil of heat. The air outside the car was gray with approaching rain. Dottie gripped the wheel tight, feeling the engine's vibrations running through her fingers. Behind her, to the east, sheets of lightning buckled. She felt the electricity in her own hair. She felt lit with life.

Jarvis was in the ground and she was on the road. One way or the other they were both starting over. As she drove west, into that vanishing blacktop, Dottie felt suddenly as if she were driving into pure space, with nothing above her and nothing below her, nothing at all.

Rapunzel

All of Claire's friends breathed a sigh of relief when, on a pink and blue April Saturday morning, she began dating Ian. Finally, they all agreed, Claire had found someone nice.

Ian was an orthodontist—what could be more respectable? He lived in a spacious condominium (so different from Claire's own rattily furnished studio apartment on the wrong side of Nob Hill) across the bay, on the thirty-third floor of a concrete-and-glass waterfront tower. On the ground floor below, amongst shops and cafes, he kept his orthodontic office. He was tall, tan, with a hawkish face and a serious air. He knew how to wear clothes, how to choose wines. He was something of a collector. Interesting sculptures twisted from scavenged hunks of metal; pre-Columbian figures; unpolished semi-precious stones. The Maserati safely garaged, the sensible Volvo sedan for every day. He took Claire to outdoor performances of Shakespearean comedies. He bought her lilies. He spoke her name in a way that delighted her: instead of accenting the hard first consonant, he drew out the vowel sound in a long breath, so that her name sounded like a wish.

Exactly what she needed, everyone agreed, after Kenny.

Claire herself, however, was not so sure. Six months ago she had been in love. Being in love had been like swimming through thick oil. Love coated everything—her skin, her hair, her mind. It slowed time, slowed movement, slowed thought. In love, her hands lost their light flutter and weighed heavily on her wrists. In love, she was languid.

Being not in love was a relief that had arrived slowly. Gradually the thick oil had dissipated. Not in love, she'd lost weight sauntering through the glimmering damp streets of the city. Not in love, she'd feel the strength in her thighs as she crested the top of a brilliantly lit hill, looked out at the black horizon beyond the white city towers, and imagined her arms light enough, strong enough, to lift herself right off the ground. She imagined herself winged and soaring between the jeweled windows, landing here, landing there, touching only who and what she wanted to touch, lifting off again.

The truth was, Kenny had been a shit. He was English— not the Royal Family kind of English, but the rugby lad, six pints of Watney's kind of English. He drove a beat-up Morris Mini, with its right hand drive, aggressively through the streets of the lower Haight, where he and Claire had lived. He had a job delivering overnight mail, and a vocation blowing glass. Graceful, ethereal vases; tiny glass eggs nesting inside other tiny glass eggs, fragile in his hands, which were surprisingly small-boned and pale. He insisted Claire wear a pager. He insisted she carry a cell phone. He insisted he know at all times where she was and whom she was with and what she was doing. In love, his conditions had not seemed more than she could manage. The first time he'd hit her, after she was an hour late coming home from a movie and her cell phone had been inexplicably turned off, she'd been so stunned, she told her friends, she could barely inhale, much less react.

She'd made excuses for him. She'd covered the bruise on her cheekbone with make-up. He'd apologized. He'd let her cry into his shoulder while he told her over and over how sorry he was, and then she'd let him make love to her.

The second time he didn't hit her. He grabbed her by the arms and shook her back and forth, shouting. Her head rolled on her neck, her teeth clicked, she bit her tongue so hard it bled. He shoved her away and stomped out of the apartment, and she fled to the locked safety of the bathroom.

The second time she wasn't sure what she'd done to provoke him.

Claire's friends decided she might forgive the first incident. After all, people do make mistakes. And afterward, they can atone.

But the second time?

The problem for Claire was this: when she thought of Kenny, she didn't think of his fists in her face or his fingers clamped on her shoulders. What she thought of was a black August night, fog raining down like silver needles as they tramped along the neon streets after a movie, a pizza, a bottle of Chianti. Both of them walking with that hurried, strained pace of two people about to make love. Kenny stopping her, turning her, pressing her back against a brick wall, his two hands pinning her wrists, desire flattening his eyelids, the shudder of her breath waiting for him to kiss her.

The third time, Kenny threw her to the floor and kicked at her legs while she rolled herself into a small, tight ball.

After the third time, she called her friends, who rushed right over, horrified, to help her pack.

Not in love, Claire studied art history. She studied paintings. She stood in museums and looked at them. She smelled them, imagining the pungent smell of oil and turpentine decades, centuries, old. She imagined she could breathe from a painting the layers of breath exhaled by everyone through time who'd stood admiring that painting before her.

Not in love, she'd quit worrying about whether or not she was attractive. She'd found such relief in that when she considered a painter to concentrate on, she found herself drawn to De Kooning. She liked his ugly women. She took to cutting her hair herself, ragged short razor cuts that, with her strong facial bones, her long nose, her slim hips, gave her an androgynous appearance. She wore black everywhere, and her skin took on a greenish cast from so much time at the library. She looked, she thought, like a witch. And she didn't care.

But Ian penetrated her disguise. That April morning, Claire had been sitting, reading at a coffee bar, her glasses sliding down her nose, her ragged hair unbrushed and dirty, her face drawn and shadowed by too little sleep and too much caffeine. He sat down across from her, cleared his throat, and then diffidently told her she was beautiful, taking her by such surprise, she couldn't help herself, she flushed. She stopped reading, looked out the window at the pink and blue morning sky, at daffodils trumpeting spring, at red tulips opening, and then she smiled. And so he said more. He commented on the planes of her face, the delicacy of her eyebrows. He asked intelligent questions about her reading and she answered with a wit she thought he evoked. He told her of the pieces he collected. He showed her photographs of several sculptures he was considering. One piece in particular made the hair on the back of her neck stand straight up. A woman's face in hammered blue metal. Emerging or retreating? The lips parted. The eyes—startled? feverish? anticipating? Hair jagged and burnished, like sparks erupting. Claire put her finger on the photograph and said, that one.

"Yes," Ian said. "Exactly what I thought."

Ian, Claire's friends agreed, was a vast improvement over Kenny.

Slowly, Claire unfurled into this new relationship. She began to speak to her friends not of herself, but of Ian-and-her. Ian-and-her at a picnic. Ian-and-her gallery hopping. Ian-and-her taking the Maserati out for a spin in Sonoma. She found herself shopping for two again, but this time at a fancier grocery store. Two artichokes, two salmon steaks, two raspberry tarts. She put on a little weight—not much. Just enough to soften the hard angles of her face.

Kenny, though, did not disappear. Several times he came knocking at Claire's apartment. She refused to open her door to him. She wasn't so much afraid of him as she was of herself. Of the tightening in her breasts as he knocked at her door. One evening, he refused to leave. Claire watched him from the second story window as he sat out on the cracked marble steps of her building, just sitting, the curve of his shoulder firm under leather. Claire called Ian and forced herself to chat casually with him about his day at the orthodontic office.

When she was with Ian, Kenny stayed away.

Summer came. Claire's semester at the university ended, leaving her with sheaves of notes for her thesis and an urgent need for a job. She called on galleries: the upscale on Geary, the avant-garde south of Market, even the touristy Ghirardelli Square shops. But though she was well equipped for any of the positions she applied for, there was an uncertainty, a way she had of never quite meeting an interviewer's gaze, that caused potential employers to pass her over in favor of more straightforward applicants.

She ended up with a summer job she'd had before, standing guard at the Hindu and Buddhist wing of the Asian Art Museum. She wore a boxy black uniform and thick-soled shoes. Ian was certain she could find better. The work was boring. It was well beneath her capabilities. But though she'd worked hard all her years in school, though she'd spent so many nights scribbling notes, studying slides and books and journals—there was a part of her that felt that Claire the student, Claire the future curator, Claire the woman Ian bought lilies for, was a construct. The real Claire was a girl curled up in a ball on the floor, protecting her head. And so she liked the solitary still safety of her job.

Late Saturday morning. She and Ian lay under white down on his bed, beneath a huge plate glass window and a vast spread of blue sky beyond.

"If it's a question of money," Ian said. "I've got plenty." He sounded frustrated with her and, because she was beginning to love him, she wanted to please him.

He pulled her on top of him. A shaft of sunlight glinted golden on her head and he toyed with the strands of her hair, which now nearly reached her shoulders. "Don't ever cut this again," he said. The commanding tone in his voice thrilled her.

She would let her hair grow and grow and grow.

Several times in July, Kenny showed up at the museum. He'd sit on the padded leather benches, with a large sketch-pad on his lap, ostensibly studying the bronze figures of Kali, studying Claire. His mouth would twist with amusement; his eyebrow would arch in something like sexual invitation as he shifted his gaze from the full-breasted, round-hipped bronzes to Claire in her black uniform and her clumpy black shoes. She'd feel a bead of sweat trickle down her rib cage, feel a flush heat her chest. She'd feel uncomfortably ripe, and then she'd want to cut her hair again.

She complained to the museum management. But the museum was a public place; Kenny had paid his admission fee; he had never threatened her. Surely she was overreacting.

Maybe, Claire's friends suggested, she should just find another job. Maybe Ian could help her.

"How about this?" Ian suggested. He needed help at the

office. Billings, charts, insurance paperwork. His previous girl had had a baby and quit. Ian had been doing much of the work himself. The files were a mess. Claire could help him.

Helping him was the exact proposition she could not turn down.

Ian was right; the files were a mess. She ushered patients, answered the phones, slowly cleaned up the records. An assembly line of dental chairs sat ranked in front of windows so that patients could lean back and gaze out over rippling water, sailboats, and the fog-shrouded spires of the city across the bay. Ian swiveled from one chair to the next, tightening, straightening, perfecting. Claire felt good to be so helpful and competent. With some of the money Ian paid her, she bought a few dresses. Not black. With that red-gold hair of hers, which now draped between her shoulder blades, Ian said she was born to wear pink.

Someone stole Claire's little yellow VW bug. The police found the car at the bottom of a hill. The glass had been shattered, the cracked vinyl seats set on fire. Kids, the police officer said, shaking his head. Seen it a million times. Kenny? Claire wondered. City life, her friends assured her. "When you need a car," Ian said consolingly, generously, "you're welcome to use my Volvo."

Working at Ian's was tiring in a way the museum job had never been. Patients (or their parents) could be unreasonable. Insurance companies could be obtuse. In the evening, after a long bus ride home to her studio apartment and after a hot shower, the ringing of the office phones would still ring in her ears. She would stare at her thesis materials and tell herself to get back to work, and then she'd sink heavily into her one good armchair and watch TV.

It was so much easier not to go home. It was so much more comfortable, at the end of the day with Ian, to ride the elevator up thirty-three floors to his condominium, to toss together a Caesar salad in his stone-tiled kitchen, uncork a bottle of Brunello, relax with the Goldberg Variations or a movie on the DVD. She'd sit at Ian's feet while he taught himself to braid her hair.

She spent more and more nights at Ian's and fewer and fewer nights at her own apartment. Her thesis languished.

It was while she was at Ian's, on a hot August night lit by a fat, full moon—so hot that Claire and Ian slept on plain white sheets, the white comforter kicked to the floor; so hot the waterfront teemed with people out strolling, carousing, peddling, making music—when someone broke into Claire's apartment. What little she had to interest a thief had been taken: her tiny TV, a pair of garnet earrings, a slender gold chain. The neighbors all claimed to have heard nothing. The front door lock had been smashed. Her ramshackle furniture had been kicked to bits. It was as if a giant had stomped destruction through the apartment. Most disturbing of all, the contents of her dresser drawers had been strewn about. Searching for hidden jewels, the police said. Kenny? Claire wondered. All the black lace bits she'd worn for him had been slashed.

Ian fingered the slashed underwear and looked sick. "You can't stay here," he said.

Claire felt sick, too, for different reasons. She felt shame, seeing Ian so elegant in his raw silk blazer and slim gold watch, fingering that cheap nylon lace. The police finished a cursory inspection and then she scurried around, stuffing everything into huge green trash bags. She would throw it all away. Everything truly good she owned was already at Ian's.

Except for her thesis notes. She boxed those up and stowed them in the trunk of the Volvo.

Privately, Claire's friends began to speculate about wedding plans.

Ian's bookkeeping was so poor that in September, Claire signed up for a basic accounting class. A night class, so that she could continue her office work for Ian. The teacher was a disappointed man in his late forties who wore sagging tweed jackets. After her third class, he stopped Claire as she was leaving, placed a hand on her shoulder, and asked if they'd met somewhere before. Then he asked her out for a drink. She tactfully declined his invitation. The college was set near the ocean and the fog could be thick. Claire was always careful to park under a streetlight. She kept close to other students.

But one night, on her way from class to Ian's Volvo, she heard footsteps striking like flint on the pavement behind her. When she stopped, the footsteps stopped. When she started again, they resumed. Was someone following her? Kenny?

In the damp, foggy dark, her heart began to flutter like a trapped bird. Panicked, she stepped up her pace. Panicked, she heard the footsteps behind her step up their pace. She ran to the Volvo, started the engine, backed out with a screech. She nearly sideswiped her teacher, who shouted and smashed his fists against her side windows. Tiny cubes of glass fell into her lap. Ridiculous, she told herself. She rubbed her hand over her fluttering heart. She tugged her hair back from the breeze riffling in through the broken window. No one had been following her at all.

Then, on the Bay Bridge, a pair of high beams accelerated up behind her, glaring into her rearview mirror. Coming close, falling back, coming close again. Kenny? Behind her, the high-riding, battering-ram grille of a Dodge truck. Where would Kenny get a truck like that? Why would he ever get a truck like that? She pushed her speed to sixty-five, to seventy. The beams closed in on her again and then suddenly cut over to the other lane. The truck sped past her, glossy and gold and stuffed with teenage boys. One hung out the window and waved at her as the truck rocked by.

Not Kenny. But she couldn't slow her heart. She couldn't help driving faster and faster. Toward Ian's condominium— the locked safety of thirty-three floors above ground. Every light she saw shone with menacing intent. Every fear heightened every other fear. Every car beside her swerved too close. She struggled to breathe. It wasn't Kenny, she thought. It was the whole world. The whole world and its dangers. She drove faster and faster, night and light smearing together as she came down off the bridge. She cut across three lanes of traffic, hearing a horn blow behind her, and then, just at the exit, a low sports car moved into her lane, cutting her off. She braked, she yanked the wheel of the Volvo, she spun around and around, thinking, a Maserati? Ian? Two cars behind her plowed into the Volvo's spinning metal frame and in a split second, Claire thought she would die. And found not terror or panic but relief in that final safe place.

Thank God, her friends said, for Ian's Volvo. Thank God for airbags. The only injuries she sustained were minor cuts and a fractured tibia. The car was hauled off, limp and broken, to be sold for salvage.

Thank God, her friends said, she had Ian to take care of her.

The college was understanding. So was her thesis advisor. Most of all, Ian was understanding. "All that matters to me," he said, "is that you're okay."

Each day he drove the Maserati to various shops to buy her gifts: lilies, pink silk nightgowns, ribbons for her hair. A silver-backed hand mirror. Glossy art books. She could not drive anywhere with the thick cast on her leg. But she could hobble around the condominium. She could change from one pink nightgown to another. She could lie on Ian's suede sofa and page through the art books while he brushed out her hair, which hung now, a shimmering red-gold curtain, to her hips.

In the evenings, she'd hobble out to the terrace that afforded such commanding views of the bay and the city and the island prison between. Just before she opened the sliding glass door, she'd see her reflection in the plate glass, but she wouldn't recognize herself. In her pink nightgown, with the gold-braided trim at her wrists and neckline, with her rippling drape of hair—she'd become beautiful. As beautiful as a princess.

Then, at the end of October, her cast came off to reveal a yellowed, shriveled, bony shin covered in thick black hair. So different from her other delicately muscled, pale, waxed leg. Carefully she circled the condominium, testing her weight, veering toward her beautiful reflection and then away again, and then out onto the terrace, and back inside. The ugly leg began to ache with strain. She would have to work to strengthen it. As she circled, testing the leg, she frowned. Because each time she caught sight of her reflection she thought the woman in the glass knew something she did not. Or recognized something she didn't know she herself recognized. Ian had gone out in the Maserati to buy her more gifts. Claire stared and stared at her beautiful reflection. A princess in a pink gown, with long, shimmering, red-gold hair. Not her reflection, but an image.

And then she knew. She felt it like a boot in the gut. Like she'd been kicked. Just to make sure, she grabbed an art book off the sofa and flipped through photographs. The Pre-Raphaelites. And there she was, on page 242: Cowper's *Rapunzel*.

Her stomach hurt. She couldn't breathe. She needed air. She limped out onto the terrace and looked straight down as, thirty-three floors below, people bustled about the waterfront sidewalk, jugglers juggling, peddlers peddling. A street musician's notes fluted up toward Claire high in her tower. Her bony, weakened leg throbbed. If she was Rapunzel, who was the witch? And where was the prince? A fat, gold moon rose up over the city, lighting a path across the bay to the city's lit towers, to the black winding streets disappearing into the hills. Claire leaned out over the terrace. Her hair had grown so long, so fast. Even so, it would take forever to grow down thirty-three floors.

Below, on the busy street, she saw Ian's white Maserati waiting at the light to turn into the parking garage. Quickly she braided her hair into a thick fat rope. There was no prince. There was no witch. There was only herself, and she would have to make her own way. In the kitchen, she found a pair of silver shears. She bent again toward her reflection, watching light flicker off those scissors as her image snipped that braided rope of hair off at her neck. Was it a trick of the light, or did her reflected skin take on a green-ish tinge? Quickly she shucked her pink nightgown, easing her yellowed leg into an old pair of black jeans. She ran her fingers through her raggedly cut red-gold hair. Her thesis notes—she had so much work to do. She'd have to spend hours in the library.

That thick rope of braided hair lay coiled by the glass. She thought about leaving it for Ian. She thought about stepping out onto the terrace and casting her hair from the tower as a kind of offering to the dangerously alive streets. But instead, she picked up that braided rope and knotted it around her waist, her own magic belt. The path she had to travel was treacherous—love lurked in every café and classroom—and she still limped. She would keep the hair she'd grown for Ian just until she was healed and strong enough,

again, to saunter the city, crest a hill, and, not in love, imagine herself with wings.

The Goat

The new kid had long hair, black, curly. He wore blue jeans and a T-shirt like everybody else, but his were funny, shiny and crisp, like they were made out of plastic. His teeth were awful—brown and jagged. He smelled strange—like cheese and dead flowers and blood. Around his neck he wore a tiny stone goat on a cord.

"Tell us about the goat, Pavi," the teacher said, prompting with a fake, encouraging smile. Gold half-glasses dangled down her flat chest.

Pavi frowned. "It is part of my religion."

At that, Eamon Wills, sprawled at a desk in the last row, leaned forward and hissed into Jimmy Crawford's neck, "Goat-fucking."

Shocking Jimmy at first. Then exciting him. He'd never heard of such a thing. He was only in sixth grade. He'd barely figured out about people-fucking. His answering laugh was a small and disturbed yelp.

But a gratified one, too. Eamon Wills had made a joke to him, Jimmy Crawford. Jimmy Crawford, who was all wrong. A wrong person. He only half understood all his wrongnesses. He was clumsy with a ball; he was big in all the wrong places. Big ears, big feet, big jutting elbows.

Eamon Wills, on the other hand, was a stocky, pudgy shrimp of a guy, with fat little fists like a girl's. He lived alone, in an apartment, not a house, with his mother—who wasn't like any of the other mothers. She wore leather pants and bright blue eye shadow and so far she'd had three husbands, one who drove Eamon around in a Porsche, one who'd taken him out of school for a week's trout fishing, one who'd played first base for the Reds' farm team. Right now, she was still divorced. At least once a day, Eamon Wills would cut a juicy fart and gross everyone out.

Still, everyone loved Eamon Wills.

And no one loved Jimmy Crawford.

But looking at Pavi talking about his country—some place Jimmy had never heard of and didn't know where it was—his goats, the inn in his village—like an inn was a big deal—and hearing Eamon Wills snickering behind him— Jimmy Crawford thought that now, with Pavi around, he, Jimmy Crawford, might just be okay.

At home he tried not to let his parents see what a wrong person he was. At home there were his brother and his two sisters, all younger than he was. The youngest, Cilly, short for Cecilia, was still in diapers. There was Bear, their big, clumsy St. Bernard. The kids were all three years apart. For as long as Jimmy could remember, there had been a baby wrapped around his mother. For all he knew there might be still more—Cilly wasn't yet three.

He tried to help out at home. He tried to be good. He double-knotted his brother's tennis shoes. He wiped jelly from Cilly's hands. He'd mind his manners at supper, hoping his parents would notice how much more polite he was than the little kids. They'd all be gathered around the maple dining table, Cilly in her booster seat. His mom, plump and roughened, changed out of her too-tight work clothes into sweats, her graying hair piled up on her head, her glasses low on her nose. His dad, tie loose, sleeves rolled up, talking about the day's headlines. Sometimes Jimmy would interrupt, would announce confidently, "Poor people aren't criminals," or "Taxes, taxes, taxes!" Which made his parents smile. Which made him try to think of other pronouncements to make.

It was a Thursday when Eamon Wills proposed the spy mission. "Everybody get supplies," he ordered. He said this in the general direction of a pack of boys gathered at the lockers, Jimmy behind them. Close enough that he could pretend to himself he'd been included in Eamon's plans. The boys rummaged in their lockers for chewing gum, for spitwad straws, for rubber bands. Jimmy had a pocketful of rocks. He tagged along behind the five or six boys following Eamon Wills and no one stopped him.

Eamon Wills wanted to see where Pavi lived. He had the idea that Pavi lived in a tent. Or a hut. Or a weird igloo kind of thing.

The boys tracked Pavi down the wide sidewalks of Cooper Boulevard. At the Chevron, they stopped to buy jawbreakers and grape soda, except for Jimmy, who had only rocks in his pockets and no quarters. Thirsty, wishing someone would share, Jimmy followed the boys following Pavi. They passed the Hojo where the geezers sat for hours over coffee. They passed Jimmy's mother's friend's dumb and hopeful children's bookstore with its cardboard hippos in the window. Jimmy ducked his head, so his mother's friend wouldn't call out to him, wouldn't embarrass him. Wouldn't remind the guys that he was with them. They passed a mailman wearing those dorky knee socks and safari hat.

All the while, Pavi walked along fast, unswerving. Jimmy didn't think Pavi lived in a tent or a hut or an igloo. He figured Pavi lived in one of those rickety houses where people with no money lived, where the windows were broken out, and at Thanksgiving carloads of families like Jimmy's would drive by with blankets and turkeys.

Pavi never varied his pace. Still, there was something in the determined way he walked, in the way he kept his arms stiff at his sides as he marched along, that made Jimmy

Crawford think Pavi knew the boys were following him.

Eamon Wills made all the guys stop at the Marine Recruiting Center on Cooper Boulevard to admire the sword in the window. Once, back in third grade, Jimmy had been to Eamon's apartment to build a solar system for a science project. The place had been pretty bare—good stuff mixed with stuff Eamon's mother bought at garage sales. A torn and tweedy brown sofa, a glass coffee table with one leg propped up on cork coasters, a brand new 36-inch TV set. On top of the TV there was a framed picture of Eamon's older brother in his uniform, with its fancy braid and shiny sword. Eamon Wills adored his brother.

After a mile or so, the storefronts and awnings of Cooper Boulevard dissolved into weed-strewn lots, into a couple of dingy bars, into auto parts stores. A ramshackle restaurant with a tin roof and a buzzing blue neon sign missing one letter: "Pizz Parlor."

Pavi turned into an alley just beyond the pizza place.

Hunched over, like a spy, Eamon followed Pavi and led the guys and Jimmy across the street. They knelt at the corner of the crumbling bricks and peered around the edge of the alley. Trash tumbled out of a dumpster beside a back door to the Pizz Parlor. Rusty water dripped into a barrel at the base of a downspout. For no reason at all, Jimmy felt scared. Like he had dropped into a spooky movie. He half expected Pavi to turn around, to have become some hockey-masked, knife-wielding creep. To lunge after them all. Jimmy felt himself breathing too fast, and he puffed his cheeks, held his breath, so he wouldn't get the hiccoughs and embarrass himself.

At the dead end of the alley, a crooked set of wooden stairs climbed to a door at the second story. At the base of the stairs, Pavi had stopped. He knelt, stroking something.

A dog? Jimmy leaned forward to see better, letting his

breath out in one loud gasp, earning a sharp look from Eamon Wills. Grit pocked Jimmy's kneecap through his blue jeans. Jimmy heard a little bell and funny stamping little steps. Then Pavi moved past the dumpsters into the pizza parlor, and Jimmy could see what he'd been petting.

A goat. A baby goat. A kid. It saw the boys, or it smelled them. Its nose twitched. It pranced a few steps toward them before the rope around his neck halted it. It had stubby little horns and a fuzzy chin. It bleated at the boys.

"What did I tell you?" Eamon Wills said, delighted. He clapped Jimmy on the back. He pumped his fat little fist. He lifted one haunch and farted in pure joy.

One evening at supper, his mother asked him, "Do you know a Pavi Movic at your school? He's in your grade."

"Yeah." They were having beans and franks that night, and Jimmy watched Cilly pick up a bean, carefully squash it between two fingers, and then stick it in her mouth.

"I met his mother today, at the office. She was looking into English lessons. How's Pavi's English?"

"Okay, I guess." Jimmy didn't want to talk about Pavi. It always made him uncomfortable, a little suspicious, when his mother started talking about other kids at school. Like maybe she'd heard something about him. Like maybe she expected something from him. He thought about telling her what had happened today, Eamon Wills' latest, how Eamon had cut up in science class, calling the girls like they were dogs. *Here Cheryl, sit Kathy, good girl. That's a pretty pup, Marcie.* A few of them had been outraged. But most of them had been delighted, wagging their tails, playing along. Later, at his locker, Jimmy had tried to do the same thing while Marcie banged around in her locker next to his. He told her she had pretty fur. She looked at him like he was a fungus. She told him he was nasty. Leaving him feeling miserably confused by the whole world.

Not a story to tell his mother.

"Maybe you could invite Pavi over some time, to play. Him and some of the other boys—he could learn English while you learn about his customs." His mother said this while she wiped bean juice off Cilly's fingers, so she couldn't see the red tide of rage Jimmy felt flooding his face.

What other boys? Didn't she see that he never had friends over? She just mixed him in with all the other kids, his brother and his sisters and their dumb friends, Cilly with her preschool play dates. Part of him was grateful: even his own mother didn't see how wrong he was. But mostly he was angry: she was supposed to see. That was her job. If she saw, maybe she could help him. Maybe she could tell him how to be different. And for a moment, his head felt heavy. He wanted to let it fall, right onto the table, onto his plate of beans and franks. He wanted to rest his head and let himself cry out his misery and let himself be soothed by her hand on his neck.

But she was prattling on about Pavi's country, about war there, and fighting, and Jimmy stayed stubbornly angry at her. It was just like her to care about people hurt a jillion miles away and not even see her own son, bleeding.

He shoved himself from the table, went out back, to his rock collection. He pulled a half dozen jars from the recycling bin and set them up on the rickety wooden picnic table. One by one he hurled his rocks at the jars. He liked the satisfying noise of the plink of stone on glass. He felt eased by the clattering shattering sound a jar made if he hit it just right, and it exploded.

In the autumn, the sixth grade boys played football in P.E. They played in the morning, first period, when the grass was still wet and the sun still hung watery, weak, and only halfway up the sky. The gym teacher led them out onto the field with the doleful air of a bloodhound still waking up. He sipped coffee from a thermos while they moved through their conditioning drills and then into scrimmages. He watched with a dull disinterest.

Jimmy Crawford was too raw-boned and clumsy to play any position but kicker. Even then, half the time when he kicked the ball it lumbered off stupidly in whatever direction.

But Pavi couldn't play either. He didn't understand the game. At first he chased anyone with the ball. Then he'd wrestle the ball away and run around in circles. With Pavi on the field, the other guys didn't complain so much about Jimmy's bumbling kick-offs and shanked punts. The gym teacher sighed, pulled Pavi aside, tried to explain the game. He showed Pavi how to throw the ball, how to place his fingers on the laces.

Surprisingly, Pavi had a good arm. Watching him throw, the gym teacher woke up a little. Jimmy heard him ask Pavi something.

Pavi's teeth stuck out in a jagged smile—giving the sharp bones of his nose, his cheeks, a predatory look. "In my country," he explained, "lots of fighting. We throw rocks. We throw bottles. We throw grenades, if we find them. My people, very fierce."

Eamon Wills, nearby, snorted. "Nothing a platoon of marines couldn't handle. Then you'd see some ass-kicking."

"Yes, yes." Pavi danced over to Eamon, his face eager. He plucked at Eamon's T-shirt. "Always we hope, the Americans will come. America will save us."

Eamon shook Pavi off. "Go save your own pussy selves." His face was twisted, disgusted looking. He kicked a clod of dirt into the air and watched it spatter to the ground while the gym teacher blew his whistle and tried to get everyone lined up for a final run around the field.

Jimmy thought then that Pavi had gotten the better of Eamon Wills. He couldn't quite say how or why. But he looked at Pavi and didn't see the weird kid with the long hair and the bad teeth and the strange smell. For just a moment, he admired Pavi and felt ashamed of Eamon.

"Jimmy," Pavi said, skipping over to him now with that jangly energy he had. Leaning in too close. "In my country we play kicking game too, with bladder of goat. I can show you."

"Show him what?" Eamon said. "This is football, not fucking goat ball. Come on, Crawford."

Jimmy was tempted to stay. Maybe Pavi could show him a better way to kick. Maybe then everyone wouldn't get so annoyed with him. He imagined a football game, tied, in overtime, and he, Jimmy Crawford, kicking the winning field goal. The cheers, the slaps on the back. A scoreboard, even, flashing his name in lights.

But Eamon Wills had already joined his pack of boys. Jimmy could hear them all laughing. And so he had to shove Pavi aside, he had to trot over to Eamon and the other guys to keep them from laughing at him.

Jimmy Crawford's birthday fell in the last week of October. In years past, he'd had limp little birthday parties with a couple boys from school, boys whose mothers were friends of his mother and so had to come to Jimmy's party. His mother would bake a pumpkin-shaped cake and set up cheesy Halloween games with Jell-O brains and olive eyeballs.

If Jimmy could design his own birthday, he'd have it at a carnival. Or a wrestling match. Or at an auto race, where if he was lucky, a car would spin out and catch fire right where he and all the guys could see the driver crawl out.

His mother said she'd take him and his friends out for pizza.

Which was okay with Jimmy, until he found out where.

Pavi's family's place. The Pizz Parlor.

"NO!" Jimmy protested. "They make their pizza out of...out of goat poop!"

"Don't be ridiculous." They were in the kitchen, dirty dishes spilling out of the sink, tomato bits stuck to the Formica countertops. His mother stirred noodles in a pot on the stove. The kitchen smelled of steam and tuna fish. "I've been there. The pizza's perfectly good. And it would do them a favor—I saw Mrs. Movic last week and I know they could use the business."

Jimmy slammed out the door, into the backyard. He gathered up his rocks from the heap by the fence. The recycling bin on the back stoop was overflowing with his dad's beer bottles and his mother's Diet Coke cans. He dumped them into a pile on the crabgrass and took aim.

Wasn't that just like her. Nevermind what he wanted—it was only his birthday. Better to do a favor for some goat-fucking strangers from some goat-fucking country than make her own son's birthday—his thirteenth birthday, for Christ's sake—special. One by one he hurled his rocks at the pile of cans and bottles. Denting the aluminum, chipping the red paint. Breaking the bottles. He didn't know which he liked better—the metallic thunk of rock on can, or the satisfying explosion of glass.

The next day at school, Pavi had already heard about Jimmy's birthday. He smiled joyfully. "We will make you a fine party."

Jimmy braced himself for scorn from the guys.

But Eamon Wills surprised him. He clapped Jimmy on the shoulder. "Crawford, you're smarter than you look with those big dumb ears of yours. This will be our chance. We can catch those goat-fuckers in action." He gathered five or six other guys around and began organizing the mission. They would need a camera. A mini tape recorder. He himself would bring his brother's old Swiss army knife.

Pavi's family had strung red and white construction paper rings around the windows of the Pizz Parlor. Red balloons were carefully taped to each of the chairs at the tables pushed together for Jimmy and his guests. Iced pitchers of root beer and ginger ale dripped condensation onto a brand new crisp paper tablecloth. The chairs were torn and taped red vinyl. The floor was peeling squares of black and white linoleum. Only one other table was occupied, in the corner, by two bearded men hunched over an ashtray, smoking cigarettes that smelled like burning hair.

Pavi and his parents greeted Jimmy excitedly. "Come in, come in." Weird jangling energy, breathing too close, seeming to demand something. Jimmy could feel himself leaning backward, away. The mother and father both looked exactly like Pavi, only taller and stouter. The same curly black hair, the same predatory bones, the same jagged teeth. Wearing the same kind of denim that had a strange sheen to it.

Jimmy and Eamon and five other boys all filled the chairs at the balloon table. The Movic parents bustled back behind the stainless steel counter, pulled pizzas from the giant oven, sliced them with long knives.

Nervous, the boys sat waiting. Eamon Wills had already checked that everyone had brought their supplies. One boy had brought a tiny folding pair of binoculars that Jimmy thought was pretty cool. They had the camera, of course, and the tape recorder. Eamon's Swiss army knife. Another boy had brought a bag of ball bearings to throw down on the sidewalk, in case of pursuit. Jimmy hadn't had anything really good to bring, only his rocks. But he'd sorted through his collection for the smoothest, the weightiest.

Pavi, uncertain, stood beside the stainless steel counter,

his hands clasped behind his back. There was no place at the table for him.

"Sit, Pavi," Jimmy's mother said. "You're at this party too." She tugged a chair from another table and squeezed it in next to Jimmy.

"Wait, I have a gift," Pavi said. He hurried through the back door into the alleyway and a few minutes later returned with a small bundle wrapped in tissue and tied with twine.

Jimmy felt embarrassed. None of the other guys had brought birthday presents—they didn't do that kid stuff anymore. But still, he felt touched. The truth was, he liked presents. It didn't even matter what they were. He just liked being given something, having it to hold in his hand.

"Come on, open it," Eamon Wills urged. The other guys echoed him, bouncing in their seats. There was a greedy eagerness in Eamon's eyes that made Jimmy hesitate, made him think he should take the present home and open it later, in private.

"Yes," Pavi said, leaning his face in too close to Jimmy's. "Open it."

As much to regain distance from Pavi as anything else, Jimmy bent over the knotted cord and worried it free. The paper fell open. Inside was a carved stone goat, the size of Jimmy's palm. It looked old. It was scratched and rubbed in places. It looked like it meant something.

Eamon Wills and the guys burst out laughing. The table practically exploded off the floor with their hilarity. But Jimmy couldn't laugh along with them. He liked the smoothness, the heaviness of the stone goat in his hand.

Jimmy's mother looked at the goat, interested. "What does it signify, Pavi?"

"Sorry?"

"The goat. Is it a symbol? Does it mean something?"

"Yes, yes. A goat is special." He looked up at Jimmy's mother, his face earnest. He completely ignored the laughter at the table, the boys' whoops and elbow jabs. "In my country, if a family has a goat, the family will always have food. Milk and cheese, at least. If necessary, meat. Even in the bad places, where the land is too rocky to farm, you can raise goats."

Pavi's mother was just setting two cut pizzas on the table. She moved to her son, placed a callused maternal hand on his shoulder. "Goats mean enough to eat. Enough to eat means peace. As long as a village has its goats, the village will have peace."

Jimmy's mother beamed. Her glasses beamed. Her eyes behind the glasses beamed. "Well," she said, as if overwhelmed, "you should be very proud to receive such a fine gift, Jimmy."

"Sure, thanks." Jimmy felt mulish at her prompting. Felt embarrassed at the gift. It was too much. He felt embarrassed for himself and for Pavi both. And embarrassment for Eamon Wills and the guys. For his mother and her round, beaming face. For Pavi's parents with their hands scarred from God knows what. He felt such embarrassment for the whole stupid world, he wanted to sink into his seat, into the floor below, into the earth, so that he'd come out on the other side of the planet in another country where everything would be different.

"We have another goat," Pavi said, his teeth poking out in a shy, jagged smile. "You want to see?"

"Yeah, show us," Eamon Wills said, still laughing.

"That's a good idea," Jimmy's mother said. "The pizzas are still hot. You boys go look at Pavi's goat while they cool." She seemed to think everyone wanted to be Pavi's friend, and in that moment, Jimmy hated her. Hated her for everything that was about to happen. He didn't know specifically what it would be, but he knew it was going to be awful. Silent, stubborn, resentful, resigned, Jimmy Crawford followed the boys all following Eamon Wills following Pavi out of the pizza parlor and into the alley.

"Goat!" Eamon cried out.

"You like her?" Pavi smiled his crooked smile. "Her name is Lady. Our cousins gave her to us when we came here—to welcome us." Pavi unhooked her rope from the rickety back stairs and cradled her in his arms. Her busy nosed twitched, sniffing at him. Her little goat lips nipped at his sleeve.

"Let me hold her," Eamon said.

Pavi hesitated for just a second. Then he handed Lady over. He kissed her on the nose as she settled into Eamon's arms. The goat lifted her furry gray head to study Eamon's face, and bleated.

The alley was damp; small pools of water collected here and there on the concrete. A few beer bottles rolled at the edges of the brick building, and garbage tumbled out of the dumpster. It smelled terrible. Like animal and mold and dead things. Jimmy waited with the other guys to see what Eamon had in mind, all the while trying to breathe only through his mouth.

"What do you do with the goat?" Eamon asked. His tone was leering, suggestive. Lady had started to squirm in his arms and he tightened his hold on her, his forearms gripping her under her belly, confining her legs.

Pavi stroked Lady's head, just between the two stubby horns. "We eat her."

The boys all stepped back, an involuntary backward movement. Jimmy looked at the goat's ribs and felt like he was going to throw up.

"You're shitting me," Eamon Wills said. In his voice was a kind of respect.

Pavi answered in all seriousness. "In spring, in my country, we have a goat festival. We put flowers on the necks of the goats and we dance with them around a big fire. There is always a goat that is chosen. That goat, we roast."

"How do you choose which goat?" Jimmy asked. The idea of roasting this little baby goat appalled him.

"Sometimes the other goats choose. They will not mate with her and at the dancing, they eat the flowers from her neck and nose her from the circle, even though she fights them, butts them, bloodies them. But sometimes the goat chooses herself—she shakes the flowers off, she comes to the stone, she lifts her head to the sky and bares her throat to what is to come. She welcomes it. Then we are happy. We know it will be a very good year when that happens."

"Right," Jimmy said. "Chooses her own self to be roasted and eaten. What goat would do that?"

Pavi just shrugged.

But Eamon had recovered from whatever flicker of admiration he'd felt for Pavi. He set Lady down on the ground, still holding the rope. "We know what else you do with the goats. My brother told me all about it—horny sheepherders up on the hills, no girls around."

"No, we have no sheep," Pavi said.

Jimmy tugged at Eamon's arm. "Come on, let's go back and eat."

"No way. I want to see some goat-fucking. Think I came here for your stupid party? Do it, Pavi. Show us."

The other guys in the alley had swarmed behind Eamon and now they began to chant: *Goat-fuck, goat-fuck, goat-fuck.*

Pavi bit his lip with one jagged tooth. "I'm sorry, I don't understand," he said, and Jimmy felt bad for him. Or maybe he just felt mad at Eamon because his comment about the party stung.

"Just leave the guy alone," Jimmy said. "Give him back his goat and let's go eat."

Eamon's eyes narrowed. He clenched his pudgy little fists. He turned on Jimmy. "Then you," he said. "You're the birthday boy." The other guys standing around all shifted, so that Jimmy now stood in the middle of them. Eamon pushed the goat toward him, turned the hind end toward Jimmy's thighs. The goat's tail stood straight up, a rigid tuft. Beneath that, the goat's butt was pink, barely furred. The goat bleated and its anus clenched and released, a tiny, pursed little mouth.

One of the guys started a new chant and the others joined in: *Jimmy and the goat, sitting in a tree, f-u-c-k-i-n-g.*

"Quit it!" Jimmy shouted. He pushed at the goat, at Eamon.

All around him he heard guys laughing. From inside the pizza parlor, he heard his mother laughing. He heard Pavi's parents laughing. The laughing wasn't like a sound, it was like a vibration, like a wave traveling up underneath his skin, along his nerve endings, into his brain. He felt hot. He felt like he was boiling over. The laughter, the vibrations, were heating him up and his muscles jerked and quivered. His fingers found the rocks in his pocket, dug one out. He turned and hurled the rock at an empty beer bottle lying against the alley wall, and the glass exploded with a crash.

"Hey, chill out, Crawford," someone said, but the others only laughed harder, and Eamon kept pushing the goat ever closer to him. The goat spun around on her rope, prancing, bleating, her bleating sounding like laughing, or crying, or both.

Crawford's got a girlfriend, Crawford's got a girlfriend.

"My brother says fucking a goat's better than fucking a chick because a goat can't talk about lo-ove."

"Stop!" Jimmy dug another rock from his pocket. He didn't notice Pavi backing away from him, he didn't notice

Eamon and the other guys. He just saw the goat, prancing, and each time she turned, that pink pursing anus. He didn't want anything like that near him. It was disgusting. It was revolting. But Eamon had put pictures inside his head and inside he felt sick—he was wrong again. They were all laughing because they knew he was all wrong inside. This time he threw his rock at the goat. It hit her on the back, on her spine, and she bleated, and spun around again, and little round turds spurted out of her butt.

"Hey, Crawford, don't go postal," he heard someone say, and so he threw another rock and then another one. And each time he threw, the rage in him boiled up hotter and redder, the rocks struck harder and harder. With killing rage he threw his rocks into her dense belly, into her spindly legs, one onto her forehead. She bleated louder and louder, her hooves scrabbling, frantic, knocking like wood on the concrete, her panic and fear making the sound of the rocks, the sound of his own blood, clang in his ears as he pinned her down under a hail of stone, throwing with all his strength. Will all the strength he wished he had with a football, with Eamon, with all the force and determination and conviction he wished he had every other moment of his life.

The goat fell over on the ground, bleating only softly now, bleeding.

"Jesus Christ," Eamon said.

"You made me," Jimmy said. Tears burned his cheeks. His voice was thick and choked. "Look what you made me do."

"I didn't make you do jack," Eamon said.

The other guys stood in a quiet, somber knot.

Pavi knelt down beside his goat, touched the wounds on her side, on her face. He wasn't smiling now, but his bones stood out sharply in his face. "Stay here," he said, in a voice that made them all obey without question. Pavi ran light-footed up the stairs, into the apartment, and returned quickly. In his hand, tucked against his leg, he carried a long, curving knife.

Pavi knelt again at the goat. He spoke to her, in his language. He petted the tiny little beard at her chin. He bent to nuzzle the spot just between her two stubby horns. Then he stretched her head and with one slicing motion slit her throat.

Eamon Wills, standing behind Jimmy Crawford, hissed. A quick, awed intake of breath.

Then Pavi stood, placed a hand on Jimmy's shoulder and gave him a gentle squeeze while he wiped his knife clean on his funny blue jeans. It wasn't so much Eamon's hiss as it was the knowingness of Pavi's touch, the rage clotted around his own throat, and the scent of blood boiling in the air, that made Jimmy reach out a finger and stroke the sharp blade of Pavi's knife. Jimmy knew he had been chosen, and he knew, too, that it was not going to be a good year.

Mimosa

All Nicky Whitman had ever wanted was everything. Moonlight, magic, mimosa. Raised to perfection by two behaviorist parents, she was twenty-four years old, with long curly dark hair, straightened white teeth, and a healthy, rangy body; and she had, since she was fourteen years old, displayed a spectacular talent for straight *A*s and older men. Both of which seemed to require the skills she'd honed through a childhood of effort and reward: that she simply be and do whatever someone else required. But all this spectacular talent had gotten her so far was a Phi Beta Kappa key and no degree, a job as a secretary to an obscenely wealthy Cuban exile, an insomnia problem, and a very bad habit of swallowing too many pills whenever she was upset.

And who was she, she thought, to feel so wretched? Three dead men for every square foot of ground on the muddy battlefields of Verdun; six million Jews dead in the Holocaust; twenty million Russians dead fighting Hitler, never mind those extinguished by Stalin; however many millions dead in Cambodia and sub-Saharan Africa; and then, of course, the crusty, bearded, homeless man she walked past every evening on her way home from work as he huddled into sleep in a Valencia Street doorway. He'd disappeared, and where had he gone? She had six pairs of shoes, four kinds of loose tea in her pantry, a secret stash of several different prescription drugs, and thirteen hundred seventy-two books—so who was she to waste her life or throw it away on rotten men? And thinking that only made her feel worse.

She was jangled and edgy. Gavin was at the lab, guillo-tining rats and osterizing their brains. He was a shit, but the kind of uncomplicated shit whose requirements didn't wear her out. He was a neurobiology graduate student who sup-plemented his teaching assistant income with the occasional sale of federally-controlled substances, and for two years he'd demanded only one thing of Nicky: that she fuck only him. He never ever told her he loved her.

She was such a terrible sleeper. Alone, at night, in her and Gavin's two-room apartment, the white-plastered walls suffocated her. Wide-open windows and pots of chamomile tea were no help. Not even *The Charterhouse of Parma* lulled her to sleep. She threw the book against the suffocat-ing wall. The city had all-night basketball—why didn't they have all-night libraries? A place she could go to curl up in a big leather armchair and page through a light romance all the way to a happy ending.

Sometimes she thought she'd die for lack of lightness alone—the bubbles that make champagne champagne. Oh, champagne, she thought; she did love champagne. One glass only, to help her sleep. And just that fast she was down the stairs and out on the sidewalk, breathing in the sharp, cold, January night, walking the three blocks to the Red Stone, her favorite neighborhood bar. It was just after mid-night and the streets were quiet. The four restaurants on the corner—one Asian-Italian, one French-Vietnamese, one Irish pub, and one burrito take-out—were closed for the night. The homeless man, she saw, had still not returned to his print shop doorway. She hoped he'd found a shelter. Or at least a warmer doorway.

The Red Stone was nothing but a black Formica slab of a bar, with a half dozen tables squeezed between narrow brick walls. It was dimly lit and usually busy and noisy with after-dinner crowds, which was why Nicky liked it. But tonight only one table was occupied, with four men who looked like spokesmen for German cars. Sleekly graying, they seemed made of cashmere and suede and polished steel. Nicky sat at the bar, sipping a very cold glass of Chandon, her long curly hair tucked behind her ears, the better to overhear their conversation. They were talking about poetry. Who could they be? What were such magnificent men doing in this Mission District dive talking, of all things, about poetry? One of them lit a Sobranie; one of them sipped a glass of red wine. The other two drank Czech beer. A few years ago, Nicky would have joined them. A few years ago, she could have joined them. She could have slid off her stool and onto a lap and stuck one of those Sobranies into her mouth and stolen a sip of red wine and pressed her lips to one of those clean-shaven throats to take a strong male voice into her own.

But she'd lost that kind of courage. Or that kind of stupidity. She knew, too, exactly where she'd lost it—on the seventh floor of the humanities building where she'd gone every Tuesday and Thursday after her social thought seminar to lie down on an oriental rug beneath a visiting professor from Chicago, who told her over and over how much he loved her while he jacked off into her hair. He'd been the one, she figured, who'd gotten her the Phi Beta Kappa key. Consolation for the gold ring he was unable to give, since he'd decided, after all, not to remove it from the finger of the woman wearing it in Chicago. After Nicky, furious, had swallowed a handful of Valium, the university quack had ordered her into counseling, and the newly minted M.A., whose fringed jacket smelled suspiciously of dope, had instructed Nicky to compile a list of all the things she would do to change her life. Nicky hadn't trusted that counselor one inch.

A straight *A* student, Nicky had smiled beatifically and scrawled on a legal pad in perfect penmanship: I will stop running away from my problems. I will stop climbing onto the laps of older men. I will learn to face consequences. The M.A. smiled back, pleased. Nicky had then gone straight back to her room, packed up her clothes into the white Honda Civic her parents had rewarded her eighteenth birthday with, and headed north. North only because the northbound onramp appeared first. She'd ended up right here on Gavin's lap—technically an improvement, since he was only four years older than she. After she'd moved in with him, she'd arranged to have all her books, which at that time numbered only nine hundred and sixty-three, crated and shipped to her.

Uncourageous, unstupid, she drank a second glass of champagne and tried to send waves of thought out into the world. She couldn't reach for magic anymore. Reach for me, she thought.

Someone heard her thoughts, all right. Gavin walked into the bar and slid onto the stool beside her. She still had on her work clothes—white silk blouse, black slit skirt, pearl earrings. He touched one earring and told her she looked good in drag. He had a faint growth of dark beard on his cheeks and shadows under his eyes, and he smelled strongly of soap and something else, something green, like growth or rot, underneath. He could be a spokesman, too, for a German car. For a stolen German car fishtailing down the autobahn at a hundred-forty miles an hour. He glanced over at the poetry men. "You wouldn't be cruising, would you?"

Nicky tensed. Sometimes she liked his jealousy—it felt like love. Sometimes it felt like a trap closing in on her—also love. "I wanted a drink to help me sleep," she said.

"If you need sleep, just ask me." He dug into his jeans pocket and pulled out four phenobarbs. He slid his thumb over her mouth, into her lips. He tasted the way he smelled. He ran his thumb, wet with her saliva, down her chin, her throat, to the hollow at her collarbone, down her blouse. He undid the top two buttons, ran his finger along the lace of her bra. Her nipples tightened; her breasts thrummed. Dread. Arousal. He poked the pills into her mouth.

She spat them out. She had brains enough yet not to mix downers and alcohol. He locked a hand around her wrist. She looked for the bartender, but he was at the other end of the bar, not paying attention. Purposefully not paying attention. The cashmere men all leaned back in their chairs and laughed. They were talking now about baseball. She struggled away from Gavin and her elbow knocked over her drink and she pulled and pulled and when he let go of her, her hand smashed down onto the glass. White light seared her palm.

"Shit." She cradled her hand in the other. Blood seeped into the creases.

"Let me take a look," Gavin said. "I almost went to med school."

A two-inch gash sliced down from the base of her index finger to the heel of her palm. He crumpled napkins to the cut and told her to hold her hand up higher than her heart. Then he squeezed her hand and she cried out. "What are you doing?"

"Applying pressure. Stand up." She did. He pressed her up against the bar. He pressed his hips flat against hers. She was half-aware of the poetry men half-standing. She was more aware of heat and nausea rising in her throat. Gavin kissed her palm, crushing the clotted blood into a red chrysanthemum. "Don't come here again without me," he said. He tucked the phenobarbs into her uninjured hand. He told her to go home, wrap her hand in gauze, and sleep. He had a guy to meet. She stood flat against the bar, her blouse half undone, until she heard the engine of his Kawasaki fire up and leave.

The place was completely silent. Finally, with some reluctance, the bartender asked if she wanted him to call the cops. When she said no, he poured her another glass of champagne, on the house. One of the cashmere men went over to the jukebox and filled the silence with Dave Brubeck. Nicky hated Dave Brubeck. She closed her blouse; she sat back down at the bar; she sipped her fresh drink; she pressed a clean napkin to her hand. And then she began to cry. She couldn't quite figure out how she'd ended up here, so alone. Every decision she'd ever made was the wrong one, and all the ways she'd tried to find something so basic—just someone who'd hold her at night so she could fall asleep—only landed her in worse trouble, and the truth was—the truth was, she loved Dave Brubeck.

Gavin came home two hours later and made love to her the way she liked it, demanding and rough, and then cradled her against him until she slept. When she woke, he'd already left to guillotine more rats. She lay on the white sheets in the sparely furnished, book-stuffed apartment, thinking how in the mornings she liked this apartment. She liked the warped oak floors, the windows bowing out high over the sidewalk; she liked the purple curtains she'd made out of a pair of sheets. She unpeeled the gauze from her hand and looked at the scabbed cut. She was going to have a scar, exactly parallel to her lifeline. As she wondered what that might mean to a palm-reader, the white winter sun rose to just the right low angle to cast one clear beam across her face and she thought then: she would change her life.

She threw back the sheets, jumped out of bed, and then rushed straight to the bathroom to throw up in the sink. She was so used to nausea, for all the usual morning-after reasons, that it took her weeks longer than it should have to realize she was pregnant.

From the outside, her boss's Pacific Heights home was unassuming. Two stories, crisp yellow paint, peaked roof, brick chimney, all surrounded by perky daffodils. But inside, the house was austere and imposing, constructed of great silent spaces of hardwood and glass—just like Mr. Candelaria. At five minutes to nine exactly she brewed his Earl Grey tea and poured it into his Spode teacup; at nine exactly he descended the staircase to his ground floor office, preceded by a forest-scented cologne. He was dressed as always in a dark suit, somber tie, white silk shirt, and silver cufflinks. If Nicky could paint, she'd paint him in blue lines and smudges. Blue wisps of ancient dark hair threaded over a blue skull; blue horizontal lines at his forehead; flat blue irritable lips. Ancient blue pock-marked scars, the size of nickels, were spattered here and there on his face and throat and hands.

"Nicky, the drapes," he said, pressing his irritable lips together.

She'd forgotten. Distracted, thinking about having a baby, she'd forgotten to open the drapes in his vast silent office. As she did so, a pale early spring light glimmered into the room. As always, Nicky was stunned breathless by the close-up view, practically from underneath, of the sweeping steel magnificence of the Golden Gate Bridge. She plucked the blue brocade drape to make it fall evenly— Mr. Candelaria couldn't tolerate asymmetry.

Of course she would have to get rid of the baby, she thought. Who was she to have a baby? She'd never even owned a cat before. Anyway, she couldn't think of it as a baby. It was too tiny, too unreal, for that. She thought of it more as a transparent minnow that had somehow darted into a pond where it didn't belong. Mr. Candelaria handed her the list of morning calls for her to place, and she settled herself into her cramped windowless office, where she had a sleek metal desk, a phone with three lines, and a Rolodex the size of a mini–Ferris wheel. Mr. Candelaria didn't trust computers.

She imagined calling her mother. She imagined curling up in a leather armchair and having a long, womanish conversation with her mother about pregnancy and babies. But she didn't have a leather armchair in her office, and she didn't have a mother who engaged in long conversations. She had a mother who'd sigh pointedly and ask if Nicky understood the way in which she had, once again, screwed up. As if Nicky chose to screw up. Which was, in fact, partly true. Instead of picking up the phone, Nicky picked up the phonebook to look up clinic numbers.

"Nicky?" Mr. Candelaria called out. "You have yet put no calls through to me. Is something wrong?"

She and Mr. Candelaria had a very specific relationship. She pretended to care about his needs, and he pretended she didn't have any. It was, in an odd way, like a marriage. She arranged his bridge dates, his spa appointments, balanced his bank accounts, got his cars detailed, and his shoes to the cobbler. And he paid her. He had never once made a personal comment to her, nor she to him. So now she gave him the exact answer he wanted to hear: everything was fine.

The nausea was exhausting. That alone was reason to get rid of it. A constant salty sloshing in her stomach threatened always to surge up into her mouth. She figured she was two months along, and already she'd lost eleven pounds. At that rate, after nine months she could model for Calvin Klein. All she could manage to eat were oatmeal cookies; she carried a baggie of them in her purse the way she used to carry dope. She visualized the oatmeal blotting up the sloshy liquid in her stomach. Walking home, past the four restaurants, the mingled smells of garlic and curry and ginger and cumin made vomit heave into her throat. She'd struggle to swallow it down while she struggled over what to tell Gavin.

If only she didn't mistrust her every decision. If only, at night, when the nausea at last ebbed, leaving her dry-eyed with insomnia; if only she didn't lie on her bed beside a peacefully asleep Gavin and watch the moon slide into the window between her purple curtains; if only she didn't feel such a strange tenderness. If only she didn't feel something small and furtive and dangerously like hope scrabbling inside her.

She couldn't remember when her insomnia had started. She'd never slept well. Her mother had complained over and over how badly Nicky had slept as a baby, shrieking and inconsolable at all hours. But when Nicky was twelve or thirteen, the insomnia had become something else. She would lie in her darkened bedroom beneath all her blue ribbons and listen as down the hall her parents bragged to their friends about her hair and her figure and her grades and her glittering future—doctor, lawyer, Miss America, Nobel Peace Prize winner—and she would cross her arms over her chest and pretend she was dead. It seemed the only way she'd ever get any rest at all.

Three times she'd called one of the clinics she'd looked up in the phonebook, and three times she'd hung up as soon as they answered the phone.

The truth was—she wanted this baby. She wanted it for every wrong reason on the planet—because she had nothing and no one else to fill her arms. And she wanted it for the most basic reason of all. Because it was hers.

Early in April, Gavin came home from the lab bubbling, exuberant over the progress of the research project he was on. He paced back and forth, from their dinette table to the bay window, to the brick-and-boards bookcase and back to the dinette again, where Nicky sat, amused. His excitement made him look younger and thinner, like a boy thrilled with something he'd built out of Popsicle sticks. He chattered on and on and Nicky didn't understand a word of it; she merely listened and enjoyed his enthusiasm. He'd explained before what they were doing as simply as he could: they were exploring how and where memories were stored in the brain. They were concentrating on the amygdala.

He'd explained memory like tracks laid down to make a recording. Some songs you listened to and forgot. Most songs you listened to and forgot. But some songs stuck. Bad memories played over and over and over because they were processed differently. When he was sixteen, he'd done a couple months in the youth authority for stealing cars. He'd met guys there with seriously bad memories, full of blood and body parts and sharp, shiny objects, and one or two of those guys, Gavin was sure, would kill someone someday. Imagine if there were a pill they could swallow to lay those bad memories aside.

Well, Nicky had thought—there goes art. But she'd kept her thoughts to herself to avoid argument.

Now Gavin was in such a good mood she couldn't help herself, she felt infected by his excitement and she gushed out all at once, "Talk about strange music—guess what? I'm pregnant."

Gavin stopped pacing midstride. He tilted his head like he hadn't quite heard.

"Yep," she said again. "Pregnant." She bit her lip, suddenly unsure.

"Are you shitting me?" He ran his hand through his scruffy, dark hair. He started pacing again, his boots thudding across the oak floors. Then he stopped, looked at her with shadowed suspicion. "It is mine, isn't it?"

That pissed her off. "Fuck you, Gavin." She got up from the dinette, went into the bedroom, angrily shucked out of her work clothes and into a nightshirt, and then slammed into the ancient pink-and-purple-tiled bathroom. The four phenobarbs were right there in a little baggie on the shelf inside the cracked mirrored cabinet, mixed in with her other collected vials. She could sleep through a very long night. And then she could wake up and get rid of this damn thing.

"I'm going for a walk," Gavin shouted.

But she didn't take the pills. Taking the pills would have consequences she wasn't quite ready to face yet. She lay down on the bed, listening to his footsteps disappear down the sidewalk, wondering if she'd ever see him again. Well, fine, so what, she thought. He could go fuck himself. She didn't care about him at all, why should she? He was a shit. All she wanted was sleep. And a good cry. But that was only hormones. The whole damn nonsense was only hormones. Biology's little practical joke, trying to trick her into believing things might work out.

After an hour, Gavin was back, smelling of beer. He knelt on the bed beside her and touched her stomach. "I think we could do this," he said. "We could become the kind of people who do this."

Could they? Nicky studied him. His entire face had changed, but maybe that was only the moonlight streaming in between the purple curtains. Everything shadowed in him was silvered, everything taut and wiry had smoothed. "Why do you want to?" she asked. "You don't even love me."

He kissed her hand. "How do you know that?"

"You never say it."

"Maybe what I feel and what I say are two different things." He wouldn't say any more than that, but for Nicky, right then, it was enough that he wanted to try.

After that, Gavin was everywhere. He'd show up at Mr. Candelaria's during Nicky's lunch hour, bringing her tuna sandwiches and pints of milk. "Baby okay?" was always his first question. He went with Nicky to see the O.B. and insisted Nicky have every test available and then pressed the doctor for even more information. He seemed to think that if she wanted to, the doctor could tell him the baby was a boy with red hair who'd grow up to play wide receiver for the 49ers. He bought Nicky three pregnancy books, read them as fast as she did, and then earnestly discussed the virtues of pacifiers over thumb-sucking. He told Nicky he wanted them to do everything right. Which scared Nicky. She never did everything right, and the ways she and Gavin could fuck up seemed huge and multitudinous.

They took one long drive in her Honda Civic down the central valley to visit Gavin's mother. All along I-5, Gavin pointed out family cars to her. Ford Aerostars, Dodge Caravans, Volvo station wagons. She pointed out to him the car she liked better: a yellow Saab convertible. Finally, finally, they exited onto a frontage road that wound through blossoming almond orchards and then past a brown little town that smelled of manure and up to a sagging white house on cinderblocks.

Rosalie, Gavin's mother, was a great massive mound of a woman in a flowered dress, with plump feet overflowing her shoes. She led Gavin and Nicky into a yellow-tiled farmhouse kitchen and put Gavin right to work fixing the kitchen faucet, chasing ants out of the dishwasher, chipping ice from the freezer, and changing the light bulb in the round-shouldered white refrigerator, all while she told him about her last trip to Reno. She'd won a hundred and fifty dollars at the quarter-slots and met a man who'd worked as a mailman and offered to steal magazines for her. When she came home, she discovered the neighbor lady had got herself a new Lhasa, which yapped day and night, and now she, Rosalie, was vowing to throw rat poison over the fence to that dog. She asked Gavin to get her a *reliable* poison. She said all this while she smeared yellow mustard on white bread and doled out American cheese for sandwiches.

Nicky sat at the old, sturdy kitchen table and nibbled an oatmeal cookie. At last Gavin finished his fix-it chores and sat down at the table next to Nicky, wrapped his arm around her shoulder, and interrupted Rosalie's chatter. "We have news for you. Nicky's pregnant."

Rosalie, checking the now nondripping faucet, frowned. Her mouth sank into a flat line across the fat of her cheeks. She looked pointedly at Nicky's stomach. "You can't be very far along."

"Three months," Nicky said, and then apologetically, "I've been losing weight, I can't help it, it's the nausea."

"Huh," Rosalie said. "Maybe I should try that. But you shouldn't tell anyone—not for another month at least. Skinny girls like you miscarry first time. It'll be a lot easier if you haven't told anyone."

Nicky paled. Gavin stood. His face flushed. "Oh, thanks a lot, Ma." Nicky watched him shake with the effort of controlling himself. "How about, congratulations. How about, thank you, Nicky, I'll be so happy to be a grandmother."

Rosalie pursed her lips. "I'm just being realistic. Which is what you should be, too. And don't expect me to babysit, I've got things to do, you know." Then she began asking Gavin questions about her most recent physical. Nicky pulled Gavin back to his seat and stroked the small of his back. He gradually calmed, peeled open his sandwich to scrape off the mustard, and then ate it with choked, determined bites while Rosalie complained that she'd paid her doctor three hundred dollars and he hadn't found one single thing wrong.

Nicky looked at the battered curio cabinet in the corner of the kitchen, at the little framed photographs of Rosalie blushing and slender and blonde, and she wondered if at night Rosalie wept, unable to sleep, wondering how she'd ended up here.

Her own mother told her to come home. Once Nicky was home, her parents and she could discuss the problem rationally and arrive at a rational solution. Her bedroom was there, ribboned and ruffled, just as she'd left it. Her old French teacher had asked about her. "I'll bet he did," Nicky said. She had called home from her windowless office at Mr. Candelaria's house, since Mr. Candelaria had driven down to Palo Alto for a lunch. Calling from there, though, had been a mistake. As soon as her mother started talking, Nicky felt the walls shrink around her, squeezing out the air. She should have called from her apartment—where she could open a window. She remembered that French teacher. His accent had been atrocious and his hands on her breasts fumbling.

"Well, he's quit teaching," her mother said. Now he ran an agency helping the homeless, and he'd mentioned he might be able to hire Nicky. He knew she'd had some problems.

"Problems?!" Nicky shrieked. Outraged, she traced the cut on her hand—it had healed to an angry red track.

But whatever had happened with the French teacher, her mother reminded Nicky that she herself was partly responsible. Well, Nicky knew that. She'd been the one wearing the sheer blouse and the lace bra, sitting on his lap. As in everything her mother said, there was a tight weave of true and false which was what made Nicky so crazy.

"It wouldn't hurt you," her mother went on, "to think about other people besides yourself for a change."

Frustrated, Nicky tried to breathe in chunks of air. She rummaged in her desk drawer for Tylenol. Tylenol was safe. "That's what I'm *trying* to do." Again, her mother let her know how much her schooling had cost. How was Nicky ever going to pay to educate her own child? Of course, her own child might do exactly as Nicky had—grow up with every advantage, cost her parents a fortune, and then drop out to do nothing worthwhile. Her father, on the extension, chimed in to tell Nicky that no one loved her as they did. Which only made her feel worse.

The instant she hung up the phone, Mr. Candelaria, irritated, stalked into the house and summoned her to his office. He'd received a speeding ticket on 101 for driving his Mercedes a mere eighty miles an hour. He'd told the officer the car could manage much, much greater speed, but to no avail. She was to call the court and explain that he drove at least that speed all the time on 280 and had never once been ticketed. It was outrageous that he should be ticketed for the same driving behavior on 101. If the court could not be moved, she was to call his lawyer. Also, the pencils on his desk were not sharp. Also, he was feeling a slight indigestion. The swordfish at lunch had been abominable. If she would be so kind as to mix him a bicarb.

Nicky took the ticket back to her desk along with his pencils. Before she mixed the bicarb, she opened his checkbook and paid the speeding fine, wondering how she could go about finding a doctor who'd declare her insane and send her away for a nice long rest.

Magically, in June the nausea stopped. Even more magically, her insomnia disappeared. Never had she fallen into such deep, luxurious sleep. She woke feeling stroked and pampered by sleep, like a plush golden cat. What a wonder—sleep! She told Gavin he ought to grind up pregnancy hormones into sleeping capsules. He'd make a fortune. But he told her he'd stopped selling drugs. He'd always only mainly dealt to friends. If he hadn't, God knows what shit they'd have gotten. But he wasn't taking that kind of chance anymore.

Nicky began to eat again; Gavin ate with her. They ate chicken burritos from the take-out on the corner, lemon grass beef at the French-Vietnamese place, and Szechwan calamari at the Asian-Italian place, and by July Nicky had to fasten her black work skirt with a safety pin, and Gavin had to go to the Gap for a larger size pair of jeans. Nicky could press her skirt against her belly and see a rising mound. She could feel the baby wriggling inside her. It wasn't a minnow anymore. It was a sleek slippery muscular carp.

One morning, just as she served Mr. Candelaria his Earl Grey tea, he cleared his throat, fiddled with a crystal paperweight, and then said, "I have noticed…that is…it has come to my attention…that you are in a delicate condition."

Nicky squirmed inside, embarrassed. She'd been meaning to tell him. She'd been delaying telling him. They never spoke of such things. Now his embarrassment made her embarrassed. And then she froze, suddenly afraid his embarrassment stemmed from a decision to fire her. Suddenly aware of how vulnerable she was to him.

He turned his head to look out the window. Gray strands of summer fog wrapped around the Golden Gate Bridge, shrouding the towers. "Many years ago I had a wife," he said.

This startled Nicky. She'd worked for him for two years and he'd never once mentioned a wife. She sat down in the leather chair opposite his vast walnut desk and waited, curious.

"It was in the old days," he said. By that Nicky knew he meant Cuba, in the days before Castro. He waved his hand dismissively, as if by "old days" he meant a whole other century, which, Nicky supposed, was true. "I raise the issue because I remember that when she was in a similar condition she often became fatigued in the afternoon." Now Nicky knew for sure that Mr. Candelaria was uncomfortable. Whenever he was uncomfortable his syntax became elaborately formal, so that his sentences seemed embossed with gold seals and flourishes. "I thought if you found yourself similarly fatigued you might take a few minutes to rest. It would do no harm, that is, it would be perfectly permissible for you to retire to one of the guest rooms. The bed in the white room, I believe, has the firmest mattress."

Nicky didn't know what to say. She felt overwhelmed by his concern, his generosity. Tears pricked at the corners of her eyes, catching her by surprise, and she quickly rubbed them away with the backs of her hands. Hormones, she told herself, sternly. Get a grip.

But he was right, she did get tired in the afternoons. Later that day, she took off her shoes. Asking herself, why was she taking off her shoes? Answering herself, because despite his invitation she felt she truly didn't belong upstairs. In stocking feet she climbed the stairs and then padded down the cavernous silent hall to the white room. The bed was so big she felt childlike on it. Closing her eyes, she had a vision of herself young, five or six, seated in a plastic child's chair in front of that smiling college counselor, while the counselor asked her younger self, *but who are you, Nicky? What do you want to do?* Equating "being" and "doing." Her younger self answered brightly, *I want to be an unwed mother living with a drug dealer with a jealousy problem. I want to be a handmaiden to a weird, old man.* The counselor patted her young head and awarded her a blue ribbon. *Very good, Nicky, as long as you know you can plan.*

Not likely, Nicky thought. But what if it was true? She could etch the same hopes in mirror writing. *I want to live with a brilliant future neurobiologist and bear the child of my own body and work with a man who is kind.*

Later that evening, as she was preparing to leave, she checked to see if Mr. Candelaria needed any last thing. He still sat behind his desk, staring out the window. The morning fog had cleared and then rolled in again, the first fingers of evening gloom stretching into the room. He looked bluer than usual. He looked hollow. Caved in by memory. She wondered if she should call his doctor. Or perhaps bring him soup and crackers before she left.

But he smiled thinly at her suggestions. "It is Wednesday, my bridge night. You know we always eat garlic sausage on bridge night."

Yes. She did know that. She ventured a small joke. "It's something I'm aware of every Thursday." He blinked. "Never mind," she said.

But the next morning, she noticed he'd doused himself even more liberally with the forest-scented cologne.

Summer slid toward autumn and she grew rounder, heavier, and yet felt ever lighter. Graceful. Like a balloon bobbing, carried along in currents of air. It had never seemed so easy simply to *be.* She went to work, rested in the afternoons, came home, rested in the evenings, content. Not reading, not struggling to breathe or sleep. There were things she should be worrying about, she knew. Plans she should be making. She was becoming bovine, and she didn't care. At night, Gavin came home from the lab, his hands carefully washed, and massaged her swelling feet and calves.

In September, the San Francisco days finally began to heat up. Winds shifted and blew in from the inland hills, lapping a hot, dusty breath of yellow summer over the city before the year began to burnish to October gold. Nicky lay on the bed in her apartment, in the gold and purple twilight. Even lightbulbs added to the heat. Her curtains hung limp at the open window. When the phone rang, it was almost too much effort to answer it. But she lifted her hand and then was too limp to flinch when she heard her mother asking about the baby. She knew Nicky's time was getting close. She thought Nicky might be feeling anxious. She herself didn't remember giving birth; she'd been given drugs. But again she talked about how much trouble Nicky had been, how she'd shrieked and cried for months on end. This time, though, Nicky was too content, too distant, to take offense. "Tell me more," she said instead.

Her mother hesitated. Then she tentatively admitted she'd been afraid something serious was wrong with Nicky—that she as a mother was doing something wrong. After another long moment she said, "I'd lost a child once before, you know."

But Nicky hadn't known that. Shocked, she struggled up into a sitting position, listening to the fracture in her mother's voice: she'd had a baby girl just a year before Nicky. Everything had been fine, she'd taken the baby home, and then a week later the baby died of a blocked intestine. Nicky envisioned her mother younger, her hair long and curly like Nicky's, holding a baby girl swaddled in pink, watching that baby shrivel and die. How awful it must have been; how confusing; how helpless her mother must have felt. Nicky felt that old nauseous thickening in her throat, and then realized it wasn't nausea at all she was feeling—it was grief. Her mother continued speaking, telling Nicky the doctors had assured her it wasn't her fault. But underneath those words Nicky heard her mother say that she would never ever believe it hadn't been her fault, and all the ways she'd driven Nicky to perfection took on a deeper tone. Then grief broke into a terrible sharp pain at all she and her mother had never been, and then beneath that pain swelled a tender possibility, scary and yet nice—that one day she might have her mother as a friend.

After Nicky hung up the phone, though, she lay in the darkening room, frightened by that dead baby. The responsibility—oh my God, she thought, terrified. There were so many things that could go wrong. And she was so very good at making things go wrong. The terror she felt tightened the walls of the apartment; she could feel the air disappearing. She had to get away from those suffocating white walls. She had to get out into the open air. Lightness. Champagne, she thought, desperately. But no, she couldn't drink champagne. With a glass of club soda and lime, with a little imagination, she'd have to pretend.

Outside in the hot open air, her blue maternity dress billowed around her. Relieved, she listened to the sounds of the city: from an open window in a neighboring building she heard music, laughter, a baby cry, quickly hushed. People were out sitting on steps, on cars, on the curb, drinking brown-bagged bottles of beer. Breathing deeply, carefully, slowly, she made her huge, graceful, parade-float way down the street, toward the Red Stone, and on the way, she saw that the crusty, bearded, homeless man had come back. He was settling his bedroll into the doorway of the print shop.

"Hey," she said, opening her wallet. "Where have you been? I've been worried about you." She pulled out a ten and gave it to him.

His crusty hand clutched the money, he nodded, smiled

a broken brown smile. "I almost got sober. Next time I mean to. For sure."

He might, Nicky thought. The odds were he was going to spend that ten on a couple bottles of Mad Dog. But he might buy a hamburger. He might get a bed for the night.

The Red Stone was practically empty. The dinner crowds were still in the restaurants. Nicky couldn't manage a bar stool; she sat down at the table where those poetry men had sat, all those months ago. Where had they gone? She hoped they'd come back. She wouldn't sit on their laps—how could she, gargantuan as she was? But she'd like to listen again to their talk. The bartender brought her an ice-cold club soda and since no one else was there, he sat down with her and began to chat inconsequentially about the heat, about the Giants' chances in the playoffs, about the neighborhood changing. Nicky rested her hand on her great round belly as he talked. The baby wasn't a carp anymore, it was a wriggling squirming octopus, with a slippery round head and arms and legs that jabbed her anywhere, everywhere, at random.

Rents were going up, the bartender said. The area was gentrifying. It was a good thing and a bad thing, both. He was a big ruddy Irishman from New York, and he'd lived here twenty years and it was good, he said, to see people making improvements—like that Irish pub on the restaurant corner, they served a great hamburger—but bad to see other people displaced. The burrito take-out might not make it; their rent had tripled, and you just couldn't charge that much for a burrito. "You and Gavin going to stay here after the baby's born, or move to the suburbs?"

"I…I don't know. We talk about it both ways," Nicky said, though that wasn't really true. She thought about it both ways, not sure where Gavin would be. And then she frowned, surprised, and said, "You know Gavin?"

"Sure I know Gavin. I know you, too—Nicky, right?" She nodded, pleased, flustered, that he knew her name. "What? You think I live in this neighborhood twenty years and don't know my neighbors? San Francisco ain't that big a city. Why I like it."

How strange—all of a sudden Nicky saw the Red Stone, the homeless man, the four restaurants, even the people living behind the window where she'd heard music and a baby, all of it an intricate weave that included her. How strange to feel, all of a sudden, that she wasn't alone.

She had to sip another club soda to think about that while the bartender talked about the upcoming mayoral election (Conor, he'd said his name was, and she'd been embarrassed she hadn't known that), and while she realized she'd lived here two years and hadn't bothered to register to vote, Gavin walked in. Instantly, she tensed to see him see her sitting with another man. But his expression didn't harden. His shoulders didn't stiffen, and his hands only beckoned her, eagerly, excitedly. "Come outside," he said. "I have a surprise." Nicky looked at Conor, shrugged, and then allowed Conor to help her rise from the chair and made her slow, bobbing way to the door.

Out on the narrow street, double-parked, flashers blinking, stood a brand new silver Chevy Lumina minivan. "Ta-da," Gavin said, waving his hand with a flourish at the car. "I wasn't going to be able to take the baby on my bike, so I sold it. I got a great deal and a loan—someone thinks I'm a good credit risk." He slid the sliding door back and forth; he folded the built-in baby seat up and down; he pulled the cup-holder in and out. Anti-lock brakes. Power door locks, power windows. Four-speaker, built-in CD player. "What do you think?"

She had to laugh. It was the ugliest car she'd ever seen. She was going to need major parking karma to ever parallel park that thing in the city. But he was so excited, so proud of all the gear, it made her think of the boy he'd been, hotwiring cars just because he could. And, after all, there wasn't anything felonious in buying an ugly car.

He had to boost her up into it. She sat up in the plush, gray, upholstered seat feeling like the captain's mate on the Titanic as he steered the thing down the side street, out onto Valencia Street. They drove past the homeless man, sleeping. They drove past a party spilling from the building next door to theirs out onto the hot, glimmering sidewalk. They circled for twenty minutes looking for a parking space. But Gavin didn't care, he didn't curse or bash the steering wheel or flip anyone off—he only circled and fiddled with the stereo, circled and played with the power windows, until a space magically opened up right in front of their building.

Up in their apartment, Nicky changed into a big, floppy nightshirt and lay on her back on the bed. Gavin ran a cold wet cloth all along her swollen feet, and her flesh rose and shivered. She felt so ripe—her breasts brown and burnished and aching to be stroked, all of her joints loose, her hips loose, open, available. She felt so flushed—was this happiness? Could this ripe, flushed feeling be what people meant by happiness? Gavin slid the cloth from her foot up her calf to her bent knee. His touch was so gentle, her breath caught, her knee fell to the side. He ran the cloth up her thigh and she gasped and then breathed in one deep, warm breath and looked down at him. "Now," he said, his eyes not shifting from hers. He lifted her nightshirt and stared down at the hard mound and then traced with his finger the dark longitudinal line traveling from her navel to her panties. He put his mouth to her stomach. "Hello there," he said.

The baby shifted and Nicky knew it was responding to

Gavin's voice. Certainty chimed in her in small silver tones: this baby was a boy; it had Gavin's deep-shadowed eyes; it had his long, slender fingers; it would have his love of engines and science; she'd have to watch it didn't grow up to hotwire that Chevy minivan. She reached out her scarred hand to touch Gavin's hair. He twisted his head to listen again to the baby, his eyes again on Nicky's. He slid his hand into her panties. She moaned. "I can't. I'm so huge."

"Shh." Gavin stroked her. He kept his head on her belly, listening to the baby tumble while he stroked her. That ripe, flush feeling swelled into heat and beauty and she moaned again, helpless but held, until quietly, softly, gently, she came into his hand, heat and beauty shuddering between her and him and the baby. Then he said, "Nicky, I love you."

Hearing that, tears slid from her eyes, sideways down her face, into her hair. She couldn't stop them. They streamed and streamed, though she didn't sob; she wasn't truly crying. She was only forlorn, certain that if Gavin loved her, everything now would go wrong.

A week later, he was arrested.

She didn't know what to do. She sat at the dinette, watching gray evening darken to night. He'd called her, frantic, from the jail. She had to get him out of there. He'd been busted for possession and the coke hadn't even been his, he'd only been holding it for a guy in a bar at one of the piers when an undercover cop came in. She had to find out about bail; she had to find him a lawyer; she didn't know what to do. The baby had dropped lower in her belly. All her ligaments had softened. She felt wobbly. She felt like she'd tip right over onto her belly, like an inflatable fat man. She felt huge and helpless. She thought about calling her parents, but she couldn't bear to think what they'd say. She thought about calling Rosalie—Rosalie, what good would that do?

She sat there, anxious, unable to move, staring at the moonless black sky. She could barely hoist herself up from the chair, how could she help Gavin? It was all she could do to make sure her heart kept beating, her lungs kept pumping, her skin didn't rupture and her belly split wide open like an overripe watermelon. It was all she could do to keep herself from sliding right over a cliff into the yawning black despair that, again, she had made the wrong decision. She had made a terrible mistake, and the consequences were going to be disastrous.

With one puffy, swollen hand on the dinette table, she levered herself up off the chair. She lumbered, fat and damp with sweat, her hair limp down her back, into the ancient pink-and-purple art deco bathroom, all with a curious sense of her true, thin, un-pregnant Nicky self hovering above, watching her ridiculous pathetic body. She watched her hand, the fingers pink and stubby, open the cracked mirrored medicine cabinet. She watched her stupid hand rummage through her collection of vials saved with bits of this and that. She watched her shaking index finger count pills into her scarred, fat hand while her true, wild self skittered with a furious and frenzied excitement. Four blue phenobarb. Ten Vicodin. Synthroid. Synthroid? What the hell was she doing with that, that wouldn't do her any good, her hand threw that vial into the wastebasket. Valium, of course. Seven Percocet, five Seconals. Many Tylenol-codeines. Her little colored jelly-bellies.

Her fat, blue fist closed the mirrored medicine cabinet and as it did so, she saw her bloated, tearful, pathetic reflection swing into view, that crack slashing across her forehead and the view filled her with rage. Goddamn her for being so stupid. Rage shuddered up into her mouth, hot and red. She couldn't breathe. She couldn't breathe at all, and the muscles in her arms and legs began to tremble and the baby inside her began to skitter and the rage exploded like an orgasm in her chest and flowed hot and red into her arm, down into her hand, into her clenched fist and she smashed her fist into that face, into the crack, and the face burst, the glass burst, into a thousand shattering clattering shards and it was the noise of it, the white light searing sound of it, that woke her, that made her stop, that made her quick lick her tongue to a small, sharp slice of blood on her palm, that made her think: what the hell was she doing?

She dumped all the pills into the wastebasket, fast, like she was dropping poisonous insects. She ran her hands over the baby inside her, softly, soothing it. Soothing herself. Purposefully, she hummed Brahms. Purposefully, she went to her bed and laid down and closed her eyes and breathed in and out. In the morning, she thought, in the sunlight, she would know what to do.

But in the middle of the night, she woke, her eyes huge and parched. She went into the bathroom and collected all the pills from the wastebasket and sorted them back into their vials. She needed to know they were there.

The next day, at nine fifteen precisely, she spilled Mr. Candelaria's Earl Gray tea all over his desk and then waited for him to yell at her. But instead, he wiped up the tea with a handful of Kleenex while she apologized repeatedly, and then he said, "Nicky, what is wrong? Is it the child?"

At his question, she started to cry. "I don't know what I was thinking. I don't know how I thought I could have a baby. I don't know what I'm doing with anything."

"Oh, Nicky, sit down." He went into her office and poured from the teapot a fresh cup of tea. "Drink this," he said, offering her the Spode cup. "It will calm you."

But she couldn't. Earl Grey tea had caffeine in it.

"Ah, well, new rules." He sat back down at his desk and sipped the tea himself. "When my wife was pregnant, she enjoyed a cup of tea in the morning. She didn't know what she was doing either. None of us did."

Nicky wiped her eyes. Very softly, she asked, "What happened to her?" Mr. Candelaria looked down at his fingernails. "She didn't make it," he said, equally softly. "We had to leave, you see. I'd already been arrested once." He touched one of the small burn marks on the back of his hand. "She might have made it. She was the one who insisted we try. And really, what choice was there? Storms in the Straits are unpredictable. They gather up wild, fierce, and then die down just as fast. One patch of sky blue and serene, the next patch a whirlwind. The sails tore, the engine failed, we drifted, many days. She developed a fever. Still, she might have made it. A matter of chance." He sighed heavily. "Well. Enough."

Nicky roused herself to take down his morning's instructions. But the baby began to shift and tumble, and she said instead, "Gavin's been arrested."

Before she could tell the tale, Mr. Candelaria held up his hand "Stop. I do not need to know the details. But—Nicky, do you love him?"

She shuddered, crying hard. "Sometimes yes. Sometimes no. I don't know."

"Ah." After a long pause, he said, "My only advice is this: when you marry, marry a good conversationalist. My wife and I had many good conversations. They made the evenings enjoyable."

Nicky hiccupped and thought, a good conversationalist? Would she say Gavin was a good conversationalist? No. Except…she remembered how excited he was when work went well. Could he become a good conversationalist? It seemed possible. She could imagine long evenings, the baby sleeping, the two of them talking about....something.

"Perhaps," Mr. Candelaria said, "if you were to call my attorney he might be of some assistance."

It was what she'd been hoping he'd say, but she'd been afraid to ask, and again overwhelmed, she thanked him so profusely his blue, hollow cheeks washed a pale, pleasured pink. He straightened his tie and told her to make the call and then return in half an hour with a fresh cup of tea for him.

The attorney said he'd have one of his associates look into Gavin's situation and get back to her. Nicky sat at her desk, nervously spinning the mini–Ferris wheel Rolodex, thinking of all Mr. Candelaria had not said. The burn marks on his hands and throat. The days under the blaring sun, hungry, thirsty. Watching his wife die in fever dream with his child inside her. All his formal silences—why should he speak to her about anything? And yet he did. Aching for him, she brewed the fresh pot of Earl Grey tea with special care and carried it gently to his office, placing it before him in what she felt was too feeble an offering.

"Thank you," he said. He sipped the tea with pleasure and then began speaking. He was buying a small painting she would need to insure. He was planning a trip to a spa in Arizona. He would require as always two seats on the airline as he could not tolerate strangers beside him. He would require a backboard beneath his hotel mattress. He had a late lunch scheduled with his investment advisor. Finally, she was to draft a letter to the mayor complaining of the excessive number of fire hydrants on the sidewalks, one on every corner wherever he wanted to park his car. But as he spoke, his voice began to tighten. He looked very blue. He tugged at his tie, his mouth sucked for air.

"Mr. Candelaria?" Nicky said. She pushed herself up belly first from the chair. "Are you all right?"

"Yes." His voice was a tight wheeze. "Fine." He put his hand to his chest.

Stricken herself, Nicky grabbed the phone on his desk. "I'm going to call your doctor," she said.

Mr. Candelaria shook his head. But all of him was blue. Even his fingernails were blue. Instead of calling his doctor, Nicky called 911, and then held onto one of his blue hands for the long, long minutes until the paramedics scrambled into the office and around his body, threaded wires and tubes into his arms and mouth and nose, and then carried him off. Nicky grabbed her purse, Mr. Candelaria's cell phone, and the Rolodex card with the attorney's phone number, and drove in her white Honda Civic to the hospital.

She sat for what seemed hours on a scarred, white plastic chair in a row of identical other scarred, white plastic chairs. People came and went in all states of distress and disorder while noisy chaos clattered down a distant hallway and from somewhere Nicky smelled a constant smell of burnt coffee, and she worried that the room Mr. Candelaria was in might be asymmetrical and that they wouldn't have any Earl Grey tea for him. The glare of fluorescent light on polished linoleum hurt her eyes. She called the attorney and left a message and waited for a call back. She waited for someone to tell her what was happening with Mr. Candelaria. She worried about Gavin, in jail, having bad memories of the youth authority and the other guys there with their bad memories. All the white plastic chairs had armrests and her back ached and it was impossible to lie down and her feet throbbed and she was hungry and then an iron hand clamped down on her belly and squeezed out her breath and she realized—she was wet. Her dress, her legs, the plastic chair—everything was wet and a sea-salt, sandy smell wafted all around her.

Panicked, she thought this wasn't how it was supposed to

be. And then she thought: but for once she was already in the right place. She didn't have to call a cab or take a bus or try to drive herself. Wet, sweaty, she sat through another tight squeeze, and then carefully, gingerly, pushed herself up to stand, walking slowly to the nurse's station, a little bent over, holding her belly, afraid the baby might just bumble out of her into a bloody heap on the floor. "Could you help me?" she said, and the nurse said just a minute and after another minute she shouted down the hall for someone else and after yet another minute began asking Nicky questions and filling out forms, while Nicky's cell phone rang and she fumbled to answer it but dropped it and couldn't pick it up. A short, fat man in white helped her into a wheelchair and handed her the phone—it was the attorney speaking. She shuddered through another contraction while the attorney told her the San Francisco D.A. wasn't big on prosecuting first-time offenders and there was a good chance the charges against Gavin would be kicked down to misdemeanor, or that they would even go away. In any event, he'd be out of jail in a few hours.

Then she was being pushed down a brilliant, light hallway. Everything was a blur of green paint and stainless steel and noise, incredible noise, clamoring, echoing off the walls, the linoleum, the flickering light fixtures—equipment beeping, phones ringing, people laughing and crying, and dropping things in ringing clatter while pain gripped her in tight iron fingers and then splayed her out onto a bed. Something heavy was strapped across her stomach; white paper unfurled from a machine graphing her pain in jagged red lines, and she thought: Gavin should be here. He would like this machine.

The room was symmetrical. The walls were white and still. A nurse with daisy earrings brought her more papers to sign and Nicky scrawled her name in big messy letters and asked, "Please could you find out how Mr. Candelaria is?" and then a doctor, not her doctor, brisk and masked in green, laughed hugely and told her she was having a baby. Well, she knew that.

But she sank down into more pain and said, "No."

The doctor only laughed again and said, "That's what they all say," and settled himself between her knees. His hands were large and brown, the biggest hands Nicky had ever seen. But maybe that was shadows, because somehow it was dark outside; she couldn't think when that happened, but then more pain surged through her and she couldn't think at all.

The nurse with daisy earrings came back and said that Mr. Candelaria was stable.

Nicky breathed. "But what does that mean?"

"It means that, for now, he's stable."

And Nicky knew what that meant—no promises. Another fierce pain clenched her back. "I can't do this," Nicky said, breathing hard.

The nurse leaned over Nicky's face to wipe her lips and her daisy earrings flashed. "You'll be surprised what you can do." She took hold of Nicky's hand and fingered the scar and asked how she'd injured her hand. But Nicky couldn't answer. She couldn't remember. Vaguely, she remembered a night in a bar a thousand years ago. Vaguely, she remembered poetry and blood.

And then she remembered nothing, nothing at all. Pain swelled and broke over her. Her whole body quaked, opening, opening, shuddering. A great noise roared in her ears—her own voice. An ocean swamped her. Push, Nicky. The doctor in green. More noise. The nurse and the daisies. Push, Nicky. Breathe. It might work out. It might.

She trembled, she gasped, she flushed, she heaved, she sweated, she bled, she pushed and pushed and pushed, tear-ing open her spine and her stomach and her skin. Push, Nicky. She wasn't strong enough. Yes she was.

She felt....slippage. She didn't have any choice. There was nothing she could do—what was inside her was messy and bloody and beautiful and unstoppable. She pushed and pushed and pushed while bright shards of light broke around her, dazzling. Dimly she heard the nurse promise her breakfast in bed. Champagne. Orange juice. Mimosa. She squeezed her eyes shut and saw a full moon ripe and silver shimmering. She saw a magician in a black coat handing her a flower. She saw jagged, white pain streak through her body. And then she heard the doctor say she was almost there. If she could do this, she could do anything. She pushed and pushed and pushed, turning her own self inside out until she felt the tumble of blood and flesh between her legs. She heard the doctor cry out she had a girl. She heard him say she was perfect. She heard the baby cry, and then she cried too, both of them new born. And then Nicky reached out her two hands, which were already filled, with hope.

About the Author

As the daughter of an air force pilot, **Karen Bjorneby** grew up in various parts of the United States and Europe. She studied social thought at the University of California at Irvine. Her short fiction has appeared in various literary quarterlies and received a special mention in the Pushcart Prize vol. XXIV; her poetry has appeared or is forthcoming in *Iris*, *Literal Latté*, *JAMA*, and *The Threepenny Review*. Karen lives in San Francisco where she is working on a novel.